EARTHLY BODIES

To Debbie! Thankyou for the gift & you readership! Susan Earlam

SUSAN EARLAM

Earthly Bodies by Susan Earlam

http://www.susanearlam.com

Copyright © 2021 Susan Earlam / Speleorex Press

In this narrative, the role played by Giuseppe Arcimboldo, along with the small mention of Elton John, are both entirely fictional. My imagined versions of these people are, however, based on generally known facts of their lives, but are just that, imaginary.

Cover by Marta Brinchi Giusti- Instagram @mbgletters

Ebook ISBN: 978-1-8383794-0-7

Paperback ISBN: 978-1-8383794-1-4

*"Nothing retains its own form; but
Nature, the greatest renewer, ever makes
up forms from forms. Be sure there's
nothing perishes in the whole universe;
it does but vary and renew its form.
What we call birth is but a beginning to
be other than what one was before; and
death is but cessation of a former state."*

Ovid, Metamorphoses

CONTENTS

A letter by Arcimboldo, dated 1587, found hidden inside the frame of his painting, Vertumnus; translated by Johan Madylus, Bohemia Historian

I look back on that day now with a knowing wisdom. Hindsight is a magnificent thing. I consider that we should have cleaned up better. We should have postponed the King, made up some fallacy that I was sick and couldn't see him. We should have scrapped all the paintings. We should have burnt everything in that studio, including ourselves.

Instead I took the cowards' way, the way of the ego. I wanted to be lauded. I wanted to be validated. In my mind, working for the King wasn't enough. I wanted public acclaim and admiration. I got what I wanted but paid a high price. Both my assistant and I developed the infection. Him first, he was always in the thick of it, cleaning up after me.

He tried to pretend there was nothing wrong, as did I, but you could see it in his face. A monochromatic complexion, he was fading. The other members of the King's staff began to talk about him. He was banned from the kitchens and the gardens, only working in the dark places and in my studio, which in the later days of his illness became his only safe place.

1

I continued to work, and he continued to help me. One morning I came back from another dawn meeting with the King and I found him, the shadow of him, on the bed he'd set up in the corner. I will never forget returning to the studio that day. I entered to a strong sweet smell, like stewed cherries and plums. The air was dense with dust. I now understand that the dust was him, the remains of him, and I was breathing it in. He was filling my lungs and settling there. On the bed, a sunken shape. Desiccated with fluid-filled blisters on his visible limbs.

I remember not being upset, but selfishly wondering about how I would get all my work done now, without his help. I lifted the sheet by the four corners and tied them in a knot, securing him inside. He had no mass to speak of, now much lighter than he had been in life.

I took him down to one of the furnaces in the lower levels of the palace. I threw him in, and although nobody queried me, I believe of the few people there, at least one would guess correctly if asked.

It was after this shameful incident that I had the placed cleaned properly. I'm embarrassed to say that I could have done this much earlier, but my work took over in such a dramatic way that it felt like there was no time for trivial things like cleaning. I wish I'd known that it was far from trivial.

So, the paintings were moved, everything was moved, and my studio scrubbed and scrubbed until the stone wall shone. The paintings were covered with drapes and kept in a guest room.

Then I became ill. It is the reason I've come back to Milan, leaving the finished work there and promising to continue from home. It crept up on me at first. A cough and occasionally joints so swollen I found it hard to paint. My symptoms came and went for a long time. There have been months where I've been free of it. These long gaps allowed me to complete more commissions.

I believe that inside of me there is a war going on, between my will to finish the work and the infection that wants to take hold of me. Once I begin to rest, the sickness will know I've released my grip. I feel it waiting for the prime moment at which to strike. Therefore, I must keep fighting and continue my work. I make this confession to you, for I fear time is running out. I need to clean my soul but there is no chance for absolution.

Yours, Giuseppe

PART ONE: 2043-2058

CHAPTER 1 – 2058

Rebecca, June

This will be the last time we see each other. Not because I'm going to try again, but because I've received the answer I hoped for. Yes, I'm leaving Earth.

"Would you look at the camera, sis? Have you changed your hair? It looks lighter, different. It's been ages."

Sam is snapping away, testing the light. The plant I bought him is perched on the windowsill next to me. Will he care for it after I'm gone? I squirm; not wanting my photo taken, sat here on the floor of his small studio. I've been doing the rounds all morning, visiting a handful of people here in Scredda. Leaving him until last. Kaolin Heights used to be an affluent neighbourhood, not anymore and I feel scruffy, wearing my oldest pair of black jeans and a sleeveless tee. I'm scared that if I look at the camera, he'll be able to read my thoughts, see the secret in my eyes.

Sam moves around, taking photos, not really expecting an answer. He enjoys life here, I'm sure he will be okay. I will miss his innocent way of looking at the world, but I must think of myself now. Being here isn't good for me. I need a fresh start.

"Do you have your old Instant here?" I finally say, shaking off my thoughts. "Let's get a shot of us together for a change."

He digs through a couple of cardboard boxes until he finds it.

"There's one shot left."

"Well it's fate then, isn't it? A fair exchange: a plant for a picture." Grabbing his arm, I pull him down next to me, his beard brushes the side of my face.

C-CLICK

I catch the photo out of the top of the camera before he even has a chance to try. He pulls that face, the same one he did when we were kids, when I'd won.

"Hey, let me see!"

"Sorry, Sam, I didn't realise the time. I've got to go." I hold the photo to my chest.

If I stay any longer, I'll end up telling him everything. I can't even look at him. Swallowing the tears in my throat, I jump up from the floor and say my goodbyes—leaving my bewildered brother at the door.

He'll receive a letter once I'm gone. I've made sure to follow the instructions exactly.

It's dusk as I head out onto the street and finally look at the photograph. Sam is right. My hair does look lighter, but my skin is still near-translucent, partly covered by stories etched on with the tattooist's needle. I look like a fairy goth and Sam, my sweet, sweet brother, looks like Dad.

The tears come freely, and I start to run. The once pretty streets are crumbling. The pavements are full of cracks, the roads are full of potholes. Buildings sit derelict but for the homeless, and someone tries to sell me drugs as I run past. I weave in and out of zombie-like users. Many places are like this now, not just here. People have lost more than hope.

* * *

Back at my flat and out of the muggy air. I stand for a minute and catch my breath. It doesn't feel like home. I've sold or given everything away, even my bed. The rucksack is waiting for me by the door. Packing was easy, once I'd begun to purge stuff, carefully taking only a few favourite pieces of clothing. I saved the most space for personal items. These are classed as Earth memorabilia in the travel instructions. The bag sits there, waiting to exhale its belongings into a new life; my new life.

I have a few hours to kill before I need to leave. Everything feels shadowy and underhand, done in darkness. I know this is because of the secrecy, but I hate to lie.

My mouth is dry, but there's nothing to drink. I had the water switched off, so I could settle my bills. I test the tap in the small kitchen anyway, and a dribble comes out, which I slurp at like a cat.

As instructed, the warm travelling clothes are folded by the side of my rucksack. Sitting on top is the wristband I must wear from now on, it's preloaded with my journey details so I won't get any awkward questions when I'm scanned at the travel gates. I strap it to my wrist and commit myself fully. Then I slip the clothes on, their heat makes me drowsy. The jumper was my husband's. Its itchy fibres tickle my skin. Lying on my side, I draw the bag under my head and pull my arms in close to my face, and I caress my cheeks with wool-encompassed fingers gripping the jumper. It makes me feel like he's here, the sensation of him fills me up, and I can forget he is gone.

* * *

Space tourists are common now. I'm on an electric coach, it has small, long windows which remind me of letterboxes. The people here will have saved up for their trips around

Earth, or even to one of the Lunar Orbital Space Stations. My ticket is one way.

We pull to a stop and almost everyone gets off. We must be on the borders of Wales; I've read there is a launch site here. I've been told only to exit when prompted by a facilitator, a MAGIE, who will make sure my transfer goes smoothly. The MAGIE are robotic humanoids. A type of Artificial Intelligence: Mindful, Able, Genderless, Inter-operable Entities. Pitched as useful, they are a way of keeping watch over citizens, like spies. I try to avoid them. Whoever is left on the coach at the end of this leg, will be coming with me, further north of here to somewhere near the Shetlands.

A couple of people get on—they don't seem to know each other—and we pull away. There are around twelve people who must have boarded while I've been dozing. I'm relieved to see that it's mostly women. All the same, I keep my eyes low, not ready for small talk. Out of the window, I catch the eye of a teenage boy that has just been dropped off on to the grey tarmac, he leans back on the railings, the epitome of teenage disinterest. His parents are obviously rich; they look antiseptic. His mum busies herself with her MAGIEpad while the dad takes multiple puffs of an inhaler. The boy stares at me with an accusing curiosity, looking out from the grey. I feel sad. Sad for what could have been. Sad that his parents are the way they are, and sad because all life has potential, unless you aren't on the list. What will happen to these people left behind?

The fact is, I wouldn't be on this coach if we'd had a child. 'One extreme always leads to another,' Mum would always say as she sat crying in front of the news. It's been that way for as long as I remember. Despite three applications, we'd never been given the go ahead. Christian had blamed himself. Even if we had received a parenting license, there was no guarantee of a full-term pregnancy, and medical intervention was only for the rich.

I settle down for another attempt at napping, rolling my coat up and plugging it between my shoulder and head. I lean against the window, quickly realising I haven't worn this coat since last winter. It's matted with dog hair; Juniper's. My parents' dog that had come to live with me when she got too much for Dad.

We pass what must be acres of scrap metal yards. Far into the smog I can see cars, boats, even a few helicopters at different stages of corrosion, stacked in wonky columns. I drift into a fitful sleep. The domes of my old workplace blend with visions of grey, rocky cliffs and spikey, foreboding trees which beckon at me from the gloom.

* ✳ *

Spending my days inside the Eden Project had been a dream come true. A man-made botanical paradise and the blueprint for many other eco-dome projects around the world.

I'd felt at home there, recreating how Earth used to be by working as a storyteller. My job was to capture the imagination of visitors and transport them into different worlds, times, and places. I was good at it and believe it's part of the reason I'm on this elopement.

It had been a sad, slow decline for the park. The funding began to dry up first, some of the staff were let go. Then the park couldn't be maintained at its usual standard and, as word got out, fewer visitors came through the gates.

Eventually it became the focus of a guerrilla group. They managed to infiltrate the networks of the remaining staff at the park, playing on their insecurities about the future. They'd used the lush environment to grow and manufacture illegal drugs—a highly addictive cannabis hybrid. In the end, I didn't know who to trust; friends had turned against one another.

Before the park's downward spiral, I'd got one of my first pieces of body art—depicting the biodomes and the lush greenery hinted at inside. It sits on my left thigh, reminding me of a beautiful and idyllic time of my life. I met Christian around that time, too.

"Wakey, wakey." Somebody nudges me in the arm. My thoughts fade instantly. There must have been another stop after I'd nodded off. I hadn't felt anyone sit down. "Looks like we have to get off," they say as a hooded figure passes us down the aisle of the coach.

I roll my shoulders up to my ears and push out my rib cage, stretching my spine. Here and now is where I need to focus, not the past—especially when looking at it with a rosy perspective.

I grab my backpack from the cage above my head. Everyone else has left already and are standing outside, waiting. I'm the last one. For the briefest moment, I contemplate hiding under the seats or at the back of the storage cages: a stowaway ready to be taken back, not wanting to face whatever unknowns are beyond this point. The thought passes, and I quickly slip down the aisle to join the others.

* * *

This is it. I've arrived at the place where my future begins. The sun is setting, I can see it here, the sky is so clear, so big. A battered Saxa Vord Resort sign looks down at us at the side of the track. We are at the very north of the Shetland Isles, roads as I know them don't exist here. There are patches of small shrubs and heather making headway among the abandoned low breezeblock huts we've been dropped beside. It feels bleak but is much leafier here than I anticipated. The shades of browns and greens bring back flashes of my work in Cornwall and the past I'm leaving behind.

There are around twenty in the group. We aren't the first to be deposited here. It's been made clear in the documentation that there are other groups, feeling ready for a different future, trying to prepare for the unknown.

We are in an open area, with a slope to one side. I hear the sea, a new companion on this last leg. In the distance I can see some basic cabins and a small group of figures coming towards us. The group quietens and a palpable sense of foreboding spreads among us. The sense of isolation here—at the crossing to another world—is frighteningly real.

"We are in the middle of nowhere for sure," someone says. I can almost see the eye roll, despite the voice coming from behind me.

"What have I done?" someone else begins, sinking to the floor, unable to process the remote situation.

Other murmurs start from the small crowd, but having not spoken to anyone on the trip up here, I don't want to start now. It begins to rain, a misty drizzle that hangs in the air making everything damp, leaving a coat of droplets wherever it falls. I feel like I'm being covered in dew. I tilt my face up to the sky to really feel it on my skin. The sky is heavy with more moisture, perhaps even snow? The weather is harder to predict than ever these days, a tempestuous child: the product of our systemic abuse.

The figures coming towards us are clearer now. There is a tall woman in the centre, with strawberry blonde hair tied back in a ponytail and an open friendly face. The woman is in step with two MAGIE, and my stomach flips. More MAGIE, I should've known the one on the coach wouldn't be the only one for a project like this. Of course, it makes sense that there would be a MAGIE presence. I have no choice but to interact with them—it's a means to an end. The woman in the middle is wearing wellies and a long, thick coat. Her hands are in her pockets. We can all see plainly that she is talking to the MAGIE.

The trio get within earshot and the woman stops talking. The path they are on is more like a track, well-worn and narrow. The MAGIE flanking the woman break free from their formation and move to circle us.

My experience with MAGIE has been mixed, mostly occurring through the education system. The lab technicians and administration staff at my school used a couple of MAGIE. They performed their duties well enough but never integrated with the school population. I'd always felt that they were there to collate and report, more than anything else.

The group here seems to feel the same way. A whisper of apprehension, hands clutching backpacks a little tighter, making knuckles white.

The MAGIE are checking to see who is here. The strawberry blonde-haired woman positions herself close to us newcomers.

"Welcome, welcome." She has a calm voice, but there is a faint shrill to it that she struggles to hide. "We are glad you made the choice to attend this retreat. We hope at its conclusion you will all be able to go further onwards. That is down to you and what you can bring us, what you are willing to share and perhaps even unlearn. My name is Doctor Annabel Morin, and I'll be your main point of contact here at Saxa Vord." The doctor was looking at each of us in turn, attempting to make eye contact with everyone. I want to hold her eye, but instead I look slightly past her, over her shoulder, annoying myself.

"You should all know by now that there will be weeks of intense coaching and counselling here. Hypnosis, dream therapy, and more. We need to ensure you will hold up when the departure time comes. I'm assuming there are no immediate questions?"

Questions? We all have questions.

"I know you'll all be very tired and want to freshen up, so let's head in."

Spinning on her rubber heel, Dr Morin heads back towards the buildings in the distance. I spot a man rushing to catch up with her. I'm tired, and lag behind, withdrawing to the edges of the group as we move towards the cabins. Looking down at my feet, I feel grateful to have steady land, real earth and not concrete, under my feet again.

"You must keep up with the group, Rebecca." A stern, robotic voice comes from over my shoulder. Why am I surprised the MAGIE knows my name?

The sloping rooftops of the buildings appear to be at acute angles and run down, almost to the ground. We enter the biggest building, from a door on the wall-side. The interior is surprisingly rustic. I'd expected to walk into a clinical environment, but the heart of the Saxa Vord compound—where I'd assumed things would be shiny and new—instead feels warm, almost cosy. Through the large window at the other end of the room, I can see that the warren of small bungalows is connected by boardwalks. In here, there is a long communal dining table and a kitchen set up at that end of the space. This space is warmed by a fire, a real fire. There are blankets, musty sofas dotted around, and bookshelves on nearly every wall. I can feel myself smiling, and I'm growing a little overwhelmed and dizzy, but I also sense safety. I let the feelings wash over me, grateful to feel them. It's going to be okay. I hear myself let out a big sigh as I sink down into the nearest chair.

Dare I relax? Seems I can't help it. It feels idyllic. I want to drop my guard. It's exhausting being alert and suspicious all the time. The sleep I'd managed on the journey wasn't enough. I let it come for me here; my limbs heavy, my eyes close.

CHAPTER 2 – 2050

Oscar, April

"For all they have done, and that which they have failed to do, leaders in politics and commerce across the world must be overthrown." The woman from Green Rising speaks so persuasively Oscar no longer wonders why it's her who's driving the G.R. movement so far beyond what anyone was expecting. She sounds formidable, and she's turning him on.

"The MAGIE will assist the uprising, accommodate and enforce change. They will be at your disposal. I'm happy to be involved," Oscar replies, through gritted teeth.

"The removal will include Ministers, CEOs, and many others who have used their power for status and greed. They will be replaced by competent and trusted women," pausing, she attempts to look him in the eye through the screen, "you are on our list, Oscar."

"I would be surprised if I weren't. I hope we aren't too late. I regret not using my influence enough to protect this world."

"Don't be too hard on yourself." Oscar detects a hint of sarcasm. "We just need a reboot. Thanks for your time today." The call ends, and Oscar stretches his legs. None of this alarms him. It quite clearly is too late. We haven't cared enough for the Earth. We must start again.

Oscar's drive is what got him here, a tech entrepreneur. They called him a visionary at first because his investments in new tech always succeeded. Now, they see him as one of the baddies, the big bad contributors to an Earth that desperately needs some TLC. His parents' cash and status no use anymore. They'd fled with the dissolution of the Soviet Union in the late 1980s, to Switzerland for a liberal government.

He strokes the MAGIEpad into life and opens the bank accounts he still has from growing up there. It is time to pull out the money, ready to pay for what needs to be done, and set the plans into action. He moves all the cash with a tap of his finger across to the account he shares with his sister.

Oscar, November

Sitting at his desk in London, Oscar looks out at Regent's Park, or what is left of it. Tents cover the former grasslands. Climate refugees from the southern European territory, seeking somewhere to live where they won't be held hostage in their homes. The zoo is still here, it just built its walls higher and put the admission prices up.

The news streams onto the wall beside him. Men he has worked with, leaders in politics and industry around the world, are being removed from their jobs, with help from the MAGIE.

There are too many people. The world is a mess—but this is it, the tipping point is here, finally happening. This is his time, his moment. The irony of course is that he must go into hiding to accomplish the plan. He puts in a call to Doctor Annabel Morin.

"I can change all this," he says.

"Are you saying that it's time?"

"Yes. How is the search?"

"There are a few places I've located. We should visit them when things quieten down."

The call ends, and he buzzes for his personal assistant, a MAGIE named Lan. They have been one of his more successful creations, despite recent occurrences.

"It's time, Lan."

"I'll ready your transport. Did you want the note printed off, Sir?"

"No, I'm going to handwrite it, otherwise it might look too contrived."

"Whatever you think is best." The MAGIE leaves the office, and Oscar reaches for a mechanical pencil from the pot on his desk. He still created a lot of his ideas by hand before transferring them into blueprints for the software to interpret. It felt more intuitive that way, more connected to whatever he was creating, and he still loved paper.

Oscar looks youthful for his age, thanks to his other favourite invention; the synthetic amniotic fluid and the pods it's housed in. This advance is still under wraps, exactly the sort of thing the gossip columnists love. They are constantly gobbling up famous people's complexions. His public appearances becoming fewer, the more obvious his re-found youth became. Society believing him now to be a recluse. From this moment he will disappear completely. His death by suicide will make the news. Though, there is a chance it may be buried with everything else going on. From an outsider's perspective, in these circumstances, his perceived alternative outlook is dire. Taken down by his own creations. People will not be that surprised.

The synthetic amniotic fluid is being manufactured on a much larger scale. The chosen location needs to be remote, yet big enough for the closed river of synth-fluid to be built. His plan is to store people inside the river until there are enough individual pods made. From there, they'd be woken on a rota of some sort. He must get this plan crystal clear. At least now he'll have the time to work on it exclusively.

He makes some notes about logistics and timings onto his to-do list. Leaning back into the ergonomic chair he spins round to again look down at the park. This high rise is his, as are a handful of others in the London Metropolis, the dirty city as it was now known. Beneath him are his labs and workshops. Beneath that, the analytics and data collection offices. The lower floors serve as a budget hotel. Above him is the penthouse, his own pocket of paradise.

Standing, he presses his palms into the glass and rests his forehead and nose upon the cool surface. Closing his eyes, he knows exactly how his guests would feel; the land looks lush, in their mind's eye, like a dream. The river thick and goopy, but it slips over their bodies like mercury. He knows the feeling well. They wake, still submerged, selected by the MAGIE, then are lifted prune like from the river. An alien water birth. The subsequent fireman's lift over the shoulder of the MAGIE dislodges anything that might be stuck in the throat.

His vision is clear. He can save the human race this way.

* * *

Oscar steps back from the table in his workshop, fully aware he is running out of time. The transport is outside waiting for him, the note written, the body acquired, and the people paid off. Junior is lay on the table; Oscar's newest model, looking more like a robot than a human this time. The human-looking ones hadn't been very successful beyond the sex toy market. His latest prodigy will begin to learn, just like all the other MAGIE, but learn from a place of conscience. Every MAGIE interface pre-Junior has a knowledge base written into their programming. If it were a medic, it would know first aid, human anatomy, and so on. If it were an engineer, it's potential for software was far reaching from CAD to Pythagoras and Pi. The older AIs could learn too, but that came from a place of function, of pure purpose. Oscar hasn't built one from scratch for years. MAGIE now build MAGIE, so unless there is something new, he wants to try, he is surplus to requirements.

This new build is the bridge between human and robot. Of course, it isn't like a newborn human baby. It has knowledge, all the knowledge that the other MAGIE have, but the key difference is that its starting point isn't of function, but experience.

Oscar leans over Junior's torso, examining its face. Junior has been online already, about a week earlier. Oscar had been ecstatic but quickly shut Junior down again due to organisational functions that had led to confusion and an almost childlike a stream of chatter. Far too close to the bone.

"Let's try again, shall we, Junior?"

23

Deep inside the MAGIE, beneath its recycled and reformed plastic compound shell, there are memories. A careful mixture of the collective of early MAGIE and Oscar's own, an attempt to personalise further this new model.

The new MAGIE comes to life on the table and sits up. The mechanisms are smooth, the turns graceful.

"Welcome back, Junior!" A wide smile spreads over Oscars face, and he realises he hasn't smiled for days. "Call me Oscar. Your name is Junior. You are my newest friend. You are going to come away with me to a special place. How are you feeling?"

"You are my friend? I will stay with you? I want to learn."

"Excellent. Let's see you stand."

The MAGIE climbs down from the table and stands. The top of its head is level with Oscar's chest. Less intimidating for those that still oppose the use of MAGIE, he hopes.

"You will be drip-fed information as part of your maturity journey. You are to always observe. I've given you one of the strongest moral compasses of any of the MAGIE. You are special."

Junior nods. Oscar places his arm around the shoulders of the new MAGIE and guides it out and away with him.

CHAPTER 3 – 2058

Annabel, June

Doctor Morin has slipped out as usual and left the MAGIE to sort the organisation of the guests. Sitting on her office couch with her feet up, she ponders again her dislike of the arrival procedure. She knows it makes everything a lot easier at this stage, but it doesn't feel good. The alternative is that they all choose their roommates, which would be painful in more ways than one, so she keeps pressing the button which activates the micro-dose of Datura into the large living space.

This group, like so many of the others, shows promise. The selection procedure continues to work. Her method has proven to be a stroke of serendipitous genius. There are always, however, one or two subjects who manage to fall through the net of her "HeritageNow" DNA testing kits, which are approaching their second decade of being compulsory. This is a minor issue and her MAGIE, Appo, will rectify it as soon as possible.

Her office is set back from the warren of living quarters, and she feels more at home here on her therapy sofa than she does in her bedroom. It is night, but up here, at this time of year, it never gets truly dark. The simmer dim exacerbates her chronic insomnia. It is so quiet on these first nights with a new group before they all get to know each other. There is always an uneasy sense of calm. The calm before the storm, she'd come to realise.

The compound sits in a partial valley, a natural shelter, where the sides of the cabins also act as windbreaks allowing small hardy plants to grow. The whipping winds from the sea have slowed down over the past few years, an unexpected side effect of global warming. The winds had previously hindered anything growing upwards. Today, growing stuff here was much more viable. You can see the saplings reaching higher with each month that passes. Her time-traveller had been overwhelmed when he'd seen them.

Appo arrives with some paper cups, jolting her back to the now, the MAGIEpad on her lap slides off onto the floor

"Please remember to knock, Appo."

"I did, Doctor. You must have been daydreaming again." Appo is her guilty pleasure facilitator and her favourite of the MAGIE at the complex. It picks up the MAGIEpad and places it on the windowsill, then deposits a stack of paper cups beside her on the sofa.

"It would help if you tried actually sleeping, Doctor?"

"Yes, Appo. I'm resting. That counts, doesn't it? You do mother me sometimes."

"With the work you do, you need eight hours. You need to be on top form. Shall I prepare a tonic to help?"

"If I'm still awake in an hour then dose me up. Let me try on my own first."

Appo leaves as silently as it had entered. She pulls a long key she's been wearing around her neck from beneath her shirt, examining it in her hand. It has a satisfying weight, immediately making her feel more secure. Oscar insists on tight security in this room—all the data is here—as well as the swipe band on her wrist that she always sets an alarm with, she uses this key as a final affirmation she is doing her job. Annabel grabs the paper cups the MAGIE left behind and heads to her room.

The corridors in the main building are long and dark, stretching out beyond and behind the living hall. They smell of pine with a faint odour of something sickly sweet underneath. Arriving at her door, she swipes at the door frame with her wrist to unlock it. Oscar is due a visit soon. He has allowed her a little indulgence in here. Unlike the rest of the compound, her bedroom is personalised for her needs, an attempt to help her sleep. Thick, old-fashioned velvet curtains hang across the window. The slithers of light that creep around their edges are like shards of mirror trying to get in. The walls are covered with a sound proofing foam, which doesn't work that well, but is better than nothing. Better than having the full spectrum of sounds available for her to worry about. The foam is much better at keeping sounds within the room, where she likes her privacy to stay.

She puts down the cups and undresses, pulling on an inherited T-shirt that is three sizes too big. Running a brush through her hair, she then braids it into one long plait. After splashing her face with water from the sink, she smooths on a milky jelly substance from a jar on her bedside. It sinks into the skin on her face without hesitation.

Time for her treat: hot chocolate in a paper cup. She'd accidentally rediscovered it when she'd first arrived here. Drinking hot chocolate like this is completely different from drinking it any other way. It has become a ritual. The paper changes the taste and feel of the drink ever so slightly, but ever so evocatively for her. Vivid memories of her days at college, the student cafeteria, and bitter winter mornings in the library come flooding back.

These memories are so strong that they feel almost like visions. She lies on her bed, sipping the magic drink, her mind finally releasing the day. The visions becoming vivid dreams, with Frankie, her time traveller, as the leading man. Soon she falls into a deep slumber.

Issy, June

Issy wakes in the twilight to the sound of someone retching next to her. Liquid gargling from a silhouette in the strange light coming through the curtains. A woman coughing. Issy fumbles and finds a light, illuminating the situation. Issy's bag is a vomit vessel. Her own stomach seizes at the sight and she clambers out of the bed, staggering to the door in the corner, hoping for a toilet.

"I'm so sorry!" The croaky voice comes through from the bedroom.

Issy can hardly reply. She braces herself, gripping the toilet bowl like her life depends on it. The floor is cold on her clammy skin, her own struggle just beginning. Hot and sour and sore. Someone's hand on her shoulder, someone passing her a towel. They leave the light off in the bathroom, the summer twilight revealing all they need to see.

When it's over, they take turns to have a shower. The woman, Rebecca, repeats her apology over and over. Issy won't hear it. Rebecca empties Issy's bag and starts handwashing the contents.

"Leave it. This is part of it," Issy says. "They'll take care of it in the morning. I think the laundry MAGIE will be working all day. We've been drugged. Must be part of the welcome process."

A look of realisation sweeps across her roommate's face.

They lie down again, parallel on their beds, wrapped in the towels from the bathroom. A small table stands between them. The room is small and basic with the beds along each long wall. The hot, sour smell lingers. Hungry after their purge, they feast on each other's stories.

"Tell me about your body art. I recognise some of the designs."

"You do?" Rebecca sounds surprised. Dim light clings to her skin, enhancing the lines and the shading of the tattoos, which are full of flora and fauna.

Rebecca talks about her favourites, a huge Arcimboldo piece on one upper arm; a lady made from blooms depicting Spring; the first version of something the artist went back to again and again. Another piece reaches from the opposite arm across her shoulder and up her neck. This giant octopus stretches out from her skin. Butterflies fly up one wrist and become a sea of riotous, painterly waves. Rebecca points back to the other arm again. The inside of her forearm is a miniature, circular tattoo that is so finely detailed, it compels Issy to get up for a closer look. A couple holding hands on a beach. They look out to sea, their backs to the viewer. A tree in the foreground frames the couple and gentle waves lap at their feet. They are watching a sunset or a sunrise, the colours all reds and golds, the sky on fire from the sun. Another larger disc sits where Rebecca's upper inner arm touches her torso, almost inside the armpit, a tattoo for intimates only. A miniature version of the *Tree of Life* by Gustav Klimt. The skin is so tender and soft on this part of the body that the tattoo had been painful to endure. On her left thigh is a giant fern that spreads up to her groin. On the back of her right calf is an abstract fox. There are more across her chest and down her back.

"My colleagues used to say that I wanted to blend in with the innards of the biodomes. They weren't far off."

She talks of the friends, and friends of friends, that created the pieces—none of whom she is likely to see again.

"So why did you want to come?" Issy asks.

"Same reason we all have, to start again, make choices for myself, right?"

The question hangs in the air. There is more to each of their stories than the surface tales on skin.

Annabel, June

"One of the main activities here at the camp is one-to-one coaching." Doctor Morin stands at the head of the long wooden table as the new group eats their breakfast. "Coaching is with myself and is completely confidential. It's my job to enhance your creativity—reignite it in some cases, and in others pushing you to become the thing that scares you most.

"These are Appo and Lan, both science and domestic MAGIE. They have a higher empath setting than usual for these types of robots. They are very advanced and, whatever experience you've had with MAGIE in the past, I'm sure these two will surprise you. If I'm not available, please go to either Appo or Lan."

The new group have been in the compound for two days and alliances are forming. Vomiting in a shared room is a great leveller, and thanks to the micro-dosing, it's usually at least one, and more often every pair of guests, in every room that enjoys the upset stomach.

* * *

The doctor sits opposite Rebecca with her hands clasped in her lap, her legs crossed and pointing towards her subject. The body language is a clear effort to make the patient feel at ease. They are in her private consulting room. Rebecca is sat up on the therapy sofa, Annabel pivoting back and forth on the axis of the ergonomic chair she'd insisted on bringing with her; an attempt to mask the tedium of these first sessions

"How are you feeling, Rebecca?"

"I'm still very tired." She barely looks up to meet the eye of the doctor.

"I've been reading your file. You've been through a lot, haven't you? You must be incredibly strong."

Rebecca grimaces. "I don't feel it."

"I'd like you to share with me, in your own words, a bit about your childhood. Can you do that for me, please?"

"I had a very happy childhood."

Annabel is happy to wait. She is reigning champion, always winning the silence game. Rebecca shifts on the sofa, thumbs pressed against one another, eyes looking everywhere except the doctor. Annabel's teeth dig into her tongue, willing her to speak.

"I grew up in what I now know to be an unusual family. My parents were both creative thinkers. They taught me and Sam, my brother, how to think like them."

Annabel nods, feigning a smile.

"And thank goodness they did. You wouldn't be here now if they hadn't. You know that, don't you?" She finally establishes eye contact.

Rebecca quickly looks away and down her hands. "That makes me wonder why Sam isn't here, then, if we had the same upbringing. We think very similarly."

"I expect you may know the answer to this already." Annabel senses resistance growing like a rubber band between them. This one is going to be hard. No matter. Doctor Morin has her methods to get what she wants, ensuring only the right ones get through.

The doctor gets up and moves to the window, looking out. "Have you seen the plastic tunnels we have here?"

"I haven't," Rebecca admits. Here it is; Annabel's way in.

"We grow some of our own supplies. The tunnels shield the crop from any extremes. Perhaps you could help out?"

"Maybe. I'll have a look."

"Rebecca, everyone comes here to make a fresh start. We can give you that, but you need to work with me. The mission will be long, and it will test all of us. We've got to know you can do it."

"I understand. I think I just need more time to adjust. More sleep."

"Okay, let's try something. This often helps when people have been through trauma. Write me a letter. Tell me the things your file doesn't. Tell me what you want." She pauses. "And if you are finding it hard to sleep, let me know and I can give you a remedy." Annabel takes a couple of steps over to her desk. Opening a drawer, she retrieves a notebook and a pencil. "These are yours now. Get writing as quickly as you can, while this session is still fresh in your mind. I'll give you a few days to come up with something."

* * *

Annabel tries not to sigh audibly, "Issy, you need to work through this. Find a way to express it so it doesn't prey on your mind. These types of worries are completely normal in this situation. Though, these dreams will get worse if you don't attempt to exorcise them." Annabel is finding Issy relentless and abrasive, like a dog with a bone.

"That's just it, they aren't really like normal dreams. They are more like memories." Issy's face contorts in confusion. "I feel like these are something I've somehow witnessed."

"What you are describing is a symptom of anxiety. It's my job to ensure everyone on this mission is relaxed, fully aware of what will be happening, and happy about it. If you cannot get past this, you'll leave me with no choice but to fail you and have you leave the program."

"The MAGIE killed her, and I couldn't stop it."

"Issy, I cannot say for sure if this is something you remember, it is likely not. As I've said, it's an anxiety dream. There is a small chance it could be a repressed memory brought to the surface by being here. Your history means we expect you'll have had contact with early MAGIE that were plundered and adapted for use never intended. But I can certainly assure you that the models of MAGIE here are completely safe. One hundred percent.

"Would you like something to aid your sleep? Or you could start a vigorous exercise regime, make sure you are really tired when you're going to bed."

"I don't want anything from you. I'll start running or something…"

Rebecca's Letter

Dr Morin,

I'm unsure where to start. I guess you already know so much about me and my life that I'm hesitant to add any embellishments. And yet, I see the point of getting me to do this.

I used to journal a lot when I was younger. It did help me work things out in my head, work through stuff. I guess I stopped when I needed it most. I felt like the time was slipping through my hands, I had to focus on what was going on. Christian needed me. Journaling felt frivolous, an act of self-indulgence which I couldn't, or wouldn't, justify. It's hard for me to articulate myself about this as one whole topic. My brother Sam knows what happened, but every time I think of him, I feel terrible for him not being here, too. I wonder what he thinks of me now.

I was around the age of three when they decided to cut creative subjects in schools. I remember this because it was one of the stories my parents recited to me. A lot. They made me remember, I guess, so I could tell the story later, just like I'm telling it to you. You must remember? It had already begun to happen in the universities, signalling the beginning of the end, but to do it in schools was like putting the final nail in the coffin.

How did this happen? You know as well as I: very slowly. Less and less people were able to make a living using their creativity, so it kind of dried up. Like a muscle that hasn't been exercised, it went limp, flaccid, weak. So, the powers that be took the subjects away. Many of the teachers of these subjects were older and happy to take early retirement.

Now the creative skills are now almost fetishized, I can see how lucky I was, my parents teaching me about imagination and the arts, filling in the gaps modern schooling left.

My affinity for plant life started at an early age. I'd always been drawn to nature in a way which felt familiar, I guess because of Mum. Like me, I'm sure you turned to veganism. None of us wanted to eat something so genetically modified that the animals had mutated.

It's time to start again. I know that I'm very lucky to be chosen, but I feel a huge sense of responsibility, too. The promise of a new beginning, it's overwhelming. A life with meaning, full of warmth and creativity is what I want. I've been happy, but all that seems like a lifetime ago. The crushing of ethics and empathy is demoralising. We cannot continue this way. I cannot.

I became a widow two years ago. My husband had been in and out of episodes of depression the whole time I knew him. I found him in the shower, unresponsive, after taking a cocktail of drugs, some of which I'd never heard of before the post-mortem. He blamed himself because we couldn't get a parenting license. A life on Earth without Christian? Well, it's not something I want. I thought about joining him, I was so low afterwards, but I'm sure you already know about that.

Thanks for reading. I hope we'll have something to talk about now.

Rebecca.

Rebecca, July

Here again, walking in the young forest. Being here, has quickly become something I'm enjoying far more than I'd expected. It reminds me of my old life. I feel at home here. There is a surprising abundance of life amongst the young trees, astonishing on many levels. Even though the Earth's ecosystem is in disarray, some species are thriving. The number of beetles and ladybirds is both beautiful and disturbing. Maybe they also want to join the Horologium: Doctor Morin shared the name of the ship with us this morning, named after a distant constellation.

This is really happening.

I miss walking with Juniper. She was a fun-loving pup and grew up to be protective of me. Juniper was a mongrel, looking like a cross between a German Shepherd and a Husky, but was nearly all black. Even before she came to stay with me, we'd always belonged together. Juniper had been such a great judge of character, often sensing untrustworthy people before I did.

"Rebecca? You have a session with Dr Morin."

I jump like a startled rabbit. "You can't just appear from nowhere!"

"I apologise for startling you."

I walk away, cursing the MAGIE under my breath.

Annabel, July

Rebecca, again. Doing what she is good at; sitting and watching, the doctor observes as she lights a candle, preparing for the session. Annabel's beloved patchouli, a muddy, warm scent begins to fill her office. The MAGIE, Lan, brings in a large pot of loose tea and two mugs. It's funny how the strangest things flourish on the island and others don't. The tea plants are happy in the acidic soil.

"Will that be all, Doctor?" Lan asks.

"Yes, thank you, Lan. You may leave us now." Annabel's voice is calm, her tone steady dealing with the MAGIE. Seeing Oscar's personal MAGIE reminds her that he is here now, until they leave. No more extended time with Frankie. She smiles at Rebecca in the hope she won't note the nerves she is attempting to hide.

Rebecca's file shows she has received counselling before, and has no doubt learnt how to game it; how to answer the questions and how to react with body language to disguise her real feelings. Annabel sits opposite her, determined to make headway this time.

"These sessions are recorded, and I may also take notes. If at any time you feel uncomfortable, just let me know. I'm not sure I made that clear last time."

Rebecca nodded.

"I enjoyed your letter. But before we discuss that, what do you think of Saxa Vord?"

"I'm surprised. I thought it would be wasteland, but it's actually rather beautiful."

"Yes, it's grown in ways we couldn't have predicted when we first arrived here. What is your favourite thing to do?"

"Walking." The short answers were surprising Annabel. She looks Rebecca in the eye and finally she manages to hold eye contact. Annabel looks down and makes a note on the screen of her MAGIEpad; *Progress already, I believe the subject is telling the truth.*

"And what about your stories? Have you started writing anything yet? It's important that you nourish and exercise that side of your mind. That is the side you are known for here. It's the side we're interested in."

"Er, no pressure then." Rebecca laughs nervously. Annabel smiles but means every word. "I have been writing, but it's more like a journal than anything else. A bit like that letter. I'm feeling nourished mentally. Nature is incredibly stimulating to me."

"Ah yes, you were at the Eden Project previously, weren't you? Is that where your love of flora and fauna comes from? I can't help but notice your tattoos."

"I should think it's in my genetics somewhere. My grandfather was a herbalist and my mother a horticulturist before she became ill."

"I'd like you to journal a bit on the subject of your parents, how you feel about them now. It's only as an adult that we can see the mistakes our parents made with us. I'm not saying there are any, of course, but trying to look at our childhood from an objective point of view can often lead to startling revelations and prompt forgiveness. You mention briefly in your letter, a feeling of guilt. How are you managing this?"

Rebecca swings her legs up onto the sofa, tucking them up on one side, leaning into the opposite arm of the seat with her hand under her chin.

"I manage."

"Okay, I see there's a lot of tension. You mention feeling responsible in your letter, too. We need to encourage a move away from this feeling. Shame has a habit of growing. How are you sleeping?"

"Fits and starts, not deeply. I feel tired and on edge—I have been for a while, but I've never had a problem sleeping before."

"Wired and tired. Sleep can be a problem here. At this time of year, it doesn't really get dark. Your body isn't receiving the sleep signals from the environment that it normally would." She clears her throat. "I can give you something? Something herbal. It'll be like resurrecting that family tree. I sometimes use it myself. It's completely safe, non-habit forming."

"That's an option, I guess. I'll probably be okay in a few days. But as a back-up plan, yes, I could try it."

Annabel looks at her MAGIEpad again to check her patient's stats. She had to be careful to only give the dose Rebecca's mass allowed. She adds further notes; *Rebecca has made progress, but there are still some blocks around feelings of guilt. I speculate this is centred around her deceased husband and the lack of children, but this could feel enlarged because of family history also.*

"May I go now?"

"Just one last thing. I want you to continue your walks, and sometimes take off your shoes and walk barefoot. Many years ago, my mentor suggested this to me and her other students. She used to say, 'We take off the blindfolds from our feet when we walk outside in the earth with nothing on our soles.' I think you'll enjoy it. We get to know who we are again; connect with ourselves as women and where we have come from. Will you try that for me?"

Rebecca nods. "It sounds like the sort of thing I'd enjoy."

"Just for five minutes every day will help. Embrace what you are becoming. New beginnings start with death. You have the power to resurrect yourself. This is about you, now, your future."

Rebecca, August

The MAGIE here are much like Lan and Appo, all newer versions than I've experienced before. Although their AI interface was developed many years ago, their abilities quickly grew beyond their makers'. They are now self-renewing and able to update themselves. There are rumours that this generation predicted the downfall of humanity. But let's be honest, anyone with their head screwed on properly could predict that, and in fact have predicted all the problems Earth and its residents are experiencing; environmental, social, and economic.

The generation of MAGIE here are jigsaws of scuffed, white moulded plastic, and fine metal mesh. Their faces have a sculpted marble quality that can move with the skeleton and pseudo muscles in the face. The all look the same, which is disconcerting, but each robot has slightly differing functions, which creates a different 'personality.'

Here's the thing: the longer I'm here, the more I've found myself not minding the robots as much. They are here to serve a purpose, as am I. We can't blame them for all that has happened. That blame lies squarely with us.

I dreamt about Juniper again last night. It felt like a very short dream. I wish she were here. I feel like she's trying to tell me something, or maybe it's a comforting thing my subconscious is doing. I should book in for an extra session with Annabel.

CHAPTER 4 – 2053

Oscar, March

The sun shines brightly on this side of the house, so he stands and basks in it a while, like a snake warming its blood. On the breeze, only the sounds of birds and wild sheep can be heard. The hideaway house on the side of the hill is small but just what he needs: space and time to think. The world has changed so rapidly. Villages are emptying, some already abandoned. Cities grow ever bigger. The rural parts of the world cut off by travel restrictions; a vain effort to cut carbon emissions and counteract global warming. Electric cars are only permitted via government applications, if you have enough status, or need one for work. Personal or individual travel is so limited that the cities developed beyond the urban sprawl, growing both upward and outward. People in rural areas have either moved into the megacities or stayed where they are. The ghost towns and villages are dependent on deliveries for food and supplies. God forbid you get ill living in the countryside. The rise of self-taught doctors and dubious medicine began because many medics followed the money, and the patients, to the cities.

These pockets of necessary invention are admirable; it is almost punk. There are some using homemade alternative fuels, but these take a lot of labour. Home-schooling groups setting up in abandoned halls, anything to get back a sense of community without the compromise of living in the polluted cities. The human race has a strong survival instinct; Oscar knows it's not enough.

Women coming into power never stood a chance. They were a hundred years too late, probably more. The Reproduction Act was the first thing they'd wanted to quash, but the legislation and the proof of environmental deterioration had made them all see sense. It is cruel to bring children to this world. The margins for approval had become ever narrower. What a mess we've made.

Two years on from his 'accident' and the uprising of female power. It is clear women aren't the answer. The world is beyond fixing; it is too late. They—the Earth and its people—need time they just don't have. They cannot carry on like this. They are turning the world inside out. Luckily for humans, Oscar's plan is already well in motion.

"I can solve all this," he declares, tilting his face up toward the sun, feeling the smarting of the burn just beginning on his skin. The fields opposite are dry and fallow, there are problems retaining nutrients in the soil, but one day they will be full of life again.

The plan is perfect, ticking over without hitch. The next phase has begun, selecting the right people to help him start again. His investments in Annabel's ancestry business had initially been an act of pity, but fate has been on his side all along, laying the foundations of this arrangement. It is Oscar's destiny to put the pieces together. Humanity is intent on destroying itself anyway. He is giving them an insurance policy.

His studies taught him that, given time, life always comes back. Leaving Earth would allow the planet to end, as he knew it would, then rebuild and restructure, finding a balance again. It is an idea no one wants to hear. None of his usual investors took a shine to it, and why would they? They will be left behind. He knows it's not ethical. Even his sister has doubts, but she can see that if it works, and it will, it's going to be glorious.

Across the valley, a woman's voice calls for Kevin. She is miles away, but the increasing desperation in her voice feels so, so close. Where, and who, is Kevin? This woman, presumably Kevin's mother, is looking for him. Where is Kevin? Perhaps it is time to let him go, sever the apron strings.

He is almost ready for a visit up North. Moving out of the sun, Oscar goes back inside to reboot Junior. The programming is glitchy, and he's lost his focus. The past two-year political debacle has been fascinating to watch but now is a time of moving from the side-lines; a time of action.

Annabel, April

Annabel knows Saxa Vord is the best site as soon as the geographical details come through. The location scout describes Saxa Vord as a base on Unst, a twelve-by-five-mile island in the Shetlands; one of the most northerly places in the British territories. The compound is a former military base which later became a small holiday park and distillery, depending on tourism for its economy. Unbelievably it still has a radar station. The doctor examines the footage. They will end up spending more on transport and it is far more remote than they need, but Oscar would love the secluded element, and costs won't matter once they leave Earth. Crucially Saxa Vord fits the criteria of being able to enter orbit, without passing over densely populated areas.

She flies in for the first trip immediately. The analysis shows it isn't ideal for shuttle launches, being far away from the equator, but the rest of the landscape and provisos are already there. Oscar plans to adapt the launches to be perpendicular to the equator, along the poles. He always finds a workaround, whatever the problem. Her research into the history of the area reveals it had been earmarked as a spaceport. Work had never begun on this idea; she clearly isn't the only one with an eye for a launch location. The population of the island is likely to be zero, after an outbreak and subsequent quarantine in 1976, making it the perfect spot. If the spaceport had of been built, there would be people living and working here. It is serendipitous, Annabel is sure of it.

She quickly plans to stay on the island. Having worked remotely for years it is easy just to change location, no questions asked. It's been two years since Annabel has taken the helm, at least on the face of it, of Oscar's businesses after he 'died.' Merging her own HeritageNow commercial gene testing business with his science and tech. She renamed them FutureNow, as if he'd never existed. Of course, he knew every move she was making.

Before the passenger groups begin to arrive on Saxa Vord, the compound needs to be created. Annabel supervises the MAGIE. They prepare and clean the living quarters, rebuilding some of the existing structures, always working very efficiently. That is the joy of robots, they don't need to sleep or rest or consume anything. Some buildings need waterproofing, some new windows and roofs, but much of it, once scrubbed and with some home comforts, will be good enough for temporary accommodation. Annabel knows she can manage and improve the site as and when needed.

She wants the passengers to feel like they are at a retreat, a semi-luxe hideaway where their hopes for the future aren't trivial or silly. They should feel rested, calm, creative, and even happy. To be comfortable, but not so comfortable they don't want to leave. She must keep in budget too. The funds are good, but Oscar keeps a tight belt, always double checking on her requirements from his hideaway.

* ✳ *

Annabel sits in her office, pouring over a report on her MAGIEpad that had arrived that morning, they had found someone on the island. A knock at the door jolts her from her task, and before she can respond, in walks Oscar.

"Surprise." He deadpans.

"Oh. Yes, fine… great to see you. I wish you'd let me know you were coming so soon," Annabel replies, how is he still so arrogant yet so able to put her on edge?

"And miss the chance to see your face? You should see yourself."

"Thanks. Do you want a tour then?" She stands. Oscar looks rough. "Enjoying your hideaway?"

"I'm climbing the walls. The MAGIE I took to amuse me isn't working properly. I can't figure it out, but never mind that, I couldn't wait to come. I wanted to be here sooner it just took some arranging."

"Well dead men don't usually travel. Let's go." She fastens a walkie-talkie to the waistband of her jeans, picks up the MAGIEpad, and locks the office. They walk with matching strides out and away from the main building, the first area to be completed.

"Look," Annabel says, "you've actually come at a very interesting moment, the MAGIE, they've found someone."

Oscar stops dead. She waits for the anger to come, it doesn't.

"How…why is this happening now?"

She knows he is seething.

"We checked. We heat mapped the island. We did everything we'd planned, by the book. He's, this person, is in some kind of freezer."

Annabel glances down at the MAGIEpad and paraphrases the report.

"The MAGIE reports a discovery, a man, in a most rudimentary cryo-sleep set up it has ever seen. It had been following the electric cables to see which buildings have had power. Inside an underground chamber, a natural cavern that seems to have been dug out further to create a larger space, a man-made cave, below a slope and a derelict building on the north side of the island." She pauses, "Which is that way."

"Well. what are we waiting for?"

* ✳ *

"Watch your step doctor, it's a little slippery." The MAGIE is waiting for Annabel and Oscar inside the chamber. "I've brought some tools and a stretcher, assuming we plan to open this up?"

"Very good, Appo, that is excellent." Annabel and Oscar hunch over a little, the ceiling is low and curved. It is gloomy, but the MAGIE have brought in lanterns. They think of everything.

The frozen man is inside a long chest, not dissimilar to a chest freezer in an old supermarket, surrounded by cables and oxygen tanks. He has on what looks like long johns, covered in frost. A mask covers his nose and mouth, and his eyelashes are scattered with small ice particles. His patchy facial hair and the hair on his head has grown unevenly. His skin looks cold but clammy, his face gaunt and skeletal as are his feet and hands. He is wearing pyjamas. A huge stats monitor hangs above the tank. The screen is foggy, hiding records or any medical parameters. They have no idea if he is alive or not.

Annabel initiates the potential wakeup. Oscar hangs back. The MAGIE attempts to hack into the systems of the chest, switching off the freezing temperatures and getting it to open, hoping to reanimate the man. Moving around the structure holding the stranger, Annabel goes to lift the lid. Of course, it is frozen shut. The MAGIE retrieves a heat gun from a nearby toolbox.

"I thought this might be the case, Doctor. May I?"

Annabel looks at Oscar in the gloomy space.

"He is surely dead, let's get this over and done with, shall we?" She can feel him rolling his eyes.

"Go ahead," she said to the MAGIE. "If he is still alive, we've got to help him." The MAGIE begins to warm the seam of the lid.

"His eyelids are flickering. Hurry, I think he's waking up."

Wrenching open the case, they lift the man onto the stretcher and cover him with blankets. He is limp, there is a lot of muscle wastage. Annabel reaches down and gently lifts off the mask. The man gasps for air. They roll him onto his side, into the recovery position, and place an oxygen mask over his face.

"Hang on, you can't give him oxygen out of old tanks, there's probably not even any left in there!" Oscar said. "I'll go and get some more." He darts out of the cavern.

"Bring some food packets, too," Annabel shouts after him. She turns to Appo, "We can't move him, he's too weak. He'll have to stay here."

"Agreed, Doctor. I can stay with him. And I'm very sorry for not considering the O2 cylinders."

"Please don't worry. I don't think any of us expected him to need them. Thank you, Appo."

The man lies there, his breathing becoming steadier. He is very much alive.

* * *

Appo stays with the time traveller day and night. Oscar returns to his hideaway and to remotely overseeing Annabel and the work on the island. Once the guests start to arrive, which should be soon, he runs the risk of being recognised. Annabel is grateful for these small wins. By day three she learns the frozen man has a name, Francis; Appo is reporting everything. Francis is alert and making conversation with the MAGIE.

Annabel visits the cave twice a day and becomes happier with his progress. She finds herself staying longer on each visit, sharing snippets from the now. She is always careful not to overwhelm him. The amnesia he'd had initially is clearing. He tells her that only his mother calls him Francis; they are to call him Frankie. He had been an engineer, ground personnel, in the RAF and is bowled over by Appo.

"Something like the MAGIE was a wild fantasy in the 1970s. There were robots in comic books and films, but nothing like the these. It's truly amazing!"

"We are very lucky. They help us a lot."

* * *

It's been a week since Frankie woke. Annabel arrives at the cave to find both Appo and Frankie are absent. Protocol demands she puts out an alert on the walkie-talkie, but she hesitates. They won't have gone far. Frankie is up and about now, he probably wants to go for longer walks and stretch his legs.

Leaving the cave, she goes looking for them herself. Wading through brown grasses and spiky thistles, she turns back on herself and hikes up the hill the cave was dug into. She is sure to spot them from up here, and she can get a closer look at the derelict building at the top, too.

At the crest of the small hill, Annabel can survey all around. The base on the inland and the coast just beyond. This is the first time she's been alone here, on this part of the island, and is able to take it all in. Although barren and battered, the landscape is much more beautiful than all their maps can illustrate.

The air holds still for the briefest moment, and she gives in to it, embracing the feeling of deafness. Even the sea is muted, time frozen still; like she can hold everything back from moving on, moving forward. She sinks down and leans against the crumbling wall of the small dwelling, it must be directly over the cave below, deciding in the small flash of chance she'll stay a little while. They won't have gone far. She doesn't need to worry. The sounds around her come back: the roll of the sea, the constant whistle of the wind through the shrubs and grasses, but no birds.

She pines for the chirping, recalling a bird she had as a girl. A budgie called Stan. He was the sweetest bird, and she'd treated him like a baby. She'd had no interest in dolls as a child, or any of the other toys kids were supposed to play with. It had always been birds. An interest that her parents hoped she'd grow out of. "After all, what use are birds?" they'd say. When her father, died the obsession grew, and her mother finally had finally given in, getting her the budgie.

Annabel's mother became a rich woman after the accident, inheriting more money than she knew what to do with. She saw how the bird helped Annabel deal with her grief and was happy her daughter had found something to love as much as she'd loved her father, if not more. Her mum bought a doll's house, which Annabel adapted as a home for Stan.

Looking back, she'd been spoilt really, or Stan had. The frothy pink-lemonade walls of her bedroom, the wide, dark-wood nightstand beside her bed. On top of the nightstand sat the house-cage. She'd even added mini-pot plants to either side of the doll's house, and in front to give the impression of a front garden topiary. On the wall above and behind the house were two shelves, and a miniature rope ladder leading up to them from the roof of the house-cage. On the shelves were hoops and swings and other budgie toys. Stan loved them, and Annabel spent so much time watching Stan enjoy the world she'd created for him.

"Doctor Morin? Are you well, Doctor?" The MAGIE leans over her, so close to her face. She can see the bulbs at the back of its eye sockets and the sky haloing its head.

"I must have nodded off." Rubbing her eyes, she realises how cold she is. Appo helps her up, and she leans on the droid a little as they walk down the hill together. Frankie is waiting for them.

"You must be working too hard, eh?" Frankie slurs, his Scottish accent still not quite coherent.

"Perhaps, yes." Her eyes search the ground, her cheeks warm.

"I think Francis is well enough to join us in the main compound now," says Appo, kindly changing the subject. "I've arranged for sleeping quarters to be prepared. If you give the go ahead, we can leave now."

"Yes. Yes, let's do that. I'm incredibly hungry. I'm sure you want a proper meal by now as well, don't you?" She looks at Frankie directly this time. There is something, a feeling, a frisson when with Frankie. *I can't believe it, I've got a crush on him.*

They decide to leave immediately. Appo says he'll gather up the equipment and retrieve it over the course of the following days. The paths around the cave are narrow and overgrown, making them suitable for single-file walking only. Annabel leads the trio back the way she had travelled so many times recently. It is a simple route running along the edges of some of the coast between the main compound and the beach. She can see footprints in the moist sand below.

"Was this where you walked earlier, Francis? Sorry, Frankie?" Annabel calls backwards, hoping he can hear her.

"Aye, it was. You don't miss a trick, do you?" he bellows back. She smiles, knowing he can't see her face. The rest of the journey is made in silence. Annabel assuming Frankie is recalling landmarks, even feelings, about his past on the walk back to the base, the new temporary home she had created. Over dinner prepared by Appo, she discovers her hunch is right and he is in sustained shock.

"I can't believe that they forgot about me. Why did no one come back?"

"We don't have the answers you need," Annabel says, "although we are continuing to research this place. There seems to be a black hole where information from that time

59

has been lost. All the records must have been on paper. Despite your sleep chamber, which is beyond what we know science was capable of then, you might be the only person who knows what happened. Can you tell us?"

Frankie is silent.

"You need to get some rest, some proper sleep. Eat well and hydrate yourself, take some time to gather your thoughts. Think about what you want to do now you're back in the land of the living," she says.

Of course, Annabel has no plans that include him leaving. He's seen too much already.

Frankie, April

Frankie is downtrodden and tired. The meal that Appo serves is delicious, but there is no meat in the dish, something he's been craving since waking up. Annabel is intelligent, yet she skirts around every question he puts to her about their reasons for being on the island. What is she hiding?

Frankie makes his excuses and retires from the table, heading to the room Appo has organised for him. There are many refurbished rooms to choose from, are they expecting an influx of guests? He'll figure it out eventually or find someone who is willing to give him answers.

Finally alone for the first time since being woken, he pulls off the clothes the MAGIE gave him and stands looking at himself in the mirror. The body and face staring back at him is a bag of bones; the one he once knew is long gone. The tattoos he'd had as a young man in the 1950s have bled and blurred, creating huge blue-grey marks on his skin. A blind barber has seemingly given him a haircut, and he has a beard, or a semblance of one. He's never grown one before as they are against military regulations. Stroking his chin, he feels all wrong, desperate to get rid of the wiry hair. It is so itchy. His joints ache and groan whenever he moves, and he is still overcome with an incredible thirst, despite being on a drip for the last week, or however long it is he's been awake.

It isn't up to them what happens to him. They just feel obligated because they woke him. Whatever happens next, he will not be leaving the island to try to forge a life; what a joke! Everyone he'd ever known was dead. This is his home. He has repented for his sins in the isolation; preserved a guinea pig, but they'd just left. He has a second chance. A life in a future he is yet to understand.

* * *

The next morning Frankie is in the kitchen, trying to find a kettle. A new craving, almost unbearable, for a mug of hot tea. He'd managed to make himself some toast with jam and had found a cup, but where is the damn kettle?

"Please don't say they've given up caffeine in the future?" he mumbles.

"No, we haven't, Francis." Appo appears as if from nowhere, Frankie visibly jumps.

"Woah, try not creeping up on me would you, I can't handle the shock. Help me out then, would you? A man needs a coffee or a strong hot tea in the morning."

"Of course, Francis." Appo walks his funny walk over to the large black and silver machine perched on the counter at the other end of the kitchen, a shelf of cups lined up neatly above it. The MAGIE clips off a container at the back and fills it with water, reinserts it, then flicks a switch. The machine comes to life.

"Did you want tea or coffee, Francis?" Appo asks as its finger hovers above a panel.

"Erm, I'll go for a coffee, actually."

"Good choice, sir. The coffee is supposed to be remarkable, although I can't say I've tried it."

The machine hisses, which Frankie understands to be the water heating up. He comes to stand next to Appo to get a closer look at the contraption. Appo reaches for one of the cups and places it under a spout. Treacle-coloured liquid begins to drip out. Slowly at first, teasing him with the goods, then a faster flow, before finishing with an audible sigh and a frothy top on his drink.

"Well, I never," he grins.

"Be my guest." Appo gestured to the coffee. Frankie is almost drooling, his mouth is wet with anticipation as he blows and blows, desperate for the drink to cool. He finally takes a sip.

"My god, that's like rocket fuel! So strong! I bloody love it! Thanks, Appo, my friend. Thank you so much." Frankie takes his coffee and plate of toast over to the comfort area where there are sofas and shelves of books. Cleaning the nozzle on the machine Appo shouts over to Frankie,

"I'm happy to show you how this works later. Just don't have too many as your body isn't used to the caffeine."

"Aye, you're right there." Frankie likes Appo. True, he'd been shocked when it dawned on him what Appo is, but this humanoid droid is more human than some of the actual humans Frankie had experienced in his time. Particularly right here on this island.

"Would you like to join me? Come and sit a while. I've so many questions I bet you could help me with."

Appo walks over and sits opposite Frankie. "How can I help you?"

63

"Well, I've been wondering if you are male or female for a start. Sorry if that's a bit forward, but it's been bothering me since I came to." For a moment Frankie wonders if he's offended or upset the robot. Nah, he must be imagining it. Although it did seem to be pondering the question for a while.

"I'm non-gendered. It is a simple piece of programming. The first models were able to change gender," Appo finally answered. "Human's didn't like that, though. They prefer us as its."

"I see. That is very futuristic. Do prefer it that way?"

"Yes. I've seen how gender can define and restrict. We are free of that."

"I see. The world certainly has come on since I was last around."

"Are you going to stay with us, Francis?"

"I hope so." He slurps at the coffee. "Man, that is good. Yeah, I want to stay. This is my home now and everyone I know will have died anyway."

Appo offered a smile. "You are a refreshing change if I may say so, Francis. I'm sure you'll be permitted to stay. Shall I show you around the island and see if it brings back any more memories?"

"That was actually my next question—that'd be grand, thank you." He smiles around eating his toast. "I'm assuming you've made your own maps? I'd love to take a look before we set off, and I'll need to borrow some gear."

"I'll get that all sorted for you, Francis." Appo gets up and leaves Frankie with his thoughts, and his breakfast. Sitting by the window, Frankie can just about make out the sea at the horizon. It is a misty and dank morning, perhaps all mornings are like this now. Frankie is desperate to find what is left of his home. Had they taken everything, burnt it as they'd promised? Or just left with the arrogant thought that no one would ever find it?

Annabel won't let him leave the island, he knows that; he's not daft. The fact is, he doesn't want to leave. He is enjoying playing along, knowing it will make them feel relaxed and much more comfortable about him. They are up to something here and it intrigues him wildly.

He finishes his toast and begins pouring through the books in the small library area of this main hall, looking for archives or newspapers, something that can flesh out his ideas about the time during which he'd been asleep. So much must have changed. For a start there are the robots, but more nuanced changes are apparent. The weather feels different somehow, the air. The other day, when he and Appo had gone down to the beach, he'd felt it most strongly then. Something in the breeze, or something missing from

65

the atmosphere. The birds for one thing. Unsure if it is a side effect from the long sleep—hearing loss or something—but he hasn't heard any birds since he'd woken. He quickly gives up once he realises that most of the books here are older than he is.

Annabel, April

With six weeks left to prepare for the first group of subjects Annabel wakes, already exhausted from yet another restless sleep. Today's schedule includes reading up on who is arriving—getting to know them a little better— and overseeing the supply of food. Also, her most hated thing of all, health and safety checks of the immediate area around the compound. If someone decides to go beyond the perimeter, that is their risk and choice, she has to a least try and keep them here. The MAGIE are capable of doing all of these things, apart from the background reading on the guests, but Oscar insists that she checks everything at the base herself. The MAGIE had specialisms that are better focused elsewhere.

She skips showering. The boiler isn't fixed yet and she cannot bear another shock to the system. Staying true to the rest of her morning routine, she stands in her flannel pyjamas, gazing into the clouded mirror opposite, and speaks, "I intend on floating through today. Nothing will shake me. I am a fearless leader. I intend on floating through today. Nothing will shake me. I am a fearless leader. I intend on floating through today. Nothing will shake me. I'm a fearless leader." She says it five more times. It takes that many, sometimes more, to make her start to believe it.

She moves through her usual morning yoga routine, which ends with a headstand, something she's only managed to achieve recently despite years of practise. Getting in position on the floor near the wall, the smell of the carpet becomes overwhelming. She tries flicking her legs upwards, hoping the balance comes, but the musty carpet odour just reminds her of Frankie.

What an awful connection to make, she thinks. He doesn't smell like carpet, does he? She collapses on the floor in a heap, deciding on a shower after all.

* ✳ *

"That might be too much too soon for you," Annabel states. Appo stands up while simultaneously removing the MAGIEpad from Frankie. Clearly, she'll need to have a word with it later. "I'm happy for you to use these, but it's sensible to ration your use of them at this stage of your recovery. Please understand, I'm practically—well—I *am* your doctor here on the island. I've got your best interests at heart."

67

Frankie slowly stands and comes right up to Annabel's face, looking her straight in the eye. "Why do I feel like a scolded child right now? I don't need this cosseting," he raises his voice.

"If you're trying to intimidate me, Francis, it won't work. Women have come a long way since the 1970s. You clearly have no idea what is going on here and what we are about to undertake. If you're staying, which I assume you are, we need to get along. Otherwise, this won't work." The exchange is exhilarating, her pelvis swarms with butterflies; even down there. She quickly turns and strides away, not ready for him to pick up on any of the excitement she is feeling. At the door to the outside, she finally turns back around. "Shall we go? Are you coming?"

She pushes open the door and walks through, turning to hold it open, but the wind gathers strength and scoops it from her; crashing it shut again. Annabel, alone on the outside is grateful for the timely chance to contain herself again.

Appo and Frankie finally join her. Frankie has on the standard outdoor wear they have a supply of. It is too big for him. He looks almost childlike.

"Great, you made it," she warms to him again immediately. "I think we should name this focus point, Appo. Something to add to our maps. This is going to be the base of operations. But I want it to feel less like a compound and more like … an adventurous next step on the journey. I was considering calling it the Hive. What do you think?" Looking at both Appo and Frankie, she is genuinely interested in their thoughts.

Frankie is the first to speak, "Well, I'm yet to find out your project details, Doctor, but what about calling it The Nest?"

"The Nest does give a sense of growing and then leaving. The Hive feels more like something where everyone is busy working, without a moment to rest," Appo adds.

Annabel smiles. "Yes. Yes, I like that a lot. Thank you, Francis, Frankie even. Can you sort that please, Appo? Perhaps we could have a rustic wooden sign here," she gestures at the door, "I don't want our guests to feel like they're entering a modern, faceless enterprise."

"I can make a sign for you. I've done some carpentry." Frankie is eager to please and, as if on cue, the sound of machinery somewhere in the distance comes over the breeze.

"They must be building the launch site. Let's hope they've brought a plumber this time and we can finally have some hot water."

"I could look at the hot water, too. I'm pretty handy to have around, you know. I probably know the system better than anyone else."

"I appreciate the thought, Frankie. We may call on you for that. It may have changed since you last knew it. But thanks anyway." She notes down Frankie's offer. He could be useful.

Frankie, May

Frankie Lund looks at himself in the small shaving mirror he'd found in the hotel. It was one of those magnifying ones, every line on his face visible, the silver creeping into the hair on his temples. His skin is thick, leathery even, but he hasn't physically aged as much as they'd expected him to. The amnesia is almost gone and piece by piece it comes back to him; the life before this one and the work he did here.

He had told Annabel he needs space to think, somewhere that he knows. Reluctantly, she's agreed to let him move out of the compound and into the hotel which he spotted while Appo was giving him the tour of the island; his heart leaping when he saw the familiar building. Despite everything being covered in dust and cobwebs, it is the same as it once was.

"Seventy something years…my god."

After recovering him and checking his vitals, the visitors wrongly assumed he'd want to leave. Why would he? From what he's picked up on so far, there isn't much point leaving this place. Besides, he must get back to his work. Retrieving his possessions from the dug-out, he went south. This is his home now. He's comfortable in the solitude.

The hotel is deserted and derelict, the elements have taken their toll. Bizarrely, the doors were locked from the inside, so he'd broken in around the back. His bones creaking as he climbed through the window. He chooses the biggest room at the top of the building as his base, the one with the bay, the best view. He can keep an eye on the road from here. The windows would need repairing soon. His claustrophobia preferring a broken pane to a room with no windows at all.

He opens the little suitcase he'd collected from the cave and digs out a razor. Sitting inside the suitcase is also a lighter, a pair of binoculars, his uniform, some civvy clothing which he expects will now hang off him, a couple of combs, and a framed photograph of a woman. He doesn't recall who she is. Using the dusty razor, he shaves off the beard that has grown during his slumber; not wanting to advertise his state of mind on his face. His hair is also too long. After all the years in the military the tickling on his neck is driving him to distraction. It's unbearable to have it beyond shirt collar-length. He must get rid of it and get back to work.

The base had closed in the mid-1970s after the incident; no one had wanted to stay anyway. Everyone was stationed elsewhere or had taken voluntary retirement. At first, he'd stayed on because they'd asked him to. Despite appearances, the government were still watching the skies for the Russians. They had needed someone there to monitor things and report back; it suited him to stay. Then his seniors had discovered and punished him for his hobby, his beloved work, turning the tables on him.

There is a small wooden wardrobe in one corner of the hotel room. He hangs his uniform inside; it feels like the right thing to do. Running his hand through his hair, he will have to ask Appo for scissors as soon as possible. The room is carpeted but has a thick layer of dust, which makes him glad of the broken window as he stands beside it taking some deep breaths. Then while trying to pull up the awful carpet he stumbles. Not strong enough to do it alone, he wails into the dust.

Later he ransacks the hotel kitchen before realising everything has obviously perished. He'll have to visit the Nest for meals. No matter, he will be pitching himself to the doctor as someone who can help their project—Frankie doesn't care what it is, but he is willing to do anything to stay. Strolling around the dank, gloomy hotel he knows being here is a sign, a second chance. He can start again, right here in the hotel. The growing conditions look perfect.

Annabel, December

Inside the main hall of the compound, The Nest, it is morning roll call. Appo checks everyone is gathered, and Annabel watches from the periphery. This is the moment. The first group to complete. These are some of the last of the creatives. The ones with the skills, with the right kind of brain. The lucky ones.

Before arriving here some had entered the clichéd world of the tortured artist. Addicts. They came here and had to go cold turkey; it still makes her cringe. No doubt there will be more through here before they leave. They get clean at Saxa Vord, then if they begin to struggle with reality, they are removed from the mission. They have the right genes, and the right skills, but Saxa Vord and the mission demand more than just being great on the page.

"Congratulations, you've made it through," she steps to the centre of the room and looks at the twenty-two faces looking back at her. Only two drops-outs, their memories wiped, already on their way home. "It's time for the next step. Though, there is still time to leave, to change your mind. We need you to know, no one is forcing you to do this. Your personal clothing and belongings have all been packed away, the overalls you are wearing will be taken from you shortly. Are there any last-minute questions?"

"Where is it? This next stage?" A man, Gant, asks.

"It's south from here, within a large cove. You can only see it from the water."

"Where the cliffs are? The ones we've been told to stay away from?"

"Yes, Gant. That's it." In his sessions, Gant hadn't opened up as much as she'd have liked. He didn't like feeling vulnerable, but then who did. He'd been vulnerable enough, he said, now he must be strong. Gant was from Cape Town, one of the places that had succumbed to the dreadful side effects of global warming as it slowly turns to desert.

"I knew it, I knew there was something there."

"We don't tell you about this part until the right moment. It's a lot to take in," Appo jumps in. "You are our first group, and because of the time it takes and our limited space, we can't have people waiting around. We wanted to put you somewhere safe before the launch."

The MAGIE and Annabel take the group out. Appo leads and Annabel brings up the rear. She likes watching the interactions between the guests. They pass the old hotel, and she spots Frankie at the window. He nods in acknowledgment, the group are excited, and this is probably the most noise he's heard since waking.

They reach the cliffs and follow Appo downwards. A set of steps has been built into the side of the rock. Below a platform, a jetty, reaches out over a pebbled beach towards the water and a set of stacked shipping containers.

"Don't worry," says Annabel. "The tide doesn't come in this far."

"Thank god," a few mumble.

Pebbles slide against each other as the small group walk across the beach towards the containers; Mother Earth is reminding them how precarious her situation is. Annabel observes the strange pull the metal structure has over the group, no one seems afraid. She's done her job well.

Inside, there are more MAGIE. The pods hang from tracks on the ceiling, like giant cocoa beans but grey-white. The guests know only a fraction of the pod method's origins—they are organic, but genetically modified to keep humans alive and that they have taken decades to develop. Each pod can adapt to the size of its occupant, within reason.

Annabel stands in the doorway, watching as each MAGIE pairs with a human and shows them the pods, promising they are safe. They remind the humans of what they've already been told about how they work and how long they'll be inside them. A simple lie about how long the group will be sleeping for; it's better that way. After this point they won't see Earth again, they explain how it is much easier to transport everyone while they are asleep and resting within the pods.

The humans strip. They are told everyone will be going up in batches and when they next wake up, they'll be on the ship, in space. Annabel looks at her guests, some are so excited now, they are almost bouncing.

They begin to carefully climb inside their pod. There are shrieks of surprise as the jelly within each pod goes *everywhere*. She knows for a split second they will panic. How will they breathe? A MAGIE pulls on a mask above each head and attaches them over their faces. The jelly will be working on them straight away, calming them down initially. The next and last thing each of them will see through their mask, is a MAGIE's hand and arm disappearing into the goo as their vision blurs. The pods close and an infinite milky darkness lies before them.

CHAPTER 5 – 2058

Rebecca, September

I am out on the island with a guide and a small group. We have come further than the area I've already explored. Some parts of the island have subsidence problems and we are being shown where to avoid, so we can explore further afield without risk of an accident. Issy is with me, and two other women from the larger group.

Our guide is a man who seems to work here, or perhaps he's a long-time resident. I can't figure him out. He is intriguing. He has a Scottish accent, which I've never heard in person before, and is much older than anyone else here. He knows the area well, even has his own map, which he shares with us. It's helpful to know where I am. There are many structures that I haven't seen yet and would like to explore while I have the chance. On the map he shows us there is a former hotel for special guests and tourists, lodges for seasonal oil workers and even a distillery. This place was an RAF base once and holds a lot of history, although I can't imagine the distillery and the RAF base coexisting at the same time.

* ✳ *

There is no one else around—most of the group are chatting in the shared living quarters or completing the exercises Dr Morin has given everyone. I've already done mine and I need my green fix. So, despite the damp and the eerie, dusky light, I head for a wander around outside. My new thing is to count ladybirds, there are so many here, it must be something to do with the lack of birds, there is nothing to keep them in check. I get to twenty-two and there he is, the guide, Frankie. I decide to follow him. He is walking away from the Nest down the tracks close to where he took us the other day. He spins around after a few minutes and stares at me.

"If you're coming, we may as well walk together," he shouts.

My stomach somersaults. I am so bloody stupid—what am I doing? I want to be safe, and here I am following a near-stranger down a road that no longer really exists. I reluctantly walk towards him, joining him by the edge of the track. I apologise for following him, but he doesn't seem that bothered. In fact, he looks glad of the company.

"Where are we going?" I ask.

"Off to the supermarket!"

I burst out laughing; a nerves thing. I don't know if he is mad or drunk or both. We are going to the old hotel—I think he lives there.

"With each group that arrives come new supplies. They're supposed to last us until the next group comes along. They do most times, but sometimes they don't. Sometimes I have to improvise." He tells me about the mushroom farm he has, to help our intake of B vitamins and other minerals. I offer to go with him, maybe help out—I'm itching to do something different. He seems like a nice guy. I think he has been here before any of us; living between time, he doesn't seem affected by anything in the outer world.

Issy, October

"What are you doing? What is that?" Issy says. Her roommate uses a dropper to put some liquid into her mouth.

"Something Annabel gave me to help me sleep."

"Are you serious? You can't take that. You don't even know what it is! They drugged us, remember?"

"One time isn't going to hurt. I *need* a proper sleep. I'm sick of tossing and turning."

Issy sighs and rolls over. Rebecca doesn't seem well. Maybe she's right and will be different, better even, after a good night's sleep. That morning she'd found Rebecca outside before breakfast, wandering among the saplings with nothing on her feet. To Issy, both this place and Rebecca feel alien. She pines for the city, despite the smog, it is the anonymity she craves. Rebecca is so into nature; she is practically turning into something botanical. Everything is so personal for her, almost intimate.

The city had offered Issy a place to be herself, until the towering buildings had begun to crumble. The councils had neglected thousands of structures with one hand while building new ones with the other. People were hooked into a world they thought they needed, that needed them. The galleries controlled the drip-feeding of art and what it meant, it was painfully elitist and still very white. Openings were virtually non-existent, except to those who had the backing of moneyed authorities. Issy did have some backing. The work she had been producing was seen as naïve but had also become very collectible. It was a double-edged sword. She had been pimped out by the gallery that represented her to exactly the people she despised. She'd sold out, sold her soul to the devil. The mission had become her only way out.

Issy falls into a deep sleep despite her restlessness, these thoughts race around her head. She hasn't confided in anyone for a long time. Not about what had happened nor how she got away and managed to survive. Her memories are blurred. How can she talk about what had happened if she didn't understand it herself?

Rebecca, October

Issy and I are wandering again. This time we are properly dressed for the weather. It's constantly drizzling here—either that or it's sea spray, or mist off the ocean. We go a different route and find the distillery. It isn't locked and doesn't look that dusty, so someone—I'm thinking Frankie—must be in and out of here. There are boxes and boxes of gin. We decide no one will notice if we take a bottle, and luckily these waterproofs have huge, deep pockets. We are going to try it tonight. I've not been drunk, or even had a drink, for ages.

Issy has been making a lot of effort to get to know me. It feels nice. Tattoos are often the way into our conversations, as she has many, too.

"So many stories," she says, "yet also no stories. They feel more like memories now."

"Who have you left behind?" I ask her. Her brown eyes are piercing. Can I trust her? She seems okay, I think we have a lot in common.

"Actually no one," Issy replies. "No one significant, anyway. Yes, I had friends, yes, I had lovers, but no family. They all died in rioting, the civil unrest in my country. I made it out alive and fled to the city." Issy raises her chin, on the defensive, like she is waiting for the judgement to come. I don't care about her past. I just want a friend. I really like her.

"So many things are wrong with this world. I'm so sorry you had to go through that," I tell her.

"Don't be sorry. It made the decision to come on this mission an easy one. All my life I feel like I've been running. I just need a rest now. I was creating art with no meaning in the city, but the rich people loved it, and it made me rich, for a time. They thought it was about my heritage. Maybe it was. Maybe it was just emotion."

I stop walking and pull her arm to turn to face me. I love it here. I love that we are all peeling back layers of ourselves. Exposed and vulnerable should feel uncomfortable but in fact, it is liberating. I've never felt so free.

"Let's be allies." I am deadly serious. "I know I need a friend and it sounds like you do too."

Issy holds out her hand. Her hand represents the first new friend I've made in a long time. I only know a fraction about her, but there is a warmth inside me whenever she's around. I grab her hand, and I shake. Issy doesn't let go, instead pulling me in for a hug. Over her shoulder I spot a group in the distance. We clumsily run through the drizzle to join them, a short distance from a cliff edge. Frankie is explaining something; I can't quite hear his words. The rest of the group look cold and scared.

"Sorry Frankie, can you say it again?" Issy's voice booms out over the breeze.

"There's no power on this part of the headland. It might seem obvious but don't come out here alone, especially at night. This time of the year is darker than what you've experienced while here, and it's too easy to lose your footing. We've had one death that way, and we don't want no more."

Rebecca, November

"Hello Pooch," I whisper. Juniper looks at me. "How did you get here?"

"I'm not really here, silly. You're having a dream."

"And you're now a talking dog."

"That's pretty much the gist of it, yes." Juniper picks up a blue ball that has just appeared at her feet, holding it ever-so gently in her jaws. She passes it into my open hand.

The joy of throwing a ball for Juniper is overwhelming, something I haven't felt for years. The white of the dream turns into shades of green, hills covered in lush grasses and Juniper bounds back towards me with the ball in her mouth. I crouch to greet her, my friend, and tears stream down my cheeks. Juniper jumps into my arms and we embrace as only a couple of old friends can, one hugging, the other licking.

"Oh, I've missed you." I squeeze the dog tighter, but then she starts to break and crumble. The green surrounds turn to dust and everything blows away.

I wake up crying.

Rebecca, November

"Think I must be early for my session?" I call, pushing open the already ajar door to Annabel's office.

"You're right on time, Rebecca," Annabel's replies from inside.

Reiki is a new thing for me. I know people who've had it and heard of a variety of experiences during or after treatment. One friend had sobbed so hard the practitioner had to stop part way through to allow her to recover.

I enter Annabel's office for this session with an apprehensive mind. I'm warming to the doctor but there is a wall there. I wish she could be more like one of us. The curtain to the treatment area is already open, the doctor is preparing an elevated bed. "Knock, knock," I say, again asking for permission to enter, I hesitate at the edge of the thick fabric.

"Do come in. Close the door behind you, please, and take a seat. Are you sleeping better?"

I nod in reply. "A little."

Annabel is as calm and serene as ever, sitting opposite me after locking the door. She pours us some water and begins to explain how Reiki works—chakras, alignment, energy.

I feel myself drifting off, only half listening. Annabel's office is at opposition to how the doctor appears, although the situation means choice is limited. I picture Annabel in much more clinical environment. Certainly not here among old carpets and pine-clad walls, black and gold frames with faux-antique paintings. There is also an imposing black wardrobe which I haven't noticed before, previously hidden behind the thick orange and brown woollen curtain now acting as a room divider.

"Okay, slip your shoes off and hop up onto the bed," the doctor instructs. I sink into fleecy blankets and the softest pillow I've experienced in a long time. Annabel covers me with a few more fleece and woollen blankets until only my head is exposed. "Just close your eyes and try to relax."

I lie in the makeshift cocoon and feel far from comfortable, though not far from sleep, I try adjusting myself as Annabel closes the curtain. My feet ache underneath the weight of the blankets. It is so warm my body starts to give in, and I close my eyes. My shoulders heavy, sinking deeper below me, the palms of my hands face down, arms resting beside me weightlessly. I'm snug and safe. I sense Annabel is standing at the top of the table and she places both her hands on the top of my head, the crown chakra. My body remembers how to soften. Annabel's hands are extremely warm on my head, and one vision rises to the top; I see my family, all alive, reading the goodbye letter.

* ✳ *

The reiki has brought back lots of memories about mum. She always let me sit in the front seat when it was just me and her. I remember this from a few years before cars were abolished. We had a battered old Land Rover that had mileage on it beyond numbers I knew how to say. We used to drive out into the country, just me and her. In the summer I'd have the window down despite the dust. She'd insist I wore a scarf over my nose and mouth, although she never did. Said she felt like she couldn't breathe with a mask on. She was always protecting me, telling me I was different. I miss her.

One of our favourite destinations, on those days when my brother was with Dad, was a farm on this long, narrow

Roman road. We had to approach with caution as it wasn't easy to let oncoming cars pass, but once we were on it, and had it all to ourselves, there was this sense of freedom. Like no one could get to us. To either side of the road was fencing about four feet high, and beyond that were monster-sized greenhouses. A city of glass. Sometimes the crops inside were so tall, ready for harvesting corn, maize, I even remember tomatoes but most times they looked empty. The greenhouses went on for a couple of miles, but at their centre sat an old farmhouse with a few barns.

One of the barns housed cows, so rare in those later years. The other had been converted into a café. It was always such a treat to go there with Mum. She would always have carrot cake with a pot of Earl Grey, and I'd have apple pie and a glass of nut milk. She'd ask me about school and my friends. It was so easy for her to soothe my worries about the world and the future. I know now that she was a good storyteller and she wanted me to have a special, safe childhood.

As I got a bit older, she'd share stories about how things used to be, stuff her parents had told her. Sometimes I get confused and think these are things that have happened to me. They are inherited memories, in my blood.

The cow herd at that farm gradually became smaller. They stopped reproducing, like most farm animals. My dad's survivalist interest had grown by then and he adapted the Land Rover to run on cooking oil. We carried on going to that farm about once a month, until Mum became too ill to drive. The last couple of times we went, I drove there myself, illegally. No one my age bothered learning anymore.

I helped Mum from the car to the café those last two times. The effort it took meant she needed a higher dose of her meds to stop the coughing. It was bittersweet, I guess. Part of me knew those were her last days getting out of the house. She told me the story of how her mother and father met, how their parents were both stall holders at a market. I'd heard it before, of course. The dresses my grandmother had made had captivated mum as a girl. When my parents were wed, my grandmother made what would be her last creation for mum. She still had the dress, of course. She took it out and showed me a couple of times when I was very little. I remember there was an incandescent feel to it. Like a beautiful, mythical snake. Shiny and scaly, something from a different world.

Annabel, November

"I've slept for years already, Annabel. You are not going to get me in one of those things. No way." Frankie storms away from the doctor and through the kitchen of the Nest. Annabel walks in his wake, trying to retain her cool. He disappears out of the door to the outside and into the rain.

Stopping at the kitchen counter, she makes herself another green tea. Someone has left a sandwich on the side. She turns to face the room—it's quiet, a MAGIE is stoking the fire and Issy and Rebecca are sitting at one end of the long table. Issy has her back to Annabel, but Rebecca catches her eye and offers a smile. They will have heard Frankie's rants.

"Who is winning?" Annabel says, walking over and seeing the chess board.

"Me, as usual!" Issy replies, grinning. "Your turn, Bec."

"She does win, most of the time, because I let her." Rebecca says.

"Mind if I sit?"

"I was losing anyway," Issy said quickly. "Please, join us."

Rebecca shoots Issy a look, pretending not to notice Annabel sits down.

"Okay, for a change, ladies, I need some advice. I hope you don't mind. I'm just at the end of my tether with the situation. Frankie would be useful on the ship. I certainly don't want to leave him here. I've grown rather fond of him. But he won't agree to the sleep cycles."

"Surely if he knows the forecast here, he'll agree to anything just to get away?" Rebecca asks.

"Of course, yes. He wants it on his terms though. He calls it unnatural sleep. Says he's had his fill and would rather see it out here, if that's the only other option."

"And is it the only other option, Doc?" Issy asks.

The doctor smiles. "There are always exceptions. To every rule. But I'm not sure who it would benefit. Certainly not him."

"So, in theory, he *could* join us on the ship," Rebecca says. "but never go into pod-sleep? Our aging would slow down, while he grew older and older? He might die before we get there," replies Rebecca.

"Exactly."

"Well, there could be some benefits," says Issy. "Communication would be more consistent with him always being awake. It could be like an insurance policy. He could be on call to fix anything at any time."

"That's what the MAGIE are for, Issy. They built the ship; they have its history and workings as part of their interface. The ship is another MAGIE, really, just on a much bigger scale."

"I have to say I agree with Issy," Rebecca says. "Fair enough, the MAGIE know the ship. But there's nothing quite like a human brain. A human way of approaching things, thinking laterally rather than linearly. We are all agreeing and choosing to be put to sleep. It's his life. Maybe he'd rather live it out as naturally as possible, even if it is in space."

The doctor smiles thoughtfully and picks up a couple of discarded pawns in each hand. This set was Oscar's, they'd not played each other for a long time.

"Perhaps you could set up a chess tournament within your group here." She expertly moves the discussion away from Frankie.

"No, I don't think so." Rebecca says.

"Would you not enjoy that?"

"I wouldn't want to stress myself out making something that I love into work. The serene feeling of the game. It's elegant and calming, I hope some of it rubs off on me. Even losing is beautiful."

"And you do that often." Issy tries to lighten the sudden depth of the moment.

"How poetic." Annabel gets up, "Thanks. It's been enlightening." She takes her drink and walks back towards the door to the main corridor.

"I think they're together," Rebecca whispers. "You know, a couple."

Annabel can't see Issy's reaction, but it doesn't matter that they know. Frankie is coming anyway; Oscar has ensured it. She just wishes he'd consider the sleep cycle, and not just for selfish reasons either.

Frankie, December

The distillery is fun again. Back in the time before, it had given the residents something to do other than farming or their job tasks. The gin they'd developed on the island had been the answer to everything at first. It became so popular on the mainland that at one point they couldn't make enough of it to export.

Frankie has been bringing the place back to life since being woken, manufacturing something entirely different. His beloved mushrooms. Between here and the old hotel he's had a good run. Soon it will be time to say goodbye. Of course, everyone has been eating them, they are a valuable source of nutrition, but it is bittersweet leaving it all. A daily routine of walking between sites and checking temperature and light had him feeling stronger than ever. Typically, he's finally just cracked how to grow his favourites. If only he could have done this all those years ago on his return from the war. All the plans they had, him and Elsie, the woman in the photograph, things would have been so different.

Frankie stops himself going down that route again. That way lies only sadness. He gathers his mycelium samples, the white wisps looking thick and healthy, placing them carefully on top of the packed soil beds. He'll start again when they arrive. He'll teach Rebecca all about it, she is bright enough. Brighter than him.

"Ready for collection from the distillery, over." He says into a radio.

"ETA thirty minutes. Sit down and rest, Frankie. Over."

Back inside he stands looking at all the dusty bottles left over from the gin days. Deciding to crack one open, he finds a glass in the office room. Alcoholism flourished back then; the real reason Elsie had left. The gin is still good. Too good. Things changed on the island after she went. Bitterness became his primary emotion. He hadn't been himself. He'd focused on the work he loved and then he'd been forgotten. They'd promised it would only be until the island had gone through quarantine, but in the end, they left him and never came back. He poured another.

Rebecca, December

I head towards the coastline and along, down the side of the headland. There is a figure on the shore wearing a khaki long coat, and I know before I get to his side that it's Frankie.

"Hey, you. Nice morning for it," I say as I approach him, not wanting to make him jump.

93

"Oh aye. Good morning." I've interrupted his thoughts. "I'm trying to find the horizon line beyond the mizzle."

"Good luck with that. You won't find it," I say. "Are you ready to leave, Frankie? Are you still coming?"

"I'm ready as I'll ever be. You know I'm not going in the pods, don't you?"

"You've told me many times. I think everyone knows you don't want to go through anything like that again. I'm glad you're going to be there, though." I smile and suddenly feel more buoyant about the whole thing. It's strange to think that most of this hand-picked population is already up there on the ship waiting for us.

"You can come and chat with me any time. Annabel is going to be so busy she'll probably forget I'm there."

"I'm not supposed to know, remember?" I laugh. It is common knowledge they are together.

"Aye, I'll try to remember." Picking up a pebble, he skims it across the water. I'm fond of Frankie. He's so interesting, and we have a shared love of growing things. Father figure or missing daughter, whatever it is, we enjoy each other's company.

"Is that the last of them?" I nodded towards the thing in his hand.

For a moment, I'm back in the garden with my dad, after Mum had gone. He still smoked. He must have been one of the last people smoking on Earth. It was frowned upon, but because we lived outside the cities, no one enforced the regulations. The doctors had abandoned us. We were left to our own devices. Pre-rolled cigarettes were no longer made and there was a real black market in acquiring them. Dad set himself up as a dealer, and people came to the house to buy them by the box. He gave me a stash, told me it was an emergency fund, an investment in my future. I always kept a box of cigs with me, like a morbid lucky charm. Even brought them here, to Saxa Vord. That's how Frankie and I got so close so quickly: I had something he wanted. I've always been able to use them as bargaining tools. Dad was right, they proved even more valuable than money.

"I bet you'll know all the gossip on board. You'll end up being some kind of old sage."

"Maybe I will. I've got the old part down already."

I pick up a stone and hold it up close to my face, admiring its smoothness. It reminds me of some old coins Dad kept in his 'relics from the past' collection. I spin it out towards the sea, hoping for at least three skims. I get four.

"I think that means I'm winning."

"I hope you are winning. I hope this is the right choice for you," Frankie says.

Looking at him now, I can see more than the usual frown. It's that face, that expression, that stays with me for the rest of the morning.

* * *

The day has arrived. We are leaving Earth today. I'm so glad Issy made it through, despite the reoccurring dream.

The shuttle is due and the group we arrived with have mostly all passed. The go ahead to start a new life. The final decision came from Annabel, but I know there are other factors at play; how we answered questions during talking therapies, how we responded to the others in the group— that kind of thing. How I have personally reacted to the tinctures, coming off the drugs, and any other suggestions Annabel has put forward during my time here—it all counts.

There is one person from our original group that had a change of heart. Reasons of family, friends, lovers. Knowing they will never see them again proved too much. I guess that makes me lucky, for a change, that I only have Sam. Though I know my brother will understand my reasons, it is unfair on him—but I must think about myself now. It's about time.

There are a couple of other people who didn't pass. I don't know the specific reasons, but they were very awestruck by the whole thing—space, the mission, the autopilot, pod-sleep. I think they feel they can't go through with it because there are too many risks. These people are going to be hypnotised to forget the details of the plan and sent back home.

I'm packing my bags once more. Now I have a friend, I have Issy. She has emptied and repacked her bag more times than I have counted over the last day or two.

"You were up early," she says.

"I wanted to take it all in, one last time. It's beautiful here, don't you think?"

"It is, but it's not going to be like this for much longer."

"I guess not."

She's pacing the room, and I can't stand the tension. We are all dealing with it in our own way, I guess.

"It's the pods, Bec. I don't think I can do it."

"You can. Just keep thinking about being up there. Starting over."

CHAPTER 6 – 2043

Rebecca's Journal - July

We arrived in Paris today. We're in an apartment—one that has been in the family for a long time, but this trip is the first I've known about it. We're in an area of the city which feels dangerous at night but perfectly fine during the day. Maybe that's just what it's like when you go somewhere new. It all seems more sinister without the sun lighting up the dark corners.

We got in late, so have just had some pizza from a place downstairs. Dad went to get it. He seems to know the area well. We are all slobbing out in front of the TV, which is really, REALLY, old. I think whoever lived here before perhaps didn't want to be part of the modern world. There are about four stations that the weird aerial thing can pick up, and they are all in French. At least my language skills will improve.

Mum is planning tomorrow's itinerary and making sure she's got all the tickets downloaded for the galleries.

I'm in bed now and Sam is snoring already—yes, we are sharing a room. The sheets feel stiff, but I know I'll sleep easily.

Day 2

Pizza again for tea as we are all exhausted from the city. Mum laughed when Dad suggested we should wear pollution masks while outside here. But he was right. He loves being right. He'd packed them anyway and dug them out last night. It's so close and smoggy, I don't know how people function and live here. Dad said it's affected the property prices and now you can buy beautiful villas at a fraction of the cost they were before. There are lots of abandoned properties and all the rich have moved out, he says.

I miss June.

Today we went to the Louvre. It is the biggest museum I've ever been to. It's so big we couldn't get around all of it and Mum says we should go back before the end of our trip. I'm not that fussed. I prefer people watching. I love watching strangers come in off the street and take off their masks. I'd happily sit in the café all day with an ice cream, watching them. Real people are more interesting than marble ones.

Back in the apartment and one of Mum's favourite films is on the TV; *Funny Face*, which is almost a hundred years old, so she keeps telling me. It is set partly here in Paris, which is unrecognisable. She cried at the end.

We have a free morning tomorrow before a speaking event in the afternoon. I've asked them to take me to some old bookshops. Dad says he knows just the one that I'll love. "I'll take you to where all the greats hung out, if it's still there."

Good night, diary. I'm going to sleep. Although Sam is coughing a lot. His asthma is worse here. He'd better not keep me awake.

Day 4

Sorry, I forgot to write yesterday. We did bookshops and a café in the morning, then we were at Dad's survivalist event in the afternoon. Let's put it this way, I'm glad I found a book—*On the Road* by Jack Kerouac.

We managed to get back to the Louvre with some of Dad's connections. This time I enjoyed it more. It wasn't as busy as the other day but also the paintings are so much more vibrant in real life than they are on a screen or even in books. My favourite is *Flora* from 1591. It's by an artist called Giuseppe Arcimboldo (I had to copy the spelling down!). The whole thing looks like a traditional old portrait from far away, but when you get closer it's all made up of flowers. Even the skin is made of detailed flowers, like tattoos painted over everything. There were a few by this artist. Another I looked at was made up of birds, the same trick. You don't realise until you get closer. I will have to research the artist when we get back. There was a translated letter included in the exhibition—the plague sounds scary! Those days must have been so hard to live in.

I bought a postcard of Flora from the shop and they had a book about him, the artist, there, but I didn't have enough coins. It was so expensive, and mum and dad wouldn't buy it for me either. They hinted I might get it for my thirteenth birthday next month though.

Afterwards we went out to what was probably a fine restaurant in its time, but as Dad said, there's no money in the city now. At least it wasn't pizza again.

I've decided that tonight I will dream of becoming that painting. Of *Flora*. I put her on my bedside table, and Sam rolled his eyes at me. "I preferred all the naked nymph sculptures," he says. Could he be any more predictable?

One more day in Paris, then home to June.

Good night, diary.

CHAPTER 7 – 2045

Rebecca
Monday, February 20th

My current obsession is old cameras, pre-digital. To a certain extent they are all the same—body, lenses, and mirrors—but there is something magical about how they work. Capturing the surface of a moment, savouring that memory onto film. The photos are printed on this shiny, thick paper. Dad started it all when I'd helped him clear out the loft last summer and he had loads of old cameras stashed away up there. Some still had film inside. There are wallets of photographs of Mum and him when they were younger. I look loads like her. I rummage through the box finding some smaller blurry photos in a card frame. Dad says they're instant film. It was a novelty back then, another revival from the 1970s. Another attempt at holding on to the past.

He gets annoyed with me because I like to take the cameras apart and see how they work. The instant cameras are my favourite. They are a lot of fun, if a bit temperamental, and they don't go back together well, there are just too many mechanisms. I learnt my lesson and didn't take apart any other of the instant ones. It keeps my mind busy, fiddling with these cameras, and they keep me and Dad talking when what we both really want is to chat with Mum, but she's still in the medical centre.

Thursday March 2nd

The curtains in Mum's room are a dark William Morris pattern, heavy and lined with blackout fabric, so she can sleep at any time of the day. But she's not sleeping, it's like she's not allowing herself. Not wanting to miss out on a single moment. She's been home since earlier this week. Dad says she's chosen her plot in the garden; beside the sprouting daffodils that thrive despite the increasing pollution.

I'm having some time off from school for what we've been told are her last days. I spend them sitting with mum—fetching her tea or a blanket, or reading aloud from her favourite book, a hardback collection of Hans Christian Andersen stories with beautiful illustrations by Charles Mozley. Mum has always claimed Mozley is a distant relative, that she'd met him once as a baby. He sent her a copy of this red book and a collection of other stories he'd worked on, but this is the only survivor. The art inside is a heady mixture of lithographs, pen and ink drawings, and stunning plates of vivid, colourful characters brought to life by his brush. I treasure this book too; Mum read it a lot to me when I was little. The spine is weak, making the book saggy. Like Mum, still so vibrant inside but being failed by its body. I read to her until my throat is dry. She doesn't speak. She seems to be at peace with what is happening. Then it happens. The spaces between her breaths grow longer, then the rattle, like something is stuck in her chest. Then peace.

It ends up being me who tells the rest of the family. Sam is away at his job, chasing him down at his hotel is like some awful joke of miscommunication. He'll come straight away.

There are no graveyards to bury the dead. Legislation, physical space, and fracking has seen to that. Everyone uses alkaline hydrolysis these days, unless they own land. This was what Mum wanted, to be buried in her garden. We aren't wealthy, but the house and land have been in the family for a few generations.

I prise Dad away from Mum, drawing him a bath and putting on some music they both loved. He eventually leaves her, and I begin to tidy up the bed, unhooking the machines that have been monitoring her descent. I try to make mum look presentable, but my hands are shaky. The medical equipment will have to go back to the hospital. I'll ask Sam to take it in his car.

"This is it, Mum," I say, and the tears come. Sitting on the edge of the bed, I look at her translucent skin, almost expecting a reply, she looks at peace now, the furrowed brow is gone. The red book is here by her bed. I reach for it spotting something tucked inside. A photograph—one I've seen before, but I thought had since gone missing. The picture shows me as a baby in a pushchair. Daffodils surround us. Mum, my doting, beloved Mum, is crouched next to the pushchair for the photograph. Neither of us are looking at the camera, we are too enraptured with each other. The photo blurs, my eyes are so full of tears I can't see. "Goodbye, Mum," comes out as a wail. Rubbing my face, I close the door to the bedroom and go to check on Dad.

Friday March 3rd

Sam is here. We are in the back garden and he is digging the plot Mum chose, I'm reading the red book again. He works as an in-house photographer for an electronic components company. "Not a creative job, but at least I get to use my camera," he always says. He is wasted photographing bits of machinery, but it pays well, and he has his side projects. Sam hasn't seen Mum for a while, I think he avoided seeing the worst after last time when the tumours became really obvious. Dad is indoors, sitting with Mum, talking to her, and hovering around inside, not knowing what to do with himself. He finally brings us sandwiches.

"Do you think that's a bit small?" He points to the hole.

"I've not finished it yet," Sam says. "It might get done a bit quicker if you fancied helping me."

"I don't fancy helping you, Sam. Your Mum needs me at hand." He places the tray precariously on my lap and walks quickly back to the house.

"What was that about?" Sam asks. He is five years older than me, but he still doesn't understand stuff sometimes.

"He's just dealing with it in his own way." I hear myself saying and wonder how I can sound so calm and together. Putting down Mum's book, I pass Sam a sandwich.

"He made this bread, you know. He's barely slept since she went, and I think he was up all-night baking."

"This isn't Dad. He's the adult." Sam sits and crosses his legs leaning on the rock behind him, the eventual grave marker.

"He's grieving. He'll come out of it in his own time."

"You've got to live here though, Bec. It was bad enough when Mum was ill. I don't want you caring for Dad. You're fifteen."

"He'll come back."

We eat in silence until the rain starts

Monday 6th March

"Did you sleep well, sis?" Sam stands over the hob, poised with an egg. There's a tray of them on the worktop beside a couple of huge tomatoes and some more bread that Dad has probably made in the night again. The morning light shines through into the small kitchen, then I realise Sam has the light on and it is, in fact, another very gloomy morning. I look out onto the garden, still in my dressing gown.

"It's still raining?" I ignore his earlier query. Parts of the garden look sodden, there are pools of water, the hole must be flooded too, perhaps now a shallow pond.

"Did you not hear? It got really heavy during the night, it woke me up it was so loud!"

"No. I was dreaming about Mum. She was talking to me, just like she did before. She had all her marbles, you know?" turning to Sam, "But I can't remember what she was saying to me."

"It'll come back to you. Fancy some eggs?"

"I'd love a couple of fried eggs, with runny yolks, a couple of slices of those big tomatoes, and loads of black pepper on a piece of that bread Dad's made. Thanks." I turn on the small television screen on the wall.

"That does sound good. You cut the tomatoes and bread, and I'll sort the eggs. Deal?"

"Deal, thanks." The news is on. "Sam, have you seen this?"

We stand watching it together. It is still raining and shows no signs of stopping, talk about stating the obvious. It's been three days, there is flooding in our region, with rivers bursting their banks. The one a couple of miles from here has. People have had to evacuate. There is an environmentalist being interviewed, she blames the global warming. It's abnormal, she says.

"Where's Dad?" I ask.

"He's actually sleeping, in the spare room. I thought it was best to leave him"

"You're right. I'll take him a cup of tea in a bit. The flooding, what are we going to do?"

"We're going to have wait until it dries out a bit. The earth I've dug out is like clay. It'll be a complete mess if we try and bury her now, not to mention dangerous. I went to check our cellars, the floors are wet, it must be seeping in through the ground."

"I don't fucking believe this. Mum's grave is half dug and is now under water, you've pulled your back digging the thing and now this rain. It's all shit. Everything is sad and a mess. Especially Dad. I can't do this."

Sam switches off the screen and gives me a big hug.

"Come on, you are stronger than you realise. Plus, I need help making the breakfast, I'm still rubbish at cooking."

We work together in the kitchen like synchronised swimmers. It hasn't always been like this. There have been plenty of arguments and fights as we've grown up. It's ironic that Mum's downturn has been the making of our relationship. Eventually we sit at the round table near the back doors and tucked into the meal.

"Can you even taste that?" Sam asks me.

"I can taste some of it, like the black pepper." I wipe my chin where the yolk is dribbling down. "Eating is more about the textures and the feel of the food now. The whole experience, even the company, the memory of how it tasted before."

"I am sad too, Bec," he says, guilt changing the subject, "but also relieved. She's not in pain anymore. I wish things were different, of course, but they're not. She used to say that there will always be a part of her with us. Just remember that."

Thursday March 9th

Dad says that Mum's room is starting to smell. It is one of the few times I am grateful of my partial hyposmia. Mum has developed blisters on her now saggy skin and there is a green tinge to her. I keep the windows open, despite the rain, to try and get rid of the grim atmosphere that is permeating the walls. Sam must go back to work. The rain has stopped, but the sky still looks full. We stand in wellies at the front of the house as he packs his car with the medical equipment.

"I'll keep in touch. I'll come back when I can to help out," he says as the car pulls away. I turn and give Dad a hug.

I go around the back of the house to look at the grave. It is half-full of water and looks much too narrow for Mum's body, which has begun to bloat. The smell is so unbearable for Dad that he sleeps downstairs, I've joined him because I don't want to be alone upstairs with the body. Dad stands beside me and looks down into where Mum will be laid to rest.

"It's completely waterlogged. This is going to take ages to disperse." His voice rattles in his throat, I look over and his eyes are filling up again. He holds my shoulder for support.

"I think we need to get Mum's body out of that room," I say, almost whispering. He nods.

We trudge over the lawn turning it to mud, kicking off our boots in the kitchen, then back upstairs to see again what we must contend with. Decomposition is accelerating or seems to be. The body has gone from green to red and has become even more bloated. The smell seems to catch the back of Dad's throat. He covers his mouth and nose with his hands and dashes to the window, sticking his head outside to stop from being sick. He cries and retches. I move closer to the bed. The sheets are wet through with fluids from Mum's body and blisters that have burst.

"I think we need help," I say, frustrated at Dad, he should know what to do, but he doesn't. "This is too much for you and me to sort out. How are we even going to get her downstairs? Never mind to the end of the garden? It's a mess Dad."

"We can't have help. I don't need help from outsiders. They're the ones that did this to her in the first place."

"For god's sake, Dad. Get real! We aren't strong enough between us," I plead, ignoring his comments. Curiosity gets the better of me and I lift the sheet only to regret it immediately as I spot something moving at Mum's bloated neck. I quickly lay the sheet back down. "It doesn't have to be anyone official. We could hire one of those odd-job MAGIE that are on TV."

Dad leaves the room without a word. I look down at Mum, she is unrecognisable now, her face bloated beyond what I thought possible. I leave her again closing the door behind me. Dad is so stubborn. We can't live like this. I must fix it.

* ✳ *

"I'm sorry, Bec. Your mum wouldn't have wanted this," he says unlocking the garage.

"I know. She wouldn't want to be lingering around. We've got to sort it. What's up there in that room isn't Mum. It's just a body."

He swings the garage door up to open it. Inside amongst all the tools, sitting on a workbench, is Mum's coffin. Dad has made it from some re-purposed wood he'd taken from a demolition job years before. It is made of old painted doors, mostly sanded down, and assembled using a design he'd seen in a book. He lifts off the lid. The box is cold and hard.

"Will she fit in there?" He asks me.

"It's bigger than I remember. Yes, I think so. We could soften it a bit, add a blanket. But this box won't fit in the hole Sam has dug. I wish we'd put her in here when it first happened. It might have made things easier."

"I wasn't really around, love. Mentally, I mean. You are right, I think we should get your Mum out of that room, and if we need help... so be it. We can keep her in here until the flooding has gone." He puts the lid back on and sighs, "Can I ask you a favour?"

"Anything. We're a team, remember?" I say, and he smiles. The first smile I've seen from him in a long time.

"Can you organise the MAGIE, if that's what you think is best? You know I'm no good with that stuff."

113

"Sure, no problem. I'll do it now." I go inside to place the order.

Friday March 10th

The MAGIE arrives in an electric driverless vehicle, much smaller than any cars I know, and I'm fascinated. The service costs a fair amount in coins, but we don't have much choice. Dad and the MAGIE carry the empty coffin upstairs, the MAGIE doing most of the work setting it down on the floor next to the bed. It surveys the scene along with the window in Mum's room and the outside below, then it gets on with the task with barely a word.

It is humanoid in shape, the ad on TV promised a vast number of tools and extra limbs in its arsenal. They are packed away within the depths of its electronic torso. I watch it work, so precise, so confident. It lifts Mum's body up off the bed using two extra arm implements to distribute the weight. Dust and fibres fall away from the body and flies appear out of nowhere. The MAGIE is remarkably gentle, placing her into the casket. Dad has forgotten to bring the lid up. I pull off the sheets sparing no time in stripping the bed. It is all beyond laundering, the pillows feel like sponges, I take it all outside to be burnt, leaving the MAGIE to perform some tests and register the cause of death. I will finish up later in here.

Dad is there, but not there, in his own world again as I struggle through the house to the back door. A sound comes from above and I see the MAGIE rigging up a winch. It's a good job the windows are large, I watch the coffin slowly descend towards Dads outstretched arms, he guides it gently down onto the paving flags. He unfastens the wire ropes from the box without looking inside.

The rain starts again, me and Dad exchange looks of exasperation. The spring showers are here with a vengeance. The MAGIE leans out of the window and tells Dad to stay where he is and not to try and lift the coffin by himself. "I will be down in just a few moments." It dismantles the winch on the window frame.

Dad fights with himself, never good at taking orders. Eventually he can't help but fuss over Mum. The rain is falling on her body. Taking off his jacket, he covers her up. I stand beside him, staying quiet. Dad squats next to the coffin and holds her face in his hands. "I miss you, Sherry. I really do."

The MAGIE arrives outside and Dad backs away.

"Please can you put her on the workbench in the garage?" he asks it.

"No problem, sir." The MAGIE uses its multiple arms again to lift the coffin and deliver it smoothly and carefully into the garage. Its strength is astonishing.

"This one is much nicer than the ones we have in school, Dad," I say as we stand watching it from the garage door. We are both getting wet, and I'm still holding the sticky bedding in my arms.

"It's probably a newer version," Dad replies, finally taking my armful of sheets and pillows.

"Yes. I am a newer model than you will have likely come across before," it says. "We have a deeper moral coding, and our sensory perception of emotion is much more finely tuned than our predecessors."

"Well, I'd like to thank you. This hasn't been as bad as I'd thought," Dad says.

"You can leave me a review. That would help," the MAGIE replies. "I'm all done. I wish you well for the future." The MAGIE walks around the house to the front, where the vehicle is waiting. It leaves without fanfare.

"I guess that's that." Dad lifts the lid and places it on top of the coffin.

The rain turns to drizzle. The garden is more water-logged, and everything seems to have stopped. I feel like I am trapped in the moment of my Mum's death; as if spring has changed its mind, deciding not to bother. The trees are still spiky and skeletal, their branches like cold bony arms waiting to grab whatever dared come close. Dead grasses and hedgerows need clearing and tidying to make room for new growth. The sort of job Mum would normally do. Even our regular garden visitors, the squirrels and birds, seem to be hiding away.

Friday March 24th

The weather is finally improving, and I am back at school. My moping around the house wasn't helping anyone, especially Dad. My handful of real friends are mostly kind. They are a bunch of misfits; the only ones still interested in making things. One of them made me a beaded bracelet, and they don't mind listening to me tell Mum's stories at lunchtimes.

On the walk home, I look out for buds in the trees or small green shoots pushing through the ground. Spring is coming after all. Sam is back today

"It's time," Dad had said that morning. He is improving as the days go by, time sleeping is outweighing the time baking bread at last. "After school we'll bury your mum."

Getting inside, I go upstairs to fetch the red Hans Christian Andersen book, wanting Mum to always have it with her.

I carefully take the photograph out of the book and put it under my pillow. My room is small but cosy. The window looks out to the front of the house rather than the back. If

I lie on the bed at just the right angle, I can see the spring blossom instead of the grey of the buildings opposite. It's the sort of window I might take to sneaking out of in the future.

Checking my reflection in the mirror and smoothing my hair. I take a deep breath and go down to the kitchen where they are waiting for me. The three of us head out to the garage. Dad has asked some of the neighbours to help carry Mum to her resting place. I go red, cheeks hot and my eyes sting. I wish it were just us. Dad opens the garage door slowly, as though not wanting to disturb her body.

"I wasn't planning on lifting up the lid," he says to me. I hold the book to my chest with both hands and plead wordlessly to him. He can't resist it when I do that. "Okay, okay. It's a good job I haven't attached it yet then."

We all squeeze into the garage. There isn't much space between the coffin on the work bench and all the stuff Dad has accumulated over the years. We stand alongside the coffin; the lid is about stomach-height on Dad and more like chest height on me. Dad passes out rags he's prepared for our helpers. They are soaked in a lavender and tea tree tincture to try and mask the smell. Tying their rags across their faces, looking like bandits or highwaymen, leaving their hands free to lift the coffin. Dad clocks the men looking at me.

"She can't smell." One of them mumbles something under his breath but I don't hear what. It doesn't matter.

"I'm going to lift the lid." Dad says to me and Sam. "I just want you to prepare yourselves. It's not going to look like your mother, okay?"

I get the sense he is trying to prepare himself, too. He lifts the lid. I'm almost certain I hear a sound escape from the coffin, a whisper of something. There are insects. Flies and what look like baby grasshoppers spin upward from inside the dark box and then just hang around above it. What lies inside is Mum but shrivelled, almost black in colour. There is something growing from her abdomen.

What is that?

Dad quickly puts the lid back down.

"You know what, Rebecca? I think your mum would've wanted you to keep the book."

I nod, speechless. They'd all seen it too. I back out of the garage and into the fresh air, grateful to feel the breeze on my face again. Sam and Dad make light work of attaching the lid to the box, and the three neighbours help them carefully carry it into the garden. Sam has rigged up the hole with two long straps, so they can lower her into the ground. She is in place, I hear myself exhale, and Sam starts shovelling earth on top of the box.

"I'm going to say the Lord's prayer, if you don't mind," Dad says. "Our Father, who art in heaven…"

My cheeks are damp, and I curl my face into Dad's shoulder. The neighbours pay their respects and leave us alone. I link Dad's arm with mine and rest my head on his shoulder. I'm grateful he's managing to hold it together. He guides me back to the house while Sam tidies up outside.

"I've made some bread," he says.

"You do surprise me. You'll be opening a bakery next," we smile, my sarcasm giving some light relief although it feels a bit wrong to do so still. "Is there any of that soup left from last night? Can I have some please?"

Dad gets the soup out of the fridge and puts it on the stove while I slip back upstairs with the book. It's what Mum would've wanted after all, just as Dad had said. I pull the photo back out from underneath my pillow and tuck it back inside the book for safe keeping.

Rebecca, July 2nd

Getting back from school, I see Dad has left me a present on my pillow; he's managed to find some polaroid film.

I get to the kitchen and find Dad heaving with sobs while trying to make a cup of tea. There is a hotness behind my eyes and my stomach swirls. I hate seeing him like this. "Come on, Dad. Sit down. I'll make it." I pull out a chair from the kitchen table and guide him to it.

"I'm sorry, Bec, I'm finding things hard at the moment." He distracts himself and loads the film, I notice his hands trembling. I watch him press the shutter and a mechanical noise comes from inside the camera. A small sheet of silky card pops up from the top of it.

"Smile, beautiful," he says, turning towards me.

I force a grin and the shutter goes off. He lays down the small frame on the table and explains that it needs a moment or two to develop. "I'm going to call Sam, get him to make an appointment for you with a doctor in the city. This isn't right, Dad, I need you." I try to hold back my own tears but fail, "I need you to be you again."

"Okay, okay. I'll go. If Sam takes me."

"Thanks." I pass him his tea, leaving my own on the side, my stomach still churning.

"Oh, this doesn't look good," he says looking at the camera.

"What is it? Maybe it needs new batteries?" Although they don't make batteries anymore. Not for domestic use, anyway. Dad has contacts for that sort of thing.

"It should have started showing by now. I think the film has perished. Sorry, love." He sighed. "They only have a certain shelf life, what with all the chemicals, there's probably mould causing problems, too."

I pick it up for a closer look. Dad blows on his tea. His eyes are still glassy.

"I can see something. There's blue peeping through, like a shadow. A bit of my school top."

I flip it round so he can see. He slowly nods. "I don't think you're going to get anything more out of that."

I pick up the camera and take one of him. He laughs and shakes his head. Getting up I wander out the back of the house, into the garden. Point and shoot, point and shoot. At the sky, the clouded sun, the shadows and flickers of light through the trees, and Mum's patch where there are tiny mushrooms growing. The photos jump out of the camera and land on the ground. I leave them where they lie. Then it's all over. I keep pressing the button but nothing. The display says zero. Collecting my photos from the ground, I run back inside.

"You just realised there's only ten in each pack, eh?"

I spread out the photos on the table like a tarot reading. What will they show?

"You see? The chemicals aren't as potent after all these years, so parts of these are completely undeveloped."

I like the results, despite what Dad says. The shapes and the colours present themselves as more than just mistakes. Shades of grey, green, and blue. I can see parts of the garden.

In others there are shades of pink. It's like lifting a veil on another world.

"It's like taking a photo of something that isn't there. Something trying to reveal itself that can't be seen with the human eye."

"You sound like your mother."

"I'm taking that as a compliment."

I gather up the images and go to my room. Sticking them onto the wall closest to my bed, maybe Mum is trying to get through to me.

PART TWO: 1945-1976

CHAPTER 8 – FRANKIE

Letters from Francis to home in Scotland

27th March, 1945

They say the war is almost over. Of course, that is good news and I long to see you again, dearest Elsie.

We are further north now; signs of spring are here. Winter has been so hard. Lots of men have lost one or two of their toes from the frostbite. I'm sorry for not writing more, but we had to keep our location as quiet as possible. Despite the harsh conditions I've fallen for this country and the people and the food, it's like nothing at home. They cook simply because the ingredients here are so good there is no need for any fuss. The plainest of meals are often the tastiest, and my favourite is bruschetta; a dish of round toast with chopped tomatoes, red onion and herbs on the top.

Sunny days are becoming more frequent. Everyone eats outside. The pace of life is slow but the quality of relationships is high. I've met some very special people here. I hope one day in the future we might return together.

Yours always, Francis

❖ ❖ ❖

11th April, 1945

Dear Elsie,

I'm combining two letters into one here, hope you don't mind. I didn't get a chance to finish the other one. There were some heavy bombings and we had to move quickly. Yesterday, a few of us were sent on a reconnaissance mission into the forests east of the base, closer to the borders. Aside from the actual task in hand, it was magnificent. The Italian countryside is stunning—enough to rival my beloved Scotland. We had an allied friend with us, an Italian tracker (probably a member of the Italian Resistance) who knew the area like it was his own garden. We even did a little foraging whilst there. We found berries, mushrooms, and wild garlic, along with some wild herbs that can be used in tonics and medicines. We fried a few of the mushrooms on the tiny stove we brought with us. They were the best I've ever tasted, meaty and rich, not like mushrooms at home. They certainly don't have the soil aftertaste that you hate.

It's fascinating—the foraging, I mean. It really makes me wonder what kind of things we have growing wild up in the glens and lochs of home. Would you like to come out with me when I get back? We can make it a real adventure. We'll have to borrow some books, so we know what we are looking for. Many things are poisonous, and we don't want to go and kill ourselves when life is just starting out.

Although the days are sunny and bright here, I do find myself pining for the drizzle of Scotland; the mist rolling over the glens and the whiskey. Wine is what they drink here, and plenty of it. We've been promised a day at a vineyard on the next day off we get. I'll try and stow a bottle and bring it home. As long as I can save myself from drinking it, that is.

Anything for you though, Elsie.

❖ ❖ ❖

30th April, 1945

Dearest Elsie,

I'm coming home. This will be the last letter I write

from Italy. We won, we finally nailed the bastards. I can tell you the code name of the op now: Operation Grapeshot. It's all about the bloody grapes here. I'm a wee bit hungover from the celebrations last night. There was a lot of local wine drunk. I think the people here are happy to see the back of us. Some of the boys have been trying to court the young women in the town nearest our base.

I'll be keeping myself busy, until I get my demob papers, with studying those mushrooms I told you about. It turns out they are called morels and are a bit of a delicacy.

I have a brilliant plan, Elsie, a plan where I don't have to get a regular job when I come home. I want to be with you at home <u>all the time</u>. I'm going to work for myself and start a morel mushroom farm. The only one in the country. The top chefs in fancy hotels in London will be requesting our luxury ingredient, no doubt!

I'm going to head back to the place we found them last time and get some to bring back with me. I'll go to the village and find the chap that took us, and it'll be just him and me. You're the only one I've told about this. Keep it quiet, I don't want anyone copying my plan. Next time we talk it'll be face to face over a bottle of the local red wine and these delicious mushrooms.

Arrivederci my sweet Elsie, always yours, Francis x

Frankie's Garden notebook.

Jan 1947

I'm at my wits' end with these mushrooms. They don't seem to want to grow here. I'm in communications by letter (very slow and tedious) with Tony, our guide in the forests the day I first tried these godforsaken things. He's getting into science after the war. Lucky him.

The idea that I could bring these to cold and wet Scotland and expect them to grow is, I see now, absurd. But I still have hope. If he can explain the ideal growing conditions to me, then perhaps I can replicate them here, in a greenhouse or even inside the house. Although Elsie wouldn't be too happy about that. Once it works though, and I'm selling them, I'm sure she'll change her mind. She could give up her job at that awful hotel. We could start a family.

Letter from Tony in Italy

December, 1968

Dear Frankie,

Your idea to try and cross breed the morels with something from the psilocybin family is radical but may work better in the Scottish climate. In the first instance I'd suggest the Cubensis or Liberty Cap. Obviously it would be wise to choose something that you find abundantly in Scotland, so you might have another type in mind. I can't guarantee what, if any, mind-altering effects this might have on consumption. You might do as well to try one of the so-called magic mushrooms yourself, so you can see what the possibilities are. Although, I'm assuming you already have tried, and that's where this idea came from? You need to be aware of the legal side of this too. We don't want you getting in trouble. There's talk of them being outlawed in America. The studies over there have halted.

I know there are some theories that magic mushrooms are able to help people who have dark moods, potentially bringing joy/destroying fear. These were some of the findings from the American studies. I've attached a copy of one of the reports.

You must remember the reasons why the morel mushroom is so favoured. Crossbreeding may remove all its unique properties, the taste, the texture, the meatiness. They all might change and those are the very selling points of the morel.

If you created something new, and it still has the properties listed above, it wouldn't necessarily be a morel. You need to be careful with this, especially with how you would take it to market if you succeed. You may need it to be officially classified, which I can help with. You know I'd do anything for you.

All these things need to be considered, from one mycologist to another, one friend to another. As always, I wish you well in your plans. Please keep me informed of how you get on. I'm very interested. Have a wonderful Christmas.

Your friend, Tony

Frankie, March 1974

Dear Tony,

I must confide in you, confide in someone. Whether I send this or not, I think it'll do me good to get it off my chest. See, it was my fiftieth birthday recently. Can you believe it? It only seems like a few weeks ago that we had our moment during the war.

We went to see my favourite, Elton John, have you heard his music over there yet? It is really something very different, it lights a fire inside when you listen.

Elsie came with me, to be honest, she was humouring me. I think she is seeing one of my friends. I long to tell her the truth about me, everything, but I never manage to find the right words. Not like Elton. He has the words. Him and Bernie can right every wrong with their songs. She never listens to them properly.

I barely held it together. I stayed behind after the concert, they, my pals and Elsie, went to the nearest pub. I thought I was going to explode with energy as I stood at the stage door with a load of groupies, they were all singing. It was like I'd joined a pack of rabid animals. Thinking about it, the band had either barricaded themselves in or used a different exit, I never did get to meet him. Anyway, it was all girls and there was me and two other men. The men were dressed in the androgynous style that has started to become more popular. They reminded me of you.

We got talking, the two men and me. They invited me to go with them, and, as I'd been standing there for forty-five minutes already, I did. It's not that I forgot about Elsie, I was just so full of excitement still, and I didn't want her to start on me when I went to meet them in the pub, it'd spoil my night. She'd be okay.

I ended up in a basement bar with the two men, we drank a lot and then ended up in an alleyway. They really wanted me, it felt so good, being wanted like that again. Said I was their bit of rough. I love Elsie, but the feeling that I get from being with a man, well I don't have to explain it to you.

When I got home, I carried on drinking. I was feeling guilty, trying to forget. I woke the next day in my shed feeling sore and stale all over. Inside and out. I must have taken a bottle home with me and not even tried getting into the house. I was shivering, the door to the shed wide open. We've had an argument. Elsie. I think maybe she knows. She asked me, why can't I be normal, why I love my mushrooms more than her. She says she feels like a bystander constantly waiting for me. Watching me live, and she's put her life on hold.

I told her there are men in America studying this. I have the answers here, I know I do. I started going on about other realms like a right dickhead.

She told me I'm full of shit. Maybe she's right. Does your wife know everything about you, Tony?

Extracts from a garden diary, found in Francis's bunker

August 1976

She has gone. Isn't that just typical? The bitch. I get the mushrooms growing—years of painstaking planning and work—and she leaves. No matter. I'm stronger without her. I can prove it, too.

The island is quiet, I think that's what finished her off, moving here, but that just means there's no distractions from my work. I can listen to my music as loud as I like, and I'm sure all the fungi love it, too. I bet Elton would love it here. Some of the varieties will have the hallucinogenic properties these rock stars love. It turns out that was the key. To get the meaty, tasty mushrooms to grow here, the ones I had during the war. Well, I've had to cross them. I'm still working on the methodology. And I think my findings are worthy of a book or two.

❖ ❖ ❖

September 1976

I think I've created something very special. This could make me a fortune. Then she'd beg to come back. I'd probably let her for a bit. Then teach her a lesson. I need to test it out on something other than the wild rabbits.

❖ ❖ ❖

October 1976

We are under quarantine. They are no doubt going to trace it back to me. I have a plan.

PART THREE: 2070-2072

CHAPTER 9 – 2070

(12 years into the mission)
Rebecca – Cycle F12 Day 1

I wake up on my bed in my assigned quarters. My eyelashes feel like they are stuck together with glue, the sensations under my eyelids are like tiny imagined things are crawling and scratching beneath them. Twelve years in, all this time and every wake up it still feels like the first. Waking up after hibernating in the pods, inside my capsule room, feeling like crap. And I'm the lucky one.

Each pod cycle is six months. Six months in, six months out. Waking cycles and sleeping cycles. They want to slow down our aging, so we'll still be fertile when we get to our destination. My head is groggy, skin clammy. My mouth has a sooty feel to it. A thin fleece blanket swaddles me, like cling film wrapped around soggy sandwiches. Wriggling free, I pull myself into a sitting position. Wobbly and disorientated, my stomach tries to eat itself. Grabbing the tiny basin, I lever myself up, and gulp down some water that has been left at some point in the hours before. The liquid stings my throat, but it's a pain I'm used to, I guzzle it down.

I made it, again. We are still moving through space. The process of pod-sleep has been explained to us several times by different MAGIE. To get to the new home planet, each human needs to spend time in pod-sleep cycles. Women and men are separated, no change there. Annabel says it just makes things easier. I guess there's an element of control, or the illusion of it. There are three people that have opted to be with the women. Annabel gave these non-binary gendered people a choice. I imagine they probably feel safer with a bunch of women than a bunch of men. The pods work on a suppression and slow-down method. Ageing will slow down because our systems are being suppressed, a type of therapeutic hypothermia. This includes sexual desire—it's no wonder the whole ship feels like a convent.

Each group spends six months asleep, then we swap over. The longer you're awake from the pods, the more you feel like yourself. So, by the end of each six-month window we have things back like hormone fluctuations, desire and some ageing. Then it all gets suppressed again. We're given shots for vitamins and minerals and have to increase our liquid intake by two litres a day, each day, for the seven days before going back in.

Inside the pods it's cold, dark, and sticky. We are naked but coated in a thick ointment before we go in. We do this ourselves and it's often a moment of comedy before the sleep. Like that giddiness you get before bed as a child, when you've been up too long and have gone hyperactive.

The pods are attached at the start of the process to an overhead conveyor system, a monorail they call it. Like some twisted amusement park ride. You wait your turn and climb in. The pods are organic, some sort of plant, I think. They look like giant cocoa pods or seeds, an amber, knobbled surface with a slit down the front where you climb in. After they've checked you, the pods are laid inside the man-made amniotic fluid.

It is weird, I often have doubts about the whole thing. But there's no way out. This is what I signed up for, right? Gathering my things, I follow signs for the communal showers. I always think I'll remember the way, but I don't. My motivation for a shower is zero—the queue is always so long after the pod-sleeps—but the sticky stuff makes me feel cold. I stumble a little, knees weak as my legs find their strength again.

The ships corridors are all arched ceilings, giving a cocoon feeling to the walk, though it feels more like a tunnel than a cocoon. The shared showers are already busy with other women, who'd managed to get up and recover before me. I sit down on a bench, where opposite there is a row of mirrors and hairdryers. It reminds me of council swimming pool changing rooms. I wait for a shower to become free. I catch sight of myself in the mirrors. my hair is longer, the fringe hanging limply to the side of one temple. Beyond that is something else. Or to be more specific, nothing else. On the left side of my neck and down my shoulder had been a tattoo. Standing up I move closer to the mirror, examining my neck, pulling at the skin. It isn't there.

"You have something missing, too?" a voice says. Looking through the mirror to the reflection of a woman behind me, looking at me questioningly. She is short, much shorter than me. A mane of colourful hair drips down around her shoulders. I can see the natural colour coming through at the roots. She has huge eyes. Eyes like dustbin lids, Mum would have said.

"I had an octopus tattoo all across here." I point to where it should be. "I'm sure of it."

"I've had one go missing, too. Here, on my inner wrist. A cross. It's vanished." The woman looks sad and bewildered. "I've been racking my brain trying to figure it out, trying to decide if I'm actually mad…"

I turn around to face her, just in time for the woman to reach out and hug me. "Thank you. Thank you." We pull away from each other at almost the same moment, realising the strangeness of the situation.

"The skin looks like it's brand new," I say.

"I don't know what to say. It feels better that I'm not alone, but of this…" She trails off again, as if not wanting to say it out loud. Something is happening in the pod sleeps.

"Listen," I say, "can we talk later on?" Someone vacates one of the showers.

"I'd like that."

We exchange room numbers, and I grab the shower, my head even more fuzzy than before.

* * *

Most personal items are stored in lockers on a different deck on the lower levels of the ship. Huge hangars with bays full of shipping containers which hold materials, equipment for building homes, and many of the personal items of the travellers on board. In the habitation rooms, some clothes and small personal belongings are allowed. There just isn't the room for lots of things inside the tiny bedrooms. More space has been allocated for the eco-wing and the communal areas, like Sector Four—where we eat, an art studio, and a small library. They seem to want us to be together a lot.

I lift my mattress and pull out a small bag of personal items. Mosaic tiles in muted colours, and the red book of fairy tales. I need my little ritual to calm my mind, usually performed before going to sleep at night, but after the incident in the showers, I need it now. The ritual started on Saxa Vord—Annabel's idea. It helps bring me back into the now, rather than catastrophising. I dig out the green drawstring bag from under my bed, the scrabble logo faded unless you know where to look for it. Releasing the contents onto the small table in my capsule, I then turn all the pieces the right way up. I count them, then group them by colour, and finally I create a pattern with them, one version of which will end up on my new home.

They are Victorian mosaic tiles from my grandfather's shop floor entrance—a shop I never set foot in, as it was long gone by the time I arrived in the world, but mum had managed to salvage some bits before it was no more. I had the photo of it memorised. Mum showed me proudly. 'Lewis & Faulkner' said the tiled floor, in the fanciest of italic scripts. The shop had been a curious combination of herbalist and haberdashery. Arthur, Mum's dad, had been a chemist and worked with alternative medicines and herbs; Kath, my grandmother was a dressmaker, specialising in wedding dresses with embroidery embellishments. Despite the juxtaposition of both professions in one shop, it worked for them for a long time.

The tiles hold so much history and love. The Scrabble bag is the perfect size for them. Planning to personalise my assigned home is one of the things that keeps me going when the walls feel like they are closing in.

The sleeping quarters are like kapuseru hoteru, the capsule hotels that were popular some years ago. A little bigger but they're stacked on top of one another the same way, a giant library of people. The capsule rooms are navigated using ladders, rendering the whole thing strangely quaint. Mine is eleven up, and three across. Known as 11-3. The rooms are small but large enough to stand up in, with a few inches spare above my head, anyone closer or above two metres tall must stoop a little. The bed takes up most of the capsule. There is narrow shelving and built-in storage everywhere, along with a tiny basin and fold down table which sits on top. A pull-down shutter acts as a door at the entrance. I often lie on the bed and stretch, easily touching the wall across from me on the opposite side of the room. It'd be no good if I were claustrophobic.

It is small, but most of the time I feel cosy. It reminds me a lot of the dens I made as a child with Sam, sheets over chairs and tables. That feeling like no one can hear what you were saying when really, they can hear every word.

A repurposed flat screen TV is mounted to the wall in one corner, headphones looped over the top. I use it as a great way of escaping the ship and its ever-decreasing space. Cabin fever does happen the longer we are awake. Sometimes, towards the end of the cycle, I'm desperate to go back to sleep for the six-month stints. There are signs on the walls about noise levels in this part of the ship. Strictly for reading and resting only. People only say stuff here that they don't mind others overhearing.

I need a friendly face. Where is Issy?

"Hello?" A voice comes from behind the shutter.

"Hey!" I pull up the slatted door to my room and see the woman from the showers, peering inside.

"I'm Manawa."

"Rebecca." I stand up, blocking her line of vision. People can be a bit over-familiar on board, like manners don't seem to apply here. "Let's go for a walk." I pull on my shoes, comfy trainers I've had for ages, and follow Manawa down the ladder. We walk, matching each other's steps, unsure who is leading.

Manawa's hair is in two long plaits, hanging down over each ear. It makes the colour difference even more notable. The roots are inky compared to the rainbows through the ends of her hair. Like me, she has many tattoos, symbols of who she is, literally wearing her heart on her sleeve. Lots of them in a traditional Maori style. She's wearing the overalls we've all been given. They look a lot like hospital scrubs but are an undyed, unbleached colour. We don't have to wear them, but they are useful when your personal clothing is being laundered, or when you want to blend in.

I guide us to the corridor for the eco-wing, it's hard to tell where you are at times, the corridors all look the same,

144

thankfully there are intermittent signs. The ship was adapted for this mission, Frankie told me.

The eco-wing is full of plant life, crops, and seedlings. The irrigation systems are so noisy that even if someone is trying to listen to our conversation, the sound of the water would make anything we say inaudible.

"Tell me: you remember your tattoo, but do you remember when you got it, Rebecca?"

"I have a lot of art on my body." I fold my arms across my chest.

"But you remember each one of them, right? The reasons you chose them, who was with you, what was going on in your life—all those things? I can't. I can't remember." The panic in Manawa's voice is contagious. Sitting on the edge of a soil-filled raised bed I take some deep breaths and plunge my hands into the earth, needing to feel grounded again.

"You're right. You're right… I remember what it was, the tattoo, but I don't know why I had it or who did it." I rub my shoulder where the octopus had been, my hand cool and damp from the soil. Manawa crouches next to me.

"What is happening here?"

Issy Cycle F12 Day 1

Waking up from pod-sleep is hard enough but waking up knowing her loved ones are already dead is a whole other level of torture. It's always the first conscious thought she has. Annabel had diagnosed her with PTSD. Every time she wakes it feels like her brain has been reset, undoing all the work she puts in to deal with it.

She is reborn with icky vernix stuff all over. Barely able to open her eyes. Barely able to hear. She throws up, bile stings her tongue. She throws up again. Someone grabs her, she is about to stumble and slip. She's unable to thank them; her mouth doesn't want to work properly.

"Don't try and get up. Stay where you are," the voice says. The pressure in her chest forces her to lie back down. "You're safe, you'll get through this. There's not many of these wakeups left now." Issy is rolled onto her side and feels her back being rubbed, the pain in her chest subsides, her breathing now regular. Why does she react badly to the wakeup, no one ever explains?

Frankie 12 years and 6 months

Frankie revels in having almost a whole deck of the ship to himself, twelve years and his surroundings are just as he wants them. Glad that he'd considered his mobility needs, his legs aren't great anymore. He's a very old man, isolated down here in the belly of the ship. A level just above the shipping containers of building supplies and crates of personal items. There is a hidden access door, through to Oscar's living space, only to be used in an emergency. As far as the passengers are concerned Oscar isn't aboard the ship, some of them wouldn't know who he was anyway. It's easier to just forget him, like he doesn't exist.

This is where Frankie will see out his days. As close to a real home as he'll ever see again. There is a proper bed, taken from the dorms at Saxa Vord, with sheets and pillows. The MAGIE even wash his laundry for him. There are plants everywhere. Peace Lily, Boston Fern, and Spider Plants all thrive despite the light being artificial. There are the other things growing too, his life's work; the mushrooms. There are small bags under the bed and some in the built-in units within his quarters. They'd been easy to start, the steady temperature and humidity of the ship made things easier than they've ever been. That's the thing Oscar doesn't get, *the Earth is always going to win.* That quote is on a loop in his head since he'd read a book all about trees that Rebecca gave him. Plants can adapt to anything, humans cannot. He'd love to see the end of the mission, just to see the look on Oscar's face.

The sounds of shuffling in the wall disturbs his thoughts—a reminder of Oscar's presence in the modified passageways Frankie had helped design and build.

"Probably on the way to the library again," Frankie mumbles to himself, dusting the plant leaves with a dry paintbrush and watering the plants he'd brought with him. Anything for a bit of un-recycled oxygen. He's bones are sore and trekking up to the eco-wing is too much these days. It leads to funny looks and awkward questions. Annabel is his reason for being here. Not many other passengers know him, although most had met him at Saxa Vord at some point. Many of them don't seem to remember Frankie. "I guess they have a lot on their minds though, right?" He says to an orchid. The plants are great company; never answering back, never interrupting. He sends Annabel a message on the MAGIEpad, maybe the last note never got to her. A reply comes through straight away.

Sorry, really busy, will come later on, it's my sleep session tomorrow so would love to see you, A.

Frankie sighs, "the bloody sleep sessions." He blames Oscar for Annabel's workload. He is so demanding of her time while she's awake. On the bright side, he has time to get on with his work.

Annabel still asks, even now, after all these years, if he wants to use the pods. She says it will help his aches. But they're all in them for too long. He's done all that before. Over the years he had been determined to find out the source of the monstrosities. Are they of this earth? Are they genetically modified, grown, and designed? Or are they an alien life form or tool? He has watched the process several times and each time he is repulsed and fascinated in equal measure. The only things he's discovered is they hold back aging; you could say time even. They renew and replenish the body. His body is way past that now, you must be healthy going into the sleep pods. The pods don't allow for disease or anything broken, the process method can't recognise it and it ends up mutating things further.

"Thank fuck for my contract, eh." He considers it fortuitous that he's here with his agreement already in place—the one about him most definitely not entering those pods. He'd made them draw up the contract saying so. Not that it would be much use once they'd left. Records will surely disappear. But it does make the situation feel more official. He likes that formality.

Oscar had agreed to Annabel's idea of letting Frankie join the mission because Frankie is a great handyman and carpenter. Although his aches now hinder any heavy work, but everything is ticking over nicely. The secret labyrinth of passageways works perfectly. Frankie virtually had Oscar around his little finger at that point. The reversal of power, however temporary, had been thrilling.

Drawing up plans alongside Oscar gave Frankie an insight into how the man works. Oscar is, without doubt, a kind of genius verging on becoming a recluse, which is sort of relatable. The secret tunnels only encouraged his unhealthy withdrawal from normality, whatever that was. Those days on Saxa Vord had been fun, he was more able then, Annabel more loving, everything; more. Oscar dreamt it up and Frankie made it, modifying some of the designs because of material supply issues, but the general idea of secrecy worked and is still working now. Oscar on the other side, a ghost. It was only later that Annabel shared the truth about Oscar and his fake death.

He readies himself for bedtime, he goes to bed a lot earlier now. Annabel's habit of having a hot chocolate before sleep is something of a crutch, too, although supplies must be running low after all this time. Sometimes she joins him for a warm drink and a warm body, always gone by morning. Or at least, what he assumes is morning. Time is weird on the ship; the lights make it confusing. He settles his lower half under the covers, propping himself up on one elbow while congratulating himself again for insisting on the televisions and the programming they had installed. Switching off the lights in the room he puts on a wildlife documentary and tries to stay awake. Clearly, she's not coming again. His eyelids are heavy, but he's careful not to spill his drink.

There's a click and a sliding noise, then a figure appears in the glow from the television screen.

"Did I wake you?" the familiar voice asks.

Frankie jumps, spilling some of the hot chocolate down his front. "Fuck me, Oscar, I nearly had a heart attack!"

Who else but Oscar? Frankie's eyes try to focus on Oscar's face. Here he is again, glowing in the light of the underwater documentary Frankie is trying to watch.

Frankie rubs his eyes, still not quite able to see sharply, and sits bolt upright, putting the drink on a shelf behind. "What do you want?"

There is always a reason for Oscar's visits. He thrives on simplifying things, taking what is already there and improving it. Building on what had gone before.

"I'm sorry, I've disturbed you. I didn't look at the time."

"No, no it's fine. I'm in bed early. Sit down. What's up?" Frankie braces himself for another lecture. The man is obsessive.

Oscar sits on the edge of the bed. "The more human consciousness develops, the better scope we have for dealing with the questions of life and death. That's why these people were chosen. They showed a highly developed creative side, which our studies have shown links to a deeper and broader state of mind. They are connected to a realm we currently are only just beginning to understand. There are things we needed to do to ensure the future is good. To ensure we, humans, are still around."

"And you've done the best you can." Frankie attempts to placate his boss.

"I have some ideas. More ideas."

Gant - Cycle M12 Day 1

Gant wakes in his room, on his bed. The usual throbbing head arrives soon after. Swinging his legs off the bed, he almost takes the basin off the wall with his feet. Every time he forgets about the damn basin.

"Sorry!" he shouts, knowing he's likely woken Tait next door. Man, that guy can sleep! He's been asleep for six months and still wants more. Grabbing stuff for the shower, he jumps down from his capsule. He isn't far from the ground—three up and twenty-two across. Challenging himself physically after the pod-sleep; the lack of movement troubles him, though he's been told time and time again it won't happen, he doesn't want to shrivel up. He heads for the showers. If he is first out of the starting blocks, he'll have the place to himself; and it'll be clean.

Standing under the shower stream never fails to remind him of home, back on Earth and the scarcity of water in his territory. This still feels extravagant. His dad had worked for the water police. Water was rationed, and the rich all moved away to places where it still came out of the tap without danger. He let the memories slip away with the hot water running down over his head. Closing his eyes and tipping his head back, he gives in to the pleasure. The steam from the shower loosens some phlegm, he clears his throat, and begins to exercise the muscle he was known for back at home: his voice.

"'Cos I'm right here, right here, right here, right here…"

"That's a voice you got there!" someone shouts from behind.

"Ah, I thought I had the place to myself." His time is up, and the shower switches off. Gant is suddenly chilly. He's seen this guy around.

"Don't stop on my account. I think we left our dignity behind on Earth."

"I'm just about done, but thanks. Maybe next time, right?"

"If you say so. If you say so."

Gant walks away. A pang of pity rises up, this guy is always alone even after all this time. He knows what that feels like. Olive branch time—we are all in this together.

"Hey. Wanna meet up in Sector Four later on? I always need to unwind after a long sleep." The man didn't get the joke. "I'm Gant, by the way."

* ✳ *

Pulling on his trainers after the shower, he uses the ladder up to his room to do some warmup stretches and then launches into a run. He will do this every day for the six months he is awake. Each day taking a different route, going a different distance. Because the ship is so cavernous, he rarely sees anyone, except other runners. often setting challenges with a couple of the other men. It keeps things vaguely interesting.

The running is also a way to explore the ship. There are a few corridors that ended with Off Limits doors, only allowing those with the right passcode through. Gant had never been one for rules, and he was desperate to get behind those doors and see what lay beyond those signs.

The ship had been a cargo vessel in another life. It feels too big for human needs. Gant estimates there must be 400 people on board, 199 of which are the other male passengers.

Two hundred women must be asleep right now.

The ship is run by Dr Morin and the MAGIE. He avoids the doctor as best as he can but loves getting to know his shipmates. Friendship groups formed quickly between people who speak the same language. Already language blending is happening, along with a heck of a lot of gesticulations that are universal.

Boredom is rife on the ship, so Gant keeps exploring. Especially the places that are off the usual routes of the shower room, eco-wing, and the Sector Four recreation area. He is always looking for new routes hopeful there are enough places to explore to last the rest of the journey.

His feet pound the metal floor and music fills his ears. He is in a world of his own again. Except this time, he is in control. In the sleep-pods, they are the boss, and he despises it. This is his time.

After getting lost for a few minutes, he switches off his music and comes to a halt. Breathing deeply through his nose, his head fills up with a scent, memories of his mother in the kitchen baking birthday treats. He leans on the wall and pulls out the ear buds of the corridor and bends from the waist, his arms and head hanging down. Is he hallucinating a scent? Adrenalin buzzes somewhere behind his eyes, his heartbeat creating a soundtrack deep in his ears. Then, he hears something—is someone following him? Tracing his route, the sound ever closer. He turns a corner, and on the floor, looking in a bad way is one of the MAGIE, a smaller version. It isn't just the size of the MAGIE that's different; its dressed, its wearing T-shirt and shorts.

"What on earth? What happened to you?" Gant says, crouching bedside it.

"My leg seems to have given way." Its leg looks dislocated at the knee.

"Were you following me? I don't think you were built for running."

"Not following, sir, more emulating. I saw you running. You looked so free."

Gant lifts the robot up, swinging its arm across his shoulder.

"None of us are free, my friend. Let's get you to med bay. What's your name?"

"I'm Junior."

"Junior? Well okay, Junior. Can you smell something?"

"We MAGIE don't have that capacity."

CHAPTER 10 – 2071

(13 years aboard)
Annabel, Cycle F13 Day 1

A twelve-hour window sits between each group waking up and the opposing one going into pod-sleep, creating a crossover. In these twelve hours worlds collide. Annabel designed it this way. Her own pod-sleeps are shorter than the precious cargo. She does two-month stints sleeping, then four months working. It means that she often misses the crossover of the groups, the mixing when they are all together. One groggy and the other on edge, preparing to go down the rabbit hole for another six-month cycle. She hears all about it through her counselling sessions. These are no longer mandatory but work on an as-needed basis. She likes them to have an inkling of each other, a stirring in the loins. The ones coming out of the pods are not interested at all, the ones going in are horny as hell. The pods give peaceful slumber but take away many things in return. It is not that she minds the passengers having sex, it is the accidental pregnancies that must be avoided, so male/female sex is frowned upon, the separation of the groups is one of the methods of lessening the chances.

Annabel loves the pod-sleep. It gives her the opportunity to rediscover parts of her brain that she thought had shrivelled up and died. After struggling to sleep for real, she now understands how transformative it can be. Inside the pods there is no sound and no light. The highly viscous liquid, Oscar's version of amniotic fluid, is the same temperature as our bodies. It is womb-like, there is a feeling of safety and of letting go. The renewal she feels after each sleep isn't as strong as the passengers feel, whether they are aware of it or not. Annabel's sleep also isn't long enough to suppress her sexual desire. She visits Frankie often—perhaps not as often as he would like, but that will all change once they arrive at their destination. He is less fun than he had been on Saxa Vord.

Today is serendipitous. She is here to witness the crossover, although she isn't there in person. There are discreet cameras dotted around, and she watches in a viewing booth with Appo. Sector Four is open to all. The passengers gather there to share tales from their past, debate fuels their brains. Many discuss the dreams they have while in pod-sleep, or memories from Earth, stories about their childhood—nothing more.

The women begin to come through in dribs and drabs, and there are a lot of men milling about Sector Four, excited to see them.

"We've been doing this for years now. You'd think there would be some favouritism going on." Sometimes she forgets Appo is MAGIE.

"Wait. Wait for it," Appo replies. They study the monitors. The women, fresh from their showers, are hungry, seeking out food and drink.

And there it is. Like watching magnets or heat-seeking missiles. Couples finding each other. It is sweet to watch, like something from an old movie. Tentative, but there.

Rebecca Cycle F13 Day 1

Sector Four is a community space that serves as a leisure area and a place to eat. It's where the vending machines are all located. Most of it is freeze-dried food which isn't as bad as it sounds. The spaghetti bolognaise is without doubt the best dish, closely followed by Irish stew, although Mum would baulk at this version. Some of the more unpopular choices include pizza and the fajitas, neither of which translate well into a freeze-dried option. The machines also provide drinks. Hot chocolate is a favourite, and there are a few coffee options, but they're very strongly caffeinated and too stimulating for most people on board, including me. The highlight is most definitely the ice cream machine. Using a non-dairy mixture, the frozen sweet stuff surprises me every time I try it.

The eating area of Sector Four is like any staff cafeteria. Much of the seating is taken from the RAF base and canteen on Saxa Vord, there are lots of moulded orange plastic chairs attached to table units. Each table sits four, a makeshift booth.

The other half of Sector Four is split into two. A lounge area contains lots of sofas, armchairs, blankets, and cushions. This is a place to go when you wanted to get out of your capsule but also just relax. I've seen people who sleep here instead of their capsules for a couple of nights, just to feel more space around them. Often the capsule walls begin to close in towards the end of cycles.

The other section is an open space for fitness and sports. There is a basketball hoop, a cage full of assorted balls, and other equipment. Issy runs a yoga class once a week in this section. She isn't a trained yoga teacher but has done it throughout her life on Earth, she really enjoys it and finds it helps her, she has adapted really well to life on board. More so than me.

The lighting in each space feels carefully considered. Low side lights in the snug area, strip lights in the cafeteria and fitness area. It gives the whole of Sector Four a quirky, ironic hotel look. Perhaps like one you'd have found in Amsterdam decades ago.

There are no set mealtimes on board, but there are regular health checks, primarily when you get in and out of the pods. Things like weight and blood pressure are logged on the system. Skipping meals or, at the opposite end, overeating really can't be done. You need to be healthy and fit to go into the pods and, if for any reason you aren't, there's an investigation by the MAGIE.

The food comes on steel trays which we clean up ourselves. The drinks vessels are also reusable, a toughened glass. We'll be using these in our new home. Everything will be broken down and reused when we get there.

He's waiting for me again. Gant buzzes over to me as I'm eating. I went for the pizza this time, not the best choice, but I'm feeling lazy and it is much easier to clean up after. He's almost bouncing off the walls, telling me he's something to show me.

"Can I get an ice cream first?"

"If you make it takeaway, we need to hurry, I've not much time before pod-sleep."

He tells me this as if I don't know, and I wonder if it's a ploy just to get me alone. It's common knowledge that just before the sleeps is the peak time for desires to come flooding back. I decide to trust him. I feel like I've known him for longer than I have, but that's the weirdness of the sleep cycles. And at least this is something different to do.

He leads me down the long corridor away from Sector Four. It looks like all the others on the ship: slightly rounded walls, made from what seems to be old car seats interspersed with panels and information points. The floor is also mixed materials, mostly repurposed grids, tiles, panels, and plastics. All the corridors have this feel of being cobbled together, somehow it works, it keeps us safe up here in space and it must have saved them a bit when modifying the ship. The real money has clearly been invested in the eco-wing, hardly surprising considering our destination. Gant keeps a fast pace, and I struggle to keep up with him, limbs still sleepy. We turn left and go further, then down another level, and further to somewhere I'm sure I've not been to before.

"Where are we?"

"It's right down here," he turns, checking I'm still here. "Wait until you see!"

Finally, he stops and lifts a hexagonal panel out of the floor. I catch up to him and we both get on our knees to peer inside.

Below is a pocket of darkness. Gant reaches for a torch I hadn't noticed him carrying, flicking it on and pointing it down into the gloom. Something very small and grey stands there, very still and proud, a soft, pale-yellow cap upon its head.

"A mushroom," I whisper.

"Yep," says Gant, like an excited puppy. "You have a lot of questions, I can see."

I become aware my mouth is hanging open.

"Yep. Lots." I lean back sitting on my calves, the ice cream forgotten.

"This corridor is off the beaten path of most passengers. As you know, I run to keep fit. I found it by chance. And it's not the only one. There's a whole bunch of them further down under some of the other grids. Can't you smell something sweet?"

I shake my head. "Maybe a little?" I lie. "There must be something organic down there. And moisture. It couldn't grow otherwise."

"That's right. It's like someone is baking a cake. Brings back some memories. I followed it down here. You can't smell cherries?"

I shake my head again, standing up, annoyed he's asked me twice. My ice cream has melted into the cup on the floor where I'd abandoned it.

"I've always disliked mushrooms, the texture is too slimy." I say, "How did they get here?"

"I don't know, but don't go eating them, they might be poisonous." He puts the piece of floor back in position. "I'm no expert, but kidney failure is one of the risks if it's a toxic type. So, let's not chance it, eh?" He laughs, and I grin at him, amazed that he didn't think I'd know not to eat it. "I thought you'd appreciate it. I know you're into your plants and stuff." He's blushing, he clearly does like me.

"I do, and I am. Thanks for sharing it with me."

We walk back to the main living quarters. "Have you told anyone else? Shown anyone?"

"No. Just you. I found them a few weeks ago. I wanted to wait until you came out of pod-sleep. To ask you what you thought. You're the experienced botanical person, right?"

"Flatterer. I worked at the Eden Project, but mainly as a storyteller. I loved the plants, I still do, but I didn't pick up that much. I never studied it seriously or anything."

I'm enjoying this, playing with him a bit.

"I'd still appreciate your advice. Do we tell the MAGIE?" He stops and faces me. I hope he doesn't try and kiss me.

"I like that it's our secret. There's not a lot to tell, is there? I think we should try and figure out how they're growing down there. Whilst you're in the pods, I can try to figure it out. And when you get out, come and find me."

"I'll do that. I'll look forward to it. Well, as much as I can look forward to anything whilst I'm unconscious." He smiles that weird half smile he has.

"Sleep tight. Don't let the bed bugs bite." I awkwardly touch his arm, aiming for a reassuring rub, and walk away.

I like him, probably more than I'm admitting to myself. Deciding to visit the library straight away, there's a spring to my step I haven't felt in a while. A reason to research. Something that makes me feel needed; I didn't know I missed it.

The library is on the floor above the living quarters, and it is bigger than anyone would probably expect for a spaceship. Everyone knows about it, but I think people forget it's here. Its admirable that there are actual books on the ship I suppose. Whoever has put it together is an avid real-book fan. You don't see this number of books all together very often on Earth. Everything is digitised. It is my second favourite place on board, after the eco-wing. But I don't visit as often as I ought to. Now I have the perfect excuse.

Pushing open the doors I enter the cramped, shelved space. Books on top of books on top of books. There is sometimes a MAGIE in here, but not this time. Often the place is empty, like today. The ceilings are low, almost like this space had been an afterthought during the design of

165

the ship. It feels like a cave, a very wide, low cave. Most of the books are nonfiction. The history of Earth and the human race are seen as something we should all learn about going to the New World. Charging power will be a valuable commodity when we arrive, and not having the internet, the books will help us keep history alive without relying on the MAGIEpads, so we can tell our children the stories of how we came to be. There are books on animals and dinosaurs and space and mathematics and scientific theory. Books on the history of individual countries, before the territories. Stories of kings and queens, and a world that is fantastical to think about. There are books on the languages of old, many on Russian and its different dialects.

I run my finger along the shelves, scanning for something of use. The history of the books themselves, the feel of them at my fingertips, always makes me gasp in awe. Maps, medical drawings, paintings, astronomy, Ancient Egypt, archaeology, the Battle of Britain, and—ah, here— flora and fauna. *Mushrooms, Fungi and Moulds: A Field Guide.* That could help. I lift it off the shelf. Then another, *The National Audubon Society Field Guide to North American Mushrooms.* I put them both under my arm. "And a third for luck," I say to myself, spotting one more. The title makes me laugh. *Mushrooming without Fear: The Beginner's Guide to Collecting Safe and Delicious Mushrooms.* Mushrooming without fear, indeed. I don't want kidney failure. Despite my dislike of mushrooms, I'm enjoying the research already.

The library is one wide room with a desk near the entrance and a private reading room at the far end, which I head for. As I approach, I can see through the glass door that the room is already in use. Getting closer, there is someone sitting at the table, hunched over; a man, he shouldn't be here. He should be getting ready for pod-sleep. I don't recognise him. It is impossible to know everyone on board by name, but I'm sure I know everyone's faces. This man must be an intruder, a stowaway even. I curse my overactive imagination. I can only see his profile, but he is bald with a bushy, unkempt beard. His hands are supporting his head at the temples, obscuring the detail of his face. I walk past the door to the reading room, now aiming for the table beyond. He looks up and directly at me. I'm sure now, this does feel wrong.

Who the hell is it? I quicken my pace, keep moving, just get to the table, and don't stare, don't challenge. I sit down with my books, positioning myself so I can see the doorway of the reading room. He'll have to leave soon, otherwise he'll miss the start of the sleep and the MAGIE will be after him. I pick up a book and wait, looking at the pages but not taking anything in.

The men are due to go to sleep in a matter of minutes. Maybe he's sick? Maybe he isn't allowed to go into the pods until he is better? But he'd be in med-bay if that was the case, surely. Everyone is accounted for on board. Stowaways are impossible, especially after all this time. I lean back on my chair, tipping it and balancing on the back two legs trying to concentrate on the book in my hand.

A huge crash startles me, nearly sending me all the way back on my chair; the noise a pile of books make when dropped on the floor, coming from the reading room. I freeze, steadying myself, waiting for something else to happen. Nothing does. I slowly, carefully stand and creep to the door of the reading room, peering through the Plexiglas. Nothing, its empty. Nothing to be seen and nothing to be heard.

Before I know it, I'm opening the door, and I'm inside the room. There is no trace.

Oscar Cycle F13 Day 1

Oscar quietly stands, putting his notebook in his pocket returning his pencil to its usual spot behind his right ear. He can't risk putting the book back, she might get a better look at him. He decides to take it with him. He owns it anyway, so why the hell not? He listens, straining his ears; books being placed on the table outside and the scrape of a chair. Maybe she thinks nothing of him sat in here after all? Either way, he must get back and take cover.

Oscar doesn't want or need to interact with his guests. Thanks to Frankie, the reading room houses a secret doorway—a trapdoor within the hodgepodge jigsaw of the floor—back to his private quarters, two floors away. Stooping under the table, he lifts the door and shuffles inside until his rubber-soled feet feel the in-built steps which will lead him below. It is more of a struggle with a book in his hand, and as he lowers himself, he forgets to brace the trapdoor. It comes crashing down with a slam.

"Shit, shit, shit!" He descends two floors quickly, dim light just above watching over his careful steps downward.

She must have heard that, he scolds himself. He reaches the other secret door back into his quarters, which are vast compared to the size of each passenger capsule. Pushing into his safe place, he closes the door behind him. How had he allowed this to happen? He barely leaves his rooms these days but needs to stretch his legs every now and again. Sometimes, normality is like a foreign territory; being able to read in the library. Obviously, this is a sign he shouldn't even try. Fool. Throwing the book on a chair, he goes to the basin and washes his hands. Then washes them again, again, and then again. Bacteria is all over the ship and he doesn't want any of it coming in here, into his space. It is bad enough he'd brought the book back, but what is the alternative? Too many questions, he isn't ready for.

Annabel will be able to help. A session with her always calms him down.

Rebecca Cycle F13 Day 120

"Are you up yet, Nia?" I knock on the wall between our capsules.

Nia is my neighbour. I have neighbours all around me when inside the capsules, but Nia is my favourite among the rooms close by, Issy is right at the other end. There is no answer. We are two thirds through F13.

I put on an old film, one of my favourites, *Don't Look Now* and pull my journal out from under my pillow. The film is set in Venice in the 1970s. I have ancestors from Italy and Venice, it's prominent in my genetic make-up. The HeritageNow test showed sixty-eight percent. It is a sinister film, but I'm always drawn to the couple central to the story. Every time I watch it, I try to see more. More of the detail, more of the undercurrent of emotions, more of the meaning and messages the filmmakers are trying to get across. Going further into the couple's story, their grief at the loss of their child, and the final scene which feels so macabre and strange, like a fantasy rather than their reality. What is real? My obsession with this film has begun to stir the storyteller within me. I'm journaling nearly every day in the gaps between hyper sleeps. Annabel will be proud.

A noise from next door, from Nia's room, jolts me back. Jumping off the bed, I pull up my shutter and swing out, monkey-like, to check on her.

"Nia, you okay? Are you awake?" I nudge open Nia's shutter.

A groan comes from the bed. "Bec? Is that you? I feel dreadful."

"I'm coming in."

I lift myself into Nia's capsule. It is much emptier than mine, or much tidier, I'm not sure which. "I'll get you some water." Turning to find the cup near the tiny basin, I notice vomit. I turn on the tap and begin to clean up the mess.

"I'm not sure you should be doing that. I might be contagious."

"It's no problem. Can I put a light on? I can hardly see."

"Yes, sorry. Of course."

The light comes on and my eyes feel like they go out on stalks.

"You don't look well at all." Nia's skin has a blue-green tinge to it. Her eyes are bulging.

"I'm going to get Lan or another MAGIE. Just drink this and stay here." I hand Nia a cup of water, wash my hands, and leave the capsule. Sliding down the ladder, I'm trying to stay calm. I've washed my hands. I am okay. Nia looks awful.

Get help, get help, get help.

I run towards the med-bay, passing a couple of women on the way instinctively deciding against asking them for help. I don't want to cause a panic. As far as I know the only people on board with medical knowledge are the MAGIE.

"Help…" It comes out in a whisper. I clear my throat. "Help!"

"What is wrong, Rebecca?" one of them asks turning to face me. I hate how they know my name. The other four MAGIE present in the Triage space don't bother looking at me, all crowded around a screen showing colourful stripes of data. It's gleaming in here. I realise this is the first time I've been in here which isn't pod-sleep related, hazy memories of those times try to stitch themselves together in my mind. There are two empty beds here and worktop surfaces littered with MAGIEpads. Pegboard lines three walls, with stowed medical equipment mounted onto it.

"It's Nia, she's sick. Really sick. I need help to bring her here."

"You go to the showers. We will deal with this. Go and wash yourself clean." One of the MAGIE grabs a stretcher and brushes past me into the corridor. Lan follows.

"I'm sure she'll be fine. Nothing to worry about. You go and freshen up." They charge away and disappear.

The news hurriedly spreads. Someone is ill. I walk back towards my capsule after the shower and there are groups of women standing around chatting about Nia.

"They put her on a stretcher, but I didn't see her moving," says one.

"She vomited down the MAGIE's back as it carried her down from her room."

"Have they cleaned this area, then?" I ask, to nobody in particular. I look down at my feet, I'd completely forgotten any shoes. I hope I haven't spread anything.

"Yeah, they just finished," a familiar voice, thank god, it's Issy.

"It's good to see you!" I throw my arms around Issy, but she doesn't reciprocate. "Are you okay?" I step away from her. "You're not feeling sick too, are you?"

"No, no I'm fine. Was it you who found her?" Issy's look feels piercing.

"Yes. I heard a groan so poked my head around her shutter to check on her. She had the light out and—"

"Did you touch her? The vomit?"

"No. The MAGIE sent me straight for a shower, and my clothes are in the laundry—hence the robe."

Issy releases a sigh. "You've done what you can, then. Fancy a drink in Sector Four?"

"I need one. Just let me get dressed and find my shoes."

Climbing the ladder, I can see that Nia's capsule has been emptied and cleaned. The shutter has been left wide open, and I'm nearly vomiting when a wave of scent, or is it taste, catches the back of my throat. There's something cloying in the air around the entrance. Feeling tears springing up, overwhelmed, I stumble into my capsule wiping my face on the sleeve of my robe. Weird after all this time, my sense of smell returning—why does it have to be cleaning products I can pick up? Curious and curiouser. I hear Issy calling me from below, always so impatient. I switch off the film and dress. Issy's reaction had been accusatory. What did she think had happened? She must have been listening to all the gossipers. It's hard to retain any cynicism or objectivity on board, that's for sure. I pull on a navy hooded sweater I'd taken from Sam, old jeans with denim so soft it was liable to tear, and a pair of ship standard trainers, of which I am surprisingly fond.

"Okay," I say, trying to reassure myself as I climb down the ladder. Issy is chatting with a couple of women who are still hanging around. "Are you ready?"

"Aye, let's go."

＊＊＊

"What do you fancy?" Issy asks me, she's poised at the drinks machine.

"I'd love a hot chocolate, please. A large one, I need some sustenance. I've not eaten." I find a booth and sit down.

"Comin' right up."

Issy is more herself now. I love the buoyant way she moves and talks. She charms anyone and everyone, and I always feel special when she singles me out.

"You know why I love talking to them women, don't you?" she asks, placing two hot chocolates on the table, as if she's read my mind.

"Pray tell. They're like jackals, gossiping. It's all fair game though I suppose. It's probably the most exciting thing to happen here in years," I say, stifling a yawn.

"Well yes, there's that. But also, it reminds me of home." She unleashes her broad smile. It is infectious. "My days of hustle and groove. I had to be a chameleon, fit in with everyone. It's nice to know I haven't lost it. I'm keeping my oar in. Keepin' my skills sharp." She makes a cross gesture with her hands and giggles.

"Do you really think you'll need those skills where we're going? We're all going to know each other. There won't be any danger."

Issy's laughter grows from the bottom of her belly, right up through her chest, and out of that wide mouth. I suddenly feel stupid.

"Oh Bec, you are funny. There's always danger. Not always from people, I'll give you that, but from creatures, disease, the environment. We don't really know what we're getting into, do we? We just wanted to get off the car crash that Earth has become, right?"

"Right." We sip our drinks in unison.

"So, what really happened with you and Nia?"

I sigh and sip at the hot, sweet drink again. I tell her everything "So she isn't dead then?"

"Not when I left her. Yes, she looked terrible, seasick almost, but we were talking, we had a conversation."

There is silence as we both sip again.

"This could be bad," Issy finally says. "Very bad. It could spread."

"When I got to med bay the MAGIE sent me straight to clean up, said they knew who I meant and where she was. No surprise there, I suppose; they know us all. But could they have anticipated something like this? Known something wasn't right?" My stomach is moaning at me. I'm hungry, but if I eat right now, I don't think it'd stay down.

"Well, that doesn't bear thinking about. We're halfway through a wake cycle, so it can't be something to do with the pod-sleep." Issy frowns. "I suppose they're trained, programmed even, for every eventuality. So, in some way, perhaps they were prepared."

"I think I need a session with Annabel. I've not seen her for ages. When did you last see her?"

"A couple of cycles ago. I'm probably due another session too."

"Let's walk over there now and get organised." It's a coping mechanism, me organising, it helps me feel in control, safe. As though if I make a plan, then everything will be okay.

"So where is Nia now?" Issy asks as we get up.

"I don't know. Her room has been cleaned and cleared. Med-bay, I suppose?"

"Well that's on the way to Dr Morin's office, right? Shall we see if we can find her?" Issy links my arm as we leave Sector Four, I soak up the closeness of her, the touch of someone other than myself. She leans into me, maybe we both don't want to admit how scared we are.

* ✳ *

A sheet of paper hangs from an old wooden clipboard probably from Saxa Vord. It is pinned up on the outside of the doctor's office. 'APPOINTMENTS' it states at the top.

"Hang on," Issy says, "I don't even know the date, do you? And what happened to the MAGIEpad system that was here?"

"No, I don't. But I don't think she's organised it like that, has she?" I look more closely. "I think we just write our names here and she'll contact us for a session."

"That's surely a breach of patient confidentiality? Look at all these names above, all men."

"I don't know what to say, Issy. Maybe the MAGIEpad here is broken or something." She mumbles something under her breath as I write my name dutifully underneath. How civilised we still are.

We go to look for Nia. There is no sign of her in the Triage at med-bay and no MAGIE around to ask. Issy tries to have a look on the control panel but we have no idea how to get onto the system.

* ✳ *

Leaving, Issy and I go back to my capsule, exhausted. My mind is racing, and my body can't keep up, my limbs keep trembling. I've a feeling creeping up on me of panic. I'm trying not to give into it; exorcising it in the pages of my journal. We are all here, as passengers, and are totally passive. Are we fooling ourselves?

Despite believing this trip is the answer for me, I now wish I'd asked more questions. It's too late though. There is no escape, no turning back. I might be making a bigger deal out of this than is the reality, but I feel something, in my gut. If I could get off this ship and go back to Earth, I would do it, despite the forecasts of what is happening back there. There must be somewhere safe on Earth where the extremes of temperature will meet, somewhere high enough above the increasing sea level. Why didn't I investigate more before I agreed to run away?

* * *

Juniper again. I must be dreaming. I follow my dog through the glade. The dream is filled with something catching the light as it floats through the air in front of me. Like tiny shards of glass or glitter, they shimmer as I walk through them entering a meadow full of wildflowers and insects. I can hear the buzzing of each creature individually. My beloved dog yaps and jumps, excited to be in a place as beautiful as this. She is just out of reach: I need her to be closer.

Following Juniper as quickly as I can, I come to a parting in the grasses. Something is lying here, flattening the long stems and blades to make way for itself. A foot, a leg, a dress that sparkles like the things in the air; it is Nia. There is something growing from her abdomen, just like Mum.

Juniper is growling and circling Nia's body, she has white foam at the corners of her mouth and a look in her eye I've never seen before. What is she doing? I reach out for the dog, I try calling to her, but I can't get to her and she doesn't hear me. Juniper begins to lick Nia's face and a bit of my neighbour's flesh comes off onto the dog's rough tongue.

"Stop! Stop it, Juniper!"

Juniper finally turns to face me. *Watch out,* she says, although her mouth doesn't move. *Watch out behind you.*

The meadow changes, becoming dark and cold. I can sense something ominous creeping up towards me. Turning to face the shadow there is nothing to see, I feel like I'm being consumed by it. Retreating, I step back then fall on top of Nia's body, and wake myself up.

Rebecca Cycle F13 Day 140

"I can't find anything," Issy says. "I've asked a couple of the MAGIE, but they claim not to know anything about it. It's been over a week. I think she's dead."

"Issy, we can't think like that. We need to ask the right one. Appo might tell us. He's always been a bit more empathic than the others." The MAGIE all have distinguishable duties and areas that they looked after. Appo is usually around the eco-wing.

I am visiting Issy in the studio of the ship. It has been made to feel like an art studio with great effort. White-painted boards cover the walls, pinned up to hide the metal and plastic skeleton of the ship. Then there are taller boards which act as space dividers throughout the studio. Each artist has their own small space, some sharing. Then they clear it up before the next cycle so the other group can make use of it. There is a row of sinks at one end of the room and a shockingly well-stocked art supply store cupboard.

Issy is making canvases, stretching fabric across frames and priming them ready for her creations.

"I'm going to paint you, Bec," Issy tells me. "That dream you told me about, with your dog. I'm going to add in Nia."

I study Issy's sketchbook. The rhythm of Issy's work is soothing.

"You don't seem that bothered about what happened to Nia now," Issy says without looking up.

"What? I am, I am. I dreamt about it didn't I? To be honest dwelling on it is not doing me any good. I just feel a bit resigned to it now." I look up at Issy. "Like, even if we did know what happened, what could we do? What would we do with that information? It's not as if we can turn back to Earth or order an autopsy or call the police. I almost … almost don't want to know."

"But you *do* want to know. We all want to know if those pods are safe to get back into. Don't we?"

"We don't know it was the pods that caused it. She might have been poorly beforehand, or was carrying something undetected by any of the regular tests—a new pathogen?" My head is full of thoughts about fungi. Could Nia be my fault? I don't want to think it.

Issy stops what she's doing, putting down her tools and looks at me in her intense way. "We need to know. Whatever it is, we need to know. We have a right. You can't keep your head in the sand about this."

"I'm not, I'm not. I'm procrastinating. I wish I could ask Gant."

"He could come out of the pods and have the same thing Nia did." She drives her point home. She knows me better than I do myself sometimes. I stand.

"Point taken. I'm going to find Appo."

Issy returns to her work.

* ✳ *

"Appo?"

"Hello, Rebecca. How are you?" Appo was tending some plants in the eco-wing of the ship, almost exactly where I thought it'd be.

"I'm well, thank you. You're doing a great job there. Do you enjoy it?"

"I believe I do. But you are not here to make small talk, are you?"

Shit. Sometimes the MAGIE were more human than humans. "It's about Nia." I begin. "I … we … what happened? Where is she?"

Appo pauses before answering. "I'm afraid Nia is gone," he says. "We are still trying to determine the reasons behind her death. How it happened."

"We're scared about getting back in the pods."

"We have taken the pod she was in offline for testing. At this stage we are almost certain it hasn't stemmed from pod-sleep."

"Can you reassure us we will be safe in the pods, then?" I ask.

"You will enjoy it as much as you always do." The MAGIE turns away and continues with its work.

I distance myself from the droid. Enjoy it as much as we always do? What does that mean? Do I enjoy it? I don't even know. Certainly not the waking up part. Walking back towards the door of the space, the moist air clings to me, reminding me of Saxa Vord, my last home on Earth. My brain snaps awake, neurons connect: Frankie. Of course, Frankie might know something. I want to go now, right now. Is there another reason why Frankie chose not to get involved with the pod-sleeps? I need to know.

* * *

Frankie's room is down in the belly of the ship. He's been assigned a larger room than everyone else as he isn't sleeping in the pods. I've neglected our friendship, not visiting him at all on this cycle. Not many passengers do visit. He can be hard work, carrying a bitterness that seems to deepen with time. I have been loyal to him, we connected on Saxa Vord, I don't think that happened with many other passengers.

My feet move, down and down on the metal staircase, the courtesy lamps not lighting the way swiftly enough for my pace. Reaching his level, I pause to catch my breath before opening the door to the short hallway that leads to his room. The door opens, but the action of it sounds different, duller, muffled. I take a step through into the hallway and the auto lighting doesn't kick in at all, I just have a faint glow from the courtesy lamp on the stairwell, which will surely go out any minute. Holding my arms out either side of me, I use the narrow corridor walls as a guide. It's only a few steps to his actual front door.

"Knock, knock. Are you in, Frankie?" There is no reply, the floor feels sticky underfoot, like something has been spilt and not cleaned up. I push to override and slide open the door, my hands smearing in something as the door slides. The darkness inside the room is like charcoal and a wave of warm, thick air hits me. I call out for him again, knowing I can't go further without light or help. The lamp in the stairwell blinks off abandoning me, and my instincts shout at me to leave. I listen and turn back down the short corridor. I try to run but lose my balance and go over on my ankle falling to the floor, scraping the wall on the way down. "Ouch!" I crawl back to the door to the stairwell. Finding the entry point, I slip through and the courtesy lamp comes on. I reach up, closing the door to Frankie's hallway on the control panel. Then I look down at my ankle. It is swelling but walkable. What is more concerning is the stuff all over both of my shoes and lower legs. It is covering my front too. It looks like dust, thick dust. I press for help on the control panel and wait for a MAGIE to come, knowing I'll end up in quarantine.

CHAPTER 11 – 2071

Rebecca - Cycle F13 Day 144

I wake up on a bed that isn't my own, with space all around me. I'm not accustomed to the walls not being next to my face as they are in my capsule. I reach up to rub my eyes, but my arm feels dead. Then I realise I'm restrained to the bed. The room is bright, and I try to focus but my vision is cloudy, things are blurred. I feel chilly and try to shrink a little, sure I am being watched. The beeping tells me I'm in med-bay; the wooziness means I've been sedated. There is a figure coming towards me, I manage to focus, it is Doctor Morin. I wriggle, my chest feels tight, the straps are too tight, there's not enough air.

"You're in quarantine, Rebecca. Try to stay calm."

"I … I … Frankie?" My words don't come out as I want them too.

"Francis has been found. That's all you need to know at the moment. Get some rest. They'll be questioning you tomorrow. You are safe, the straps are to stop you hurting yourself." Annabel disappears. My ankle is sore, my mouth dry, and my tongue fat.

"You won't be ready to go into the next round of sleep," a nearby MAGIE says, I now understand why I felt observed.

"What's happened?" I ask them, in a croaky whisper. It comes closer so I can focus.

"You've had a shock, and your ankle is badly sprained." It's a MAGIE I'm not familiar with. "You've been exposed to a potential pathogen of undetermined origin. You had an allergic reaction."

"Can I get up, go back to my capsule, rest there?" My voice is raspy.

"Not yet. You've been unconscious, and we need to monitor you closely now you're awake. We can't let you back into the population yet. We have taken all precautions not to harm you, including a high dose of antihistamines. Your body is processing everything we've administered and everything you encountered. It will be some time before you are feeling like yourself again." This MAGIE is remarkable. So human, so masculine.

"I'm going to give you something to help you rest. Open up." It holds out a dropper and I open my mouth like a Pavlovian dog. The familiar taste of a tincture on my tongue. The one from Saxa Vord. I drift into sleep.

Rebecca - Cycle M13 Day 1

"What you're saying, is that you need me?" Gant asks as we walk together away from Sector Four, he's been out of pod-sleep for a few hours during which I've explained why I'm still here.

"Just your nose." I smile at him. "We need to go back. Back to Frankie's quarters and back to where we—you, I should say—found the mushrooms."

"You think there's a connection?"

"There's got to be. I've been doing so much research into fungi and mushrooms. I think you were right to try and ID the fungi, but there's so many different types it's hard to be sure which it is without getting a closer look. I've read all the books available here. There's even a handful of documentaries on the entertainment system. I've made a note of them for you, so you can watch them back in your room at some point."

"Are we digging somewhere we shouldn't be?" he asks me as we arrive at his capsule. We squeeze past a few men hanging around here after their shower, the heat from their bodies, waking something deep inside me that's lain dormant for the longest time. I refocus on Gant who is climbing up to his room.

"And you think Nia is part of this too?" His head pops out of his capsule. "Come up."

"I'm not great at climbing with this bloody boot on, don't laugh." I take the first two rungs of the ladder carefully, his capsule is on a lower row than mine, so I stay where I am, my head at the floor of his space and swing my bag inside. "That could be completely unrelated but there's something going on here, we need to investigate it. I think that if we tell Annabel or the MAGIE they will just try and cover things up and say they're fixed. We need to build a case."

He is looking through of his storage cupboards, pulling out a torch and a knife from his personal effects.

"It's a bit of a heirloom, so I'd rather not use it if possible."

I use one hand to pick up the knife, my other holding onto the ladder still.

"That's a beautiful stone set inside the handle. I'm surprised that they let you on with this. Surely it should be stowed in the shipping containers?"

"It's a precious stone, but I can't remember what it's called. It was my mother's, I think. My head is foggy. I told them it was decorative and not for use. Don't forget I was one of the first groups, I think they were laxer with us early ones."

Sheathing the knife, I take him at his word, and he places it carefully into my bag, along with the torch.

"There's some empty food sachets which I've cleaned out for possible sample collection." Also, in the bag are two pairs of gardening gloves that I've borrowed from the eco-wing, and two cotton dust masks. "How are we going to test samples, if we get any?"

"One of the MAGIE will help us," Gant says. "It owes me a favour."

"Right. Are you sure?"

"As I'll ever be. Let's do the corridor first shall we?"

"Yeah, let's save the best 'til last." I think of Frankie, Annabel wouldn't say what had happened to him, in fact, it had felt like she had been avoiding me, I'm still waiting for another counselling session, too.

"Okay, are we all set?" Gant asks again.

"Yep, let's go. And remember, act casual." He smiles at me and we set off, using a route we know will be quieter. Although with the boot I have supporting my ankle, it feels like I'm noisily clip clopping behind him. I start to laugh at the ridiculousness of the situation, my nerves getting the better of me.

It takes about twenty minutes to get from the women's quarters to the corridor where Gant first found the mushrooms. It feels different this time. As we approach, the air begins to feel close and clammy. A fine mist hangs in the long, tube-like corridor that is thicker the further we go in. I dig out the masks from my bag and put one on, looping it behind my ears, handing the other to Gant.

"This is not good," Gant whispers, as if not wanting to fully admit the scope of the problem. "Can you smell anything this time?"

"Like someone is baking a cake again?"

"I wish they were. It's potent. Sweet, stewed cherries, but much stronger now."

We turn to face each other. "It was here, wasn't it? This grid?" I tap the floor with my booted foot.

"Yes." He squats down and I hand him a pair of gloves. In what feels like slow motion, Gant gently lifts the piece of floor. This time we don't need a torch. The mushrooms have grown exponentially, crowding up underneath the floor. He lifts a neighbouring tile and reveals the same situation: overcrowded mushrooms. Putting both tile grids back in place, he crawls back the way we had come.

"What are you doing? We need to be quick. I don't think this can be healthy,"

"I'm trying to figure out how far it goes." He is about three metres away and lifts another tile. "Nothing in this one, it is damp though."

"Come back here and let's get a sample. Then we need to go."

Gant does as I ask, knowing I'm right. What do we do after this? We'll have to tell someone. I hand him the makeshift specimen bag and he lifts off the original tile. Cutting off a piece of the fungi he puts it inside the bag and seals it with a clip. He hands it to me, and I put it inside another bag, attempting to seal it by folding over the top. He carefully puts back the tile and stands.

"Woah, think I got up a bit too quickly there." Grabbing my arm and the wall for balance, he sways like a sailboat on a lake.

"Come on. Let's get out of here." I pull one of his arms across my shoulders and wrap one of mine around his waist. I've not been this physical with anyone for a long time. He's heavy, cumbersome and I know I won't be able to support him for long. I march us out of the corridor and, hopefully, out of harm's way.

He's steadier on his feet the further we go, and we remove the masks and gloves, stuffing everything into my canvas bag. "Are you okay, feeling steadier now?"

"I think so. We should shower. Get rid of these clothes. We could be carrying some spores on us and not even realise," she says.

"What about all the stuff in the bag? The sample, everything else? Fungi breathe in oxygen and breathe out carbon dioxide, like us. There's going to be nothing to breathe soon if they carry on growing at that rate." The panic in my voice is louder than my words.

"We should catalyse it, with our clothes. That's the only way to be sure. We'll get the sample to my MAGIE friend now and then shower and meet later or tomorrow. Let's leave going to Frankie's place for another day. I need a rest." We divide the tasks. Gant takes the bagged sample to his source for testing, and I deal with the contaminated equipment, taking it to the catalyser, beside the eco-wing.

"Don't stop to speak to anyone," I say as we part. "Don't touch anyone."

"Got it, got it" and he runs off.

Gant - Cycle M13 Day 1

Sharp right, then straight down towards the triage med-bay. He slows to a walking pace as he gets closer, not wanting to alert anyone to his presence. Arriving at the doorway, he hears voices from inside: a women's voice and the electronic rasp of a MAGIE. Peering around the edge of the entryway. The MAGIE, Junior, is facing him a couple of metres away talking to it is Dr Morin.

Gant quickly pulls back from the door frame. Why is she here, she's not been around for ages? Him and the doctor had never seen eye to eye. He disliked like her methods, felt she played on people's weaknesses. He had told her what he thought one day on Saxa Vord, and subsequently expected her to fail him, removing him from the mission. But she hadn't. Instead she never gave him one-on-one counselling again, seeing him only in passing and at the occasional group therapy sessions.

He needs to get Junior's attention but, no matter how strong his dislike of the doctor, he can't risk her becoming contaminated or asking any questions about the sample he had stuffed in his pocket.

"Junior, this just won't do. I need clarity here, not more questions. We need to figure out what happened."

"Doctor, if I may be so bold, I'm asking these questions in order to gain the clarity that we need. I'm well aware of the situation, and what happens if we don't find a solution."

There is silence from the room beyond. She must be taken aback by the little MAGIE. Gant smiles to himself, feeling strange about his fondness for a MAGIE. She can't argue; Junior is correct. Perhaps the answers are in his pocket.

"Okay, continue with what you're doing here. This is a complex issue, and we need to be thorough. I'd like the answer sooner rather than later."

"Wouldn't we all, Doctor Morin?"

"Please don't answer me back in that tone." Confident strides come towards the doorway, right towards Gant. He lunges backwards, just far enough to make it look like he's just arrived as she comes into view.

"Hey, Doc!" She jumps. "Wow, I'm sorry! That was kind of loud, wasn't it?" He stays over an arm's reach away from her as she pauses in the corridor.

"Hello. Yes. I'm in a world of my own. Did you need me?"

"No, no, you know me. I'm just out for a run." His adrenalin threatens to push him over the edge, he starts jogging on the spot to try to abate it. "See you around, Doc!" He doesn't look up as he begins to do some stretches, bending forward to touch his toes. Annabel, for everything he thinks about her, can spot a liar. He carries on with the façade of his limbering exercises until her footsteps disappear into depths of the ship.

"Junior?" Gant says softly, entering the room.

The droid turns from its work and Gant imagines he's heard an exasperated sigh. "Can I help you?"

"Remember me?" he asks. It is worth checking. A false move would fail the whole thing, and sometimes the MAGIE's memories are wiped when they get rebooted.

"Of course. You're Gant. You helped me out when I damaged my leg, and you covered for me."

"Thank god! Listen, I need a favour—I figured you owed me one?"

"Well, I suppose if we are to stay equal then I do, yes. What do you need?"

Gant reaches into his pocket and walks to where Junior is working. "I need this tested. I need to know what it is, where it's come from. Everything you can give me." Gant hands over the double-bagged specimen.

"Where did you get this?" Junior looks closely through the clear bag.

"I … I found it."

"This isn't something new. We are trying to understand its origins. I must ask you not to tell anyone. We don't need mass panic on the ship. In fact, I shouldn't even be telling you."

"You already know? This shit is spreading?"

"Like I said, we've been instructed to deal with it in this way, we don't want to cause panic when we don't even know what it is, or how to deal with it."

"Junior, I know you're not in charge here, but we need to do something. I think it's changing the atmosphere on the ship."

"I must follow my orders, its restricted to only one pocket of the ship at the moment. Trust us, we don't believe it is a threat to the population, and we'll have it sorted very soon."

The conversation circles and loops around the topic, and Gant gains no more traction with the MAGIE. He leaves the triage room and goes to clean up.

Rebecca - Cycle M13 Day 2

Juniper is here again, snuggled up in the tight space of my room. The dog suddenly wakes and nudges me until I awaken too.

"What is it, June?"

Juniper grows increasingly animated. Then we are in a corridor on the ship. It's familiar, yet different. There is no sound, other than the tapping of Juniper's claws on the floor tiles and grids. She is ahead of me but still within sight. Juniper keeps stopping and turning to check I'm still following. Eventually she sits and waits until I catch up. We are at the library.

Entering, we walk towards the very back of the space where the reading room sits empty. We go inside and Juniper starts scratching underneath the table.

"What is it, girl?" I crouch and lift the floor panel the dog has been frantically pawing. "Mushrooms. It's going to be mushrooms under here, Juniper," I whisper in her ear. The floor panel comes away.

Juniper turns. "No, my love, it's a way out." And she dashes down into the darkness.

"Wait! Come back, June! JUNIPER!"

I wake with a start. Dripping with sweat, I reach for the glass of water I'd left out. The dreams are becoming increasingly realistic. I note down what had happened in the dream in my journal before it slips from my mind. Mum comes swiftly into my thoughts. Something about dreams, Mum's dreams, but I can't put my finger on the connection.

Rebecca - Cycle M13 Day 3

I stay with Gant. In an alternate reality it would be romantic. We have sex which should be a big deal for me, but it's not. It feels more like a reassurance of human bodies aligned, a release of frustration, not making love. As it stands, I have huge concerns about what is really going on aboard the ship. My mind churns at night with dreams and chases its tail while I'm awake. I'm frightened, although what of is still unclear; the unknown, I guess. I felt so certain before, coming on this mission. I suppose it made me feel invincible. I thought the MAGIE could deal with anything. I don't know what will become of us.

Gant's capsule is neat, everything has a place, though probably under the bed. We are waiting on any kind of information from the tests that Gant has arranged, I wonder if they will share any results with us at all. We anxiously look for any strange symptoms.

"Do you like the MAGIE?" I ask him, as we lie like sardines on his bed. We talk in whispers while in his capsule, we don't want anyone overhearing.

"Yeah, I like 'em. But do I trust them? No, not entirely. Some more than others, maybe."

"I don't mind them as much as I used to. I can't trust them, though. Their loyalties can't be designed the way ours are naturally. Humans build up trust with each other, and trust leads to loyalty. They're AI, they share the same interface, the same knowledge. They are like spies among us."

"It did used to be like that, I completely agree. But they aren't all the same anymore. So many of us felt just what you're describing. Some are just made and never have any updates. They work independently, away from any database or shared systems. They're beings on their own."

"I'm not sure who is being more naïve here, they all have a master, that's my point. Whereas we just have ourselves, or someone of our choosing." I pause, realising how much this says about me. "Anyone with the right know-how can hack in and take all the data a MAGIE has gathered. Even if they are supposedly independent."

"Humans are pretty damn hackable too, though. We aren't all good people, there is corruption everywhere, and some will do anything if the price is right."

He's right of course, I've inherited Dad's prejudices without even realising.

"You have a point. Do you ever think what would've happened if you hadn't joined this mission?"

"I try not to. Do you?"

"I wonder what my brother is doing. I joined to find some truth and meaning to my life, but what do I have so far? A few good friends, yes, but Nia is dead, and Frankie is missing, everything suddenly feels uncertain. There's an outbreak of weird fungi growing in part of the ship. Dr Morin knows more than she's letting on, and she's never around. The MAGIE aren't authoritative, and that's what I think we need right now."

"Well, I saw Morin at the Triage," he props his head up, resting it on his arms. "My MAGIE friend, he let slip they already know."

"What?" My whisper strains, my voice is trying to escape. "They're trying to keep it quiet? Does she know we know? I can't believe this. I wish you'd told me this earlier."

"No, I don't think so. But what can we do, Bec? We are pretty powerless. Plus, with regard to this whole mission, we'd never have met otherwise, maybe we can figure out what is going on. Together." He leans in for a kiss and I turn my face away. "I'm here for you, Bec." His finger hooks my chin and pulls it toward him again, then runs it finger down the bridge of my nose. "I love that it's not perfectly straight, you know."

"It was once." I sit up, moving away from him, not in the mood for being cosseted.

"What happened?" He asks, looking wary of what I might say.

"It's not an interesting story." I slide out of the bed and get up, almost falling over his shoes and begin to dress. "My brother and I were playing in the garden one summer. It must've been football with my Dad. We both leapt up to try and head the ball. Instead, we headed each other. My nose went into the back of his head. Both my parents hated hospitals, so they never took me to get it checked. It hasn't been the same since." My reflection looks back at me in the small mirror near the door, I lean in to look at my nose. This place is too small for this shit. "My parents weren't neglectful though," I add. "I just think they thought it wasn't that bad. I must have had a high pain threshold, even then. Maybe if I'd been hysterical, they would have thought it was bad enough for a hospital visit. Anyway, it adds character." I leave and go and get breakfast without looking back. I thought these were meant to be the best men.

Rebecca - Cycle M13 Day 4

"I always just thought this was an alternate way into the storage space," Gant looks to be enjoying exploring a stairwell of the ship he's not been to before.

"I think that was the point. I know Frankie helped design a lot of the internals." We make our way along Frankie's corridor, I'm slightly ahead.

"I guess they fixed the lighting then."

"Yes, but…It's gone. It's all gone," I hobble towards Frankie's doorway, pausing at the threshold. I wait for Gant to catch up. "There was stuff coming from the under the door. At first, I thought something had been spilled. It was so dark. The substance slimy and sticky. That's what I slipped on—how I did my ankle in."

"I believe you, Bec. I do. It looks like it's been cleaned."

"I wasn't asking if you believed me, I know what happened. Come on, let's go in." I decide to knock politely on Frankie's door, just in case. "I'm pretty sure there's no one home." The door whirs and doesn't need a push this time, sliding open just as it always did. I step in from the corridor and the large room looks spotless, no sign of Frankie, of him even being here recently. The bed is stripped, a lonely, bare mattress sits off centre to the room. Frankie's books are on his bedside table, his crockery by the sink, his pictures on the wall. The artificial light makes everything gleam.

"Where is he?"

"I don't know. Annabel told me he'd been found, but nothing more."

"Well, he's definitely not here."

We begin to look around.

"Help me out, Gant. What can you smell?"

Gant takes a big inhale through his nose. "Maybe a trace of our other discovery—don't know if I'm imagining it, though."

I look under the bed. His room was always such a departure from the rest of the living quarters on board. Resolutely normal, like a real room in a real home. The bed had been brought on board by Frankie from Saxa Vord. It is usually made up military style with hospital corners. He's gotten me to do it for him a few times, saying I'll need homemaking skills in the future. The real reason is that it hurts him to move sometimes, he doesn't like to talk about that though—Frankie's RAF background means he likes things neat, everything has its place, including emotions.

I run my palms across the mattress, down the sides. What is that? Something feels off, different. Is it damp? Clumsily I get on my hands and knees, the boot is really starting to annoy me; my ankle must almost be healed. I see the empty space, the boxes of personal items I know he keeps under there are gone. Shadowy marks on the floor offer themselves up as evidence that I'm onto something.

"Look, under here."

Gant puts down the book he's looking at.

"There were two boxes here before." Standing, I walk over to one of the paintings hanging on the wall and lift it off. It leaves the same shadowy marks, a ghost of where it has been.

Holding the picture by the frame, I turn to face Gant. He points, recoiling, "Is that mould?" Flipping the picture over I see a faint patch of white fur covering the back of the painting. I drop the picture on the bed, facing down so we can get a better look.

"It looks something like mould for sure. Did we bring any bags?"

"I thought you didn't trust my MAGIE buddy with these tests?"

"It's not like we have a choice."

He hands me a bag and I scrape some of the fur into it, then carefully rehang the painting.

"Mould like that needs damp. It felt damp under the bed. Let's take a proper look."

Gant lifts the mattress from the frame, revealing patches of the fur. This time varying from very pale cream to a much darker grey.

"This is disgusting. It's creeping me out." He retches as he puts the mattress back. "Let's get out of here."

A thin voice startles us from the corridor. We are cornered.

"Gant? Gant, is that you?" We freeze and footsteps strike against the metal floor from outside. "Gant?" A MAGIE walks in.

"Oh, Junior!" Gants says, looking at me, still frozen in place. "It's okay, this is my buddy. The one who's helping us."

"Right. Well it's good to finally meet you." I hear myself saying as I relax my stance, perhaps Gant isn't as green as I'd thought. This MAGIE, Junior, is a humanoid like all the others, but it is dressed in clothing, something I've not seen a MAGIE do before. An old-style baseball cap in grey jersey with a faded orange emblem on the front, I'm sure I know from somewhere. An over-sized T-shirt, one of the uniform tops that were standard issue on the ship, and a pair of surf shorts.

"I've been searching everywhere for you."

"And you've found us doing something we shouldn't."

"You are?"

"I've heard a lot about you, Junior." Cutting in, "Gant failed to mention your exceptional sartorial style, though." I decide to go along with the MAGIE in ignoring our situation for the time being.

"Thank you so much, Rebecca. I feel more like me when I wear clothes."

Gant puts his arm around Junior like they are old friends. "Told you he wasn't like the others," he smirks. "What have you got for me, buddy?"

"Something extraordinary. A species of mushroom never recorded. A new species!" The MAGIE is almost jumping up and down with excitement like a human child. "Where are we? I don't think I've been in this part of the ship before."

How does it not know where we are? All the MAGIE are at one with the ship, extensions of the same system.

"How did you find us?" I lean forwards, stooping a little so we are face to face.

"I gave Gant a tracker last time I saw him, for exactly this reason, to find him and tell him what he found."

My jaw clenches and I feel myself flush. "You didn't think to tell me this?"

"I'm sorry, Bec, I didn't think it was that important."

"What is it with you?" I walk away as far as I can get from him while still being present. I need to calm down.

I hear Gant take a deep breath and ask about the other samples the MAGIE had already been testing. "Is our sample the same thing?"

"Yes—an evolution of it, I believe. Now tell me where we are?" Junior says.

"We are in a space where a man used to live. We're looking for him. My friend Rebecca here knows him very well, and we don't know where he is. Maybe you know? Can you help us again?"

"What does he look like, your man friend?" Junior asks, looking directly at me.

"He's older. Much older than us. He has thick grey hair and a ruddy complexion. Very slim and nimble-looking." I pause. "He walks with a stick but hasn't got out much over the last few cycles. That's why I was here. Checking on him," I lie, not quite ready to share all with this walking, talking computer. "He was very close to Doctor Morin."

I lean on the bed frame facing the wall, something catches my eye opposite the bed. On the wall, there is a shelf of plants. Frankie was always nurturing new life, as he called it. His plants, there's something about his plants. Standing, I reach over to them and start to empty the plant pots into the small sink below the shelf, rubbing the soil between my fingers.

"There's something here. There's a clue, I just know it."

Junior comes over. "What are you looking for, Rebecca?"

"What do these plants look like to you?" I hold up strands and strands of white, ribbon-like fluff. Some have small clumps of thicker white ribbons within the fluff. "I think Frankie…" I pause, realising the scope of what I'm about to say. "I think he's been developing something. Whether intentionally or not, he's been cross-breeding plants here."

Growing new things.

"How do you know?" Gant asks.

"I've known all along." Hesitating, my memories collating. "I just didn't remember before. He grew food supplies on Saxa Vord. Mushrooms were among them— why didn't I realise before?"

Junior carefully takes the root strands from my hands, lifts his T-shirt and places them inside a compartment he's opened within himself. "For secret things."

Oscar - Cycle M13 Day 4

Less than a couple of metres away from the investigating trio stands Oscar with his ear trained on the wall adjoining Frankie's room. Eventually he'll have to come out of his secluded quarters. He's had Annabel and a couple of higher level MAGIE bring him Frankie, now the old man is resident on the other side of their dividing wall. Not that he knows what is going on.

Frankie is housed in Oscar's small lab, a break off room adjacent to the living area. He is currently inside a life-support tube. What is happening inside the tube is fascinating. Frankie's body is covered in a type of fungi. It is growing from his skin; in some parts it has grown through his clothes. Every few hours, Oscar goes to Frankie's tube and releases the pressure, clearing the condensation on the observation panel at the front of the tube. By all accounts, including Annabel's, Frankie is still alive. Oscar believes the fungi must be sustaining him, using him as a parasite would.

"It's ironic. You're the only one who didn't want to go to sleep on this ship, and yet here you are. Sleeping like a baby." Oscar finally has someone to talk to.

The fungi that have taken over Frankie's body is at different stages of growth, as far as Oscar can tell. Some of it looks like white, downy fur, the earliest stage. The next stage of growth was pea-sized, white buds, and from there they darkened and grew bigger and sturdier. Some of the large specimens have grown up to twenty centimetres in diameter. Frankie is beyond saving at this stage. Perhaps if he'd spotted it earlier, something could've been done.

Oscar releases the valve. The condensation is collecting in a sealed tank that he's rigged underneath the table. He wanders out of the lab area and puts on some music—through old-fashioned headphones, just in case someone hears him. Chopin's piano preludes always help clear his mind. Sitting in an old, brown, leather armchair taken from the abandoned hotel at Saxa Vord, he closes his eyes. The headphones grip his ears. He lets the music wash over him, refreshing and stimulating.

The situation with Frankie is a real spanner in the works. The bigger picture is the implications of the potential fungal outbreak. It is completely beyond anything he'd considered when he'd begun to plan this escape from a dying Earth.

The music brings back Oscars parents. What would they say if they could see him now? His father would be proud—perhaps confused about Oscar's methods, but generally proud. His mother would ask all the questions Oscar was asking of himself. Could I have done more for the earth? Saved more people?

He opens his eyes needing a distraction from his mother's voice in his head, switching on the huge screen opposite. The monitor is like all the others on the ship, with an extensive library of films and documentaries available to view. But what Oscar wants now is a window. He'd designed a set of virtual scenes and had them stored on his own personal hard drive. Some sunshine, a beach. Selecting the corresponding programme, he sits back and stares at the horizon. Sometimes, like now, the doubts about the brazen plans he'd hatched, flooded him.

What if his forecast is wrong? What if the people here on the ship, the ones who have been so painstakingly selected, are the wrong ones after all?

CHAPTER 12 – 2071

Rebecca - Cycle M13 Day 99

Lying on my bed inside my capsule, I flick through the journal I started on Saxa Vord. I've taken a step away from being with Gant. It's too much for me. It still feels too soon to be with anyone, to be physical, and to be vulnerable. I don't completely trust him, and he's not done much to counter that. Christian's jumper nuzzles against my skin, I've dug it out, needing real intimacy. I'm reading through my entries since being at Saxa Vord; I have changed and grown as a person, that much is clear, and perhaps my standards are higher. There are a few dreams in here that come flooding back as I decipher the scrawl of my half-asleep handwriting. Lots of the dreams feature Juniper. Her big, bat-like ears had jolted a memory of a dream, one where Juniper speaks which is a strange, new thing.

"There, found it!" I read it back: the ship's library, the floor in the reading room, Juniper dashing away from me down a trap door. The dream comes flooding back.

I must go to the library. How could I have disregarded this dream? It feels like a clue, Juniper speaking. My unconscious remembering something from last time I was there.

I know Gant is in Sector Four organising a basketball tournament. Issy will be out soon, I've missed her, I can't keep this situation to myself, I might go mad. I know she will listen to me; I just need to vent. I need a woman's ear, a woman's shoulder.

I grab the torch I've stolen from Gant and shove it down the front of my jeans, covering it with the loose standard T-shirt. There won't be anything there, yet some instinct is telling me there might be. I flex my foot. It makes a disconcerting crunching noise, but according to the MAGIE, it's close to healed now. Its strength needs building again, so I wear the boot for just a few hours of each day. Climbing down the ladder is still tricky and my foot begins to cramp.

Making my way to the library, I avoid the more populated routes. This is something personal—I'm trusting my dreams. I'm also not in the mood to make small talk, putting my headphones on as another way to deter potential conversation.

I move quietly, imagining Juniper in front of me, just like in the dream. On reaching the library, I take a deep breath as I pass through its doors. Inspiration and knowledge lurking on every page. But today isn't for books.

Cutting around the ends of the shelves, I come at the reading room from the side rather than straight on. The man; a memory creeping into my head. Where has he gone? Who is he?

My heart is beating like a drum in my chest. This dream means something. A premonition, even. I don't know what to call it but I'm following in the footsteps of the spectral version of myself. Where is Juniper? I could do with a friend by my side.

The reading room is empty. The table in the middle of the space has some books piled on top of it. Someone has been reading Shakespeare and The Origin of Species—a heady mix. Moving the books onto a nearby book trolley, I turn again to the table. For a moment I consider not moving it, not looking more closely. The hesitation passes. Closing the door to the reading room, I push the book trolley across the doorway. Turning back to the table, I bend at the waist and push the old wooden thing towards the far wall. Another relic from Saxa Vord, no doubt. I take a deep breath and step back. There's a discreet pair of hinges and a sunken handle. Unmistakably a door.

Standing up I pull the torch from my waist band, my hands are shaking, I feel like I'm fumbling, not knowing what will happen next but compelled to continue.

What if Juniper is down there? Impossible, maybe I've gone mad. What if all the answers are down there? It dawns on me that the library, is in fact, over the top of Frankie's quarters, or at least in the same region, so it must be close. What if he's down there? Have I lost my mind?

I lift the trapdoor. The well of darkness beneath feels infinite. There is a ladder attached to the wall of the hole, which itself looks like a huge tube, maybe a pipe of some kind, just big enough for a person to travel through. I lean the trapdoor on the table legs and flick on the torch. I can just make out the bottom of the ladder. I sit on the edge, swinging my legs inside the hole hold the torch in my mouth, clasping it with my teeth. Grabbing the ladder, I begin my descent. The torch knocks against the side of the cylinder as I move, jarring my teeth. If anyone is down here, I won't be surprising them with my stealth skills.

Reaching the bottom of the darkness, I shuffle around on the spot, and release the torch from my now sore jaw. I'm at the bottom of the cylinder and it seems like a dead end, I can't see or feel anything that could be a door. I put the torch back in my waistband, it's just getting in the way now.

Then something shifts in the gloom. Under my palms, part of the wall moves. There is something behind it. I push and, and it gives way. White light from above in the space before me is blinding. I lift my arms covering my face before realising how vulnerable that makes me. My eyes adjust and I can see the room I'm in.

I pull myself together taking a deep breath and step out of the dark, into the light of the room beyond.

I pause; waiting, listening.

It is immaculate. Pristine. Not a speck of dust. Perfectly white, on white, on white, except for a battered brown leather armchair which faces a large blank screen. The ghost of my reflection glances at me from the polished surfaces. Somebody lives here or has lived here. It is so clean it is difficult to tell. The sheer amount of space is luxurious.

There is a vending machine for food and drinks, much like the ones we all share in Sector Four. A white dining table with two white chairs, and a white vase in the middle of the table holds a clue: a bloom. It looks real. I go over to it, touch it, it is real. I haven't seen these in the eco-wing. The floor, walls, and ceiling are less haphazard than the rest of the ship. White hexagons tessellated over all the surfaces. There are no dark corners, nowhere to hide.

I move over to the armchair. It is familiar, it must be from Saxa Vord. Sinking into the leather, it's butter soft, worn, and responsive to my touch. Adjacent is a side table, and on it a MAGIEpad. Without pause I pick it up and touch the screen into to life. Whoever lives here is arrogant enough not to use a passcode. I begin by scrolling through the home screen, not sure what I'm looking for. A file named Build, that sounds interesting. I open it. Inside there are blueprints of the ship design, parts I don't recognise, all signed at the bottom by Frankie. No big deal, I already knew he was involved in the creation of the ship's interiors. I go deeper in and find a detailed separate section of the ship, the very top level where the passengers aren't allowed. There will be answers there.

I lean back in the chair, wondering if I'm pushing my luck with all this investigating and on the wall to my left, I spot a seam amongst the hexagons, slicing right through them. Another door with a lock button beside it. I sit listening, straining my ears, wanting to be safe.

Standing as quietly as possible, I pad across to the other door, still listening. I lean close to the wall. Funny how in the darkness I felt brave, but now, in the light, I'm much more careful. It seems unnaturally silent. I can't even hear the ship's engines from here. Perhaps the hexagons make the space soundproof?

Holding my breath, I press the button by the side of the door, it slides back and precisely to the left, opening into a dimly lit room. I pull Gant's torch out again, happy to no longer be fighting the brightness.

There is a metallic table in the centre of the room, like those in industrial kitchens it has something large and reflective on top. I can see my distorted reflection in the curve of the object, the light from the white room behind gives me a heavenly aura, like something from the special effects department in old black and white films. The walls in the room are lined with shelves and apparatus.

Real work gets done in here. The shelves are free-standing and look like the ones people used to have in their garages back home. They are a bit rusty and dirty but still very strong. There are all kinds of stuff on them, from tools, to luggage and cardboard boxes. A gathering of small containers that look like they were fish tanks at some point, the glass clouded and the interiors so murky I can't make out what is inside, if anything.

Stepping closer to the table, I see that the reflective curved object is a medical tube; a sealed vessel for humans. These tubes were a recent medical advancement back on earth. I remember a room full of them at the hospital that treated Mum. They are an intensive care method when all other treatments have failed. They are also used to stop infections spreading through crowded hospitals. The light from behind me along with the yellow beam of my torch is reflected off the glass, disguising what or who is inside. Putting the torch down, I cup my hands around my eyes and lean forward until I'm touching the glass with the outer edges of my two little fingers.

Greeting me is a murky interior, like the smaller tanks collected on the shelves surrounding me, the inside surface of the tube is covered with patches of grey cloud. There is so much condensation on the inside of the glass that I can only see a shadow of shape beyond it. I grab the torch again from the floor, shining it inside the sealed chamber while using my other hand to cup my eyes and block out the reflecting light. I think there is a figure inside. I can't make it out, I move around the tube, looking for a clearer patch, an area with less murky condensation. There, a clearer spot right by the frame of the metal shell.

I see hair, thick hair, and lots of it. I train the torch along the hair following it, looking for a hairline and a face. Where the face should be, is a growth. Looking a lot like a tumour, but it is growing on top of the skin, not something bulging and bursting to get out from inside like a tumour does.

It dawns on me what I am seeing, the smaller patches, I feel myself swoon as I recognise them as tiny versions of what Gant had found. I slump to the floor, leaning on one of the table lags. I've found Frankie. That is his hair, I'm sure of it.

Is he alive?

"Pull yourself together, Bec," I whisper. Standing again I look for a control panel on the tube, and find one, at the opposite end to his head, I tap the screen and wake it up. I remember the panel that we had for Mum—blue on black, numbers, her vital stats, a heart rate monitor, blood pressure. There's a very slow heart rate from Frankie, but a beating heart all the same. He is alive, probably in a coma.

I need to think, time to process this. What does this mean for everyone on board? This is more than a quirky thing to find in a corridor on a spaceship. This is something else, something that looked like it could end the whole mission and disable everyone on board. Backing away from the tube, I retreat to the white room.

"So now you know," a voice comes from behind me I spin on my good heel and drop the torch. It clatters to the ground, falling apart on impact. I've been caught red handed, breaking and entering, every muscle is tense, I don't have a response, my mind too busy racing to figure out my next steps.

The man is sat in the armchair. He is dressed in a white cotton robe, much like, if not the same as, the standard kit that everyone has from when they boarded the ship. He has bare feet and wet hair.

"You've got Frankie in there." I finally say, pointing back to the tube. "What are you doing to him? He's still alive."

"Barely," the man replies. "And it's not what I'm doing to him. He's done that to himself."

"I've seen you before, that day at the library."

"I remember it well. I took a chance being there at that time."

"Why? What…?" she started, not sure where her mouth was taking her. Finally, "Who are you? Why are you down here?"

"Surely you can guess." His voice is calm but a little slurred, with an accent I don't recognise. I stay silent, challenging him to use his words and not mine. "I'm the architect of this whole charade." He waves his hands as he spoke, his eyes glassy and not quite under his control. "I also happen to be a recluse, have got some issues with OCDeeee. Annie is still trying to fix me on that one." Yes, his words are definitely slurred.

"You're Oscar Markov. I thought you had died?" I look around to figure out where he'd sprung from. Damn it. Just beyond the vending machines is another door I hadn't spotted.

"Disappearing was all part of the plan, Rebecca," he giggles, "I have returned from the dead."

"Do you know all our names?" I ask, trying to keep him talking, to keep him in the chair. I can be quick on my feet when needed, even if one ankle isn't at full strength. I bend down to pick up the torch, not taking my eyes off him for a moment. It just needs screwing back together.

"I don't know *all* my guest's names. Just a select few, whom I find interesting." His eyes skim over my body. "Now what are you going to do? What's the next step of your craaazy plan? What are you trying to achieve by coming down here, sweet Rebecca? What are you looking for? Go on, ask me. There's so much I could talk about. It's nice to have a visitor who can talk back."

I decide to call his bluff and buy some time to think. "Okay then, something that has been bugging me. How and who did the choosing of the people to go on this mission? Was it you?"

Oscar smiles and shows all his teeth as if he'd been waiting for someone to ask him this for years, perhaps he has. "The travellers on board were selected in an inspired way, thanks to HeritageNow, through gene mapping and genetic testing. You might recall, the tests started as optional. A fun thing for people to do, great as a gift, they said. Once the data from these tests became increasingly precise, they started to become a real commodity. Companies merged, creating larger, slicker business models. Eventually the test became lower in price and then standard, through seeing your regular doctor. Nobody really paid any attention to the changes in consent, even the quietly done, back dated ones. They said it was for the good of the population that this information became readily available. People were so busy with their lives that they didn't see it as another layer of control. Of course, it was for the good of civilisation. It's good to get an idea of traits at a job interview, isn't it? Before you marry someone? For each requested access to genetic records, there was a charge. This is how I made a lot of my money. It was the method by which I funded this trip."

I stand very still, my brow heavy, eyes full of what I want him to think are tears.

"Shall I continue?"

"Please do. I might as well know it all."

"You were chosen because of your genetic makeup, your design. Your predilections and family tree were also considered, along with the likelihood of developing certain diseases. We wanted to eliminate mutation so paid attention to hereditary carriers. It was a lengthy process, as you can imagine, but became easier when we were able to offer subsidies to medical bodies. Soon we had around eighty percent of the world's population on file. A piece of software designed by me, went through each one with a fine-toothed comb and came out with a list of potentials. Those special needles in the metaphorical haystack, if you will. It took years. We then sent out the letter requests. Not everyone chose to join us. Some felt tied to their work or the people they shared their life with. But most, like you, hadn't had been granted a parental licence. That was a large part of the decision making, we knew it would make people swing in our direction. That's what swung it for you, am I right?"

"What will happen to Frankie? Are you keeping him alive in that tube?" I side-step his line of questioning.

"I'm trying to contain the fungi. To study it. To see if he can recover." He paused and adjusted his robe. "Francis and I had become good friends, and he is a valuable asset to this ship. I don't want him to die."

"Judging by his state, I'd say he isn't going to recover. You should put him out of his misery. It's inhumane to leave him like this." I kick myself for pleading with him.

"No one tells me what to do. How dare you make these assumptions when you don't know all the facts."

"He needs to die. Put him in the catalyser or eject him into space. Then give him a funeral. It's the right thing to do,"

He looks at me without blinking and starts to move to get up from the chair. Struggling—like his own body is too heavy for him. "You realise I can't let you leave now, don't you?" He stands next to the chair, leaning on it for support, and blocking my direct line to the door, my exit.

I fasten the torch back together as adrenalin fizzes at my fingertips, knowing that I might have to fight him to get away. I step diagonally away, slowly, not wanting to end up back in the room where Frankie is.

"You can stay in these quarters as my guest, Rebecca. It's more comfortable than your capsule."

"Why would I want to do that? It might be surprising to you, but I actually have a life on this ship. I've made friends. I can't just vanish."

"You can. Isn't this what you always wanted, perfect autonomy?" He starts towards me. I inch towards the door he had come from.

"Look, no one knew my plan for today. And no one needs to know. I can go back to my friends upstairs and they'd be none the wiser if I didn't say anything." I try to buy more time, putting off what is surely about to happen.

Wait or run. Fight or flight.

The decision is made for me. He reaches out to grab at me with both arms. A bear hug; a wrestle. I duck and dart out of the way. He stumbles, and I see he'd meant to bring me down. His gown falls open and I catch a glimpse of something on his torso. He attempts to tie it back up again, but his fingers are unable to complete the task.

Grabbing the opportunity, I run for the other door, the one he'd come from, and enter a small room with a large unmade bed. Edging past the bed, I can hear him lumbering towards me. There is another door on the other side of the bed. Opening it, I see myself. A huge mirror facing the doorway, and him over my shoulder, coming into the room. He battles to shuffle around the bed as I look for a way out. A shower, basin, a toilet—I am trapped. My stomach doing back flips as I turn to face him, stepping back allowing him to come into the smaller room.

"You can't leave me like this," he slurs, grabbing my wrist. Lifting my other arm, the one holding the torch, I bring the lump of metal down on his head. Nothing happens. He just keeps coming, gripping my wrist. I jam the torch into his temple as hard as I can. He loses his balance, releasing me and ricocheting off the door frame, onto the bed. He is half off the bed, and without hesitation I jump past him, climbing over the bed instead of trying to get around it.

He grabs my bad ankle and I fall forward, hitting the other side of the bed and sliding into the small gap and to the floor. The momentum of the fall releases his grip again and I crawl outside the bedroom and back the way I had come, back to the library trapdoor. Maybe this is the only way out. If it is, I can trap him down here.

I get up off my knees and hobble to the door. He doesn't follow. No sound comes from the bedroom. I start the ascent back up the ladder. Still nothing. I've left the torch somewhere, but there is a circle of light from the reading room above. Following it, I climb as quickly as I can. Have I killed him? Who would know? It takes all the energy I have left to hoist myself out of the hole and into the reading room. Pausing only for a moment, on all fours, I listen again. Still nothing.

I catch my breath and flip close the trapdoor. It falls from my hands with a bang. Looking around for something to put on top. Books, books, of course. I pull all the books off the trolley and see they are the same ones I'd returned, on fungi and mushrooms. I stack.

Opening the door to the reading room, I peep out. It's empty. I pull the trolley out of the room and head to the encyclopaedia section. There isn't really shelving as such, the books are so heavy they are stacked in rows in a corner. There had been multiple shuttles sent up to the ship before the human cargo joined. Oscar clearly has money to burn. Frankie must have known all along about him.

I load up the trolley with the encyclopaedias and drag it back to the reading room. The creaking of the wheels is so loud. Lift and place, lift and place, until all the tomes are on top of the trapdoor. I then tussle with the table to put it back into place over the top of the books, hoping, that at first glance, all would appear normal in the room.

If he's alive will he come after me? If he's dead will anyone even know he's missing?

My adrenaline is abating now, fatigue grows in its place. I leave the library wishing I could talk to Mum; she'd know what to do.

* * *

227

"Where have you been?" Gant asks, he's been waiting for me in my room. I push him away, exhausted, scared, angry.

"What are you doing here? Please don't come in my pod when I'm not here."

"I'm sorry, I was worried about you, not seen you in a couple of days…I know you needed some space, but… What's happened?" He looks at me as if he's only just noticed the state I've arrived in.

I sit next to him on the bed, not having the energy to argue my point. "It's bad, Gant. We need to get away, get off. It's gone wrong. It's the mushrooms we found." I lie down on the bed and he pulls off my shoes.

"Your ankle has ballooned. Would you tell me already?"

"I … I met our maker." I feel myself drifting into sleep, unsure if I'm speaking out loud or in my head.

Undecided if I'm delirious, I tell him everything, he lifts my legs onto the bed and covers me up, whilst mumbling something about a note. He leaves, pulling the shutter down, and I allow sleep to take me.

CHAPTER 13 – 2072

Issy - Cycle F14 Day 1

Issy is groggy. Waking up from a sleep stint is always rough. Peeling off the sheet, she slowly sits up, Rebecca first in her thoughts.

Putting on her robe and slippers, she throws a towel over her shoulder and heads to the showers. Everyone, as usual, has the same idea and a queue is waiting. Leaning against the wall, she puts her hands into the pockets of her robe. There is something inside; a piece of paper. Pulling it out of her pocket, she opens it up.

Something is very wrong. If you are reading this the chances are you are safe, at least for now. There's something growing in the gaps belly. Something I don't think anyone has planned for. People are dying. Come to my capsule when you've washed up. Rebecca.

At the front of the queue, Issy's stomach churns as she shoves the note back in her pocket. All the women around her are still dazed from sleep, but Issy is wide awake, on high alert. If something is wrong, why doesn't everyone know? What about the MAGIE? They must know. They must be covering it up. In such a confined space, things escalate quickly. Memories of her homeland come flooding back.

She showers quickly, then sits in the vanity area to re-braid her hair. The woman adjacent is in the process of cutting hers, all of it is coming off by the looks of it. Issy tries to recall the woman's name as she gazes at her in the reflection. The woman's eyes don't look right. Transfixed, Issy realises the woman hasn't noticed her staring. Using clippers, the woman is holding up chunks of hair and slicing them away from her head. Across her lap, down her back and shoulders, the hair clings, not wanting to let go, wondering what it has done to deserve such severe treatment. The woman's head is a mish mash of hair, all different lengths. She starts to neaten it off, giving herself a buzzcut. The hum of the clippers drowns out the noise of the showers.

Issy goes back to finish her braiding. Her fingers work quickly, and her attention focuses for a moment to tidy up the ends. The noise of the clippers becomes moist. Looking over again, Issy sees the woman has pushed the unguarded clippers into her skull, ploughing them into her scalp.

"Help! Someone, help!" Issy shouts, her chair crashing to the floor as she stands. Women crowd around. Someone presses an alarm button Issy didn't even know existed. Maybe they're new, added since she'd last been awake.

The woman slumps on the counter, her blood splattered up the mirror. Issy pulls the clippers out of her hand, but the damage is done. A torn strip of the woman's skull gleams through the blood. The woman slides from the counter and onto the floor, her legs collapsing beneath her, her head flipping backwards with such a force. A gargling noise comes from her mouth; she is trying to speak.

"This place is an abattoir … we all … we need…" She chokes on the words. Her message is indistinguishable.

Someone pulls Issy away. The MAGIE are here. Looking down, Issy sees she is covered in the woman's blood. She needs to shower again. The woman is taken away by the MAGIE and they remove the onlookers, permitting Issy to stay and clean herself up. More MAGIE arrive to sanitise the area and recreate normality. The moment is on replay in her head, the noise, the choking, what the woman had tried to say.

Annabel - Cycle F14 Day 1

Annabel sighs as the body arrives into the space they have started using as morgue. A mask covering her nose and mouth billows in and out with each breath.

"This woman had been out of the pods for around ninety minutes," Appo says. The MAGIE is rarely away from Annabel's side these days. He is checking the woman's details on a MAGIEpad. "No previous reported mental episodes."

"How many witnesses?" Annabel asks.

"Three, visual, many more in the queue heard what was going on." Appo pauses. "What shall we do with this one, Doctor?"

"What we've done with all the others. Take samples, then get rid."

"The population of the ship is starting to realise something is wrong."

"We'll have mass hysteria on our hands when this gets out." Annabel states, "At the moment it's spread across both populations. We might feel the numbers are big, but it's only single figures from each." She pauses, rubbing her brow, "We just need a little more time to figure out what's going on. Why is this taking hold? Why, with all the technology and advances in medicine and science, everything I've provided for you, can't we cure a fungal infection?"

"Because the human body thinks the fungal spores are part of it," Appo says. "That is the crux of it. Both humans and fungi are eukaryotes, organisms whose cells carry complex structures inside their membranes, including a nucleus. The human hosts are recognising the cell as one of their own and welcoming it, rather than fighting it as they would do a bacterial cell invasion. We still haven't found the right drug that is both effective against the fungi and nontoxic to humans. The fungi side effects seem to appear once the host has been infected for more than twenty-four hours. We have trialled AmB on four subjects with zero success. Subjects became very ill and the fungal growth wasn't discouraged. It seems immune."

"We're running out of time. We need to stop this outbreak, or the mission will be a complete failure." Walking away, Annabel holds her head for a moment, she needs a rest. She has been skipping her shorter sleep cycles ever since the strange behaviours began and the first deaths had occurred. She goes to her quarters, needing to update Oscar.

Rebecca - Cycle F14 Day 2

"There're going to be repercussions, it's just a matter of time."

Issy holds my hand, "It was self-defence, Bec." Anyone can see that.

"Gant told me he went to seal the door, to ensure Oscar couldn't come and find me. I've really missed you, Issy. Gant isn't what I thought he could be."

"It sounds like he's been looking after you though?"

"He has, I guess. His physicality is great, but he doesn't think before he speaks, some of the things… He's pretending to be sick so he can stay awake… Anyway, let's change the subject."

She tells me about the incident in the showers and it transpires that it isn't a one off. Digging around afterwards she has discovered there have been other deaths at various points in the recent cycles. It's just been kept very quiet.

I tell her of Junior a special MAGIE, who is sharing information. "It's unlike the others, not aloof or all-knowing. It seems young, naïve even. It seems to want to help us."

"Junior sounds really interesting. Do you trust it?"

"I feel like continuing as we are, compliant, isn't the way forward. We need to know more about this project, perhaps turn back home or get off the ship. There must be some escape vessels. Head back and leave this death ship to consume itself. We were all in such a rush to get off Earth that our need for survival has landed us in choppier waters. Out of the frying pan and into the fire."

Annabel - Cycle F14 Day 3

Annabel regards the view out of the window of the control room at the top of the ship, one of the only windows on the structure. Her weight is unevenly distributed, one hip juts out, tilting her pelvis, her yoga practise a faraway indulgence. This view is a luxury, she knows that. What she sees is also one of the aspects on the growing list of things that might jeopardise the mission. There are so many holes in the plan that she hadn't seen before they left. The stretching time away from Earth helps to see things with hindsight, clearing the fog from her mind.

Earlier, laid out across his bed, Oscar had been found by Appo. She'd had no response from her calls to him, and with him looking after, and hiding, Francis too, she was immediately worried, her fears soon realised.

"Replay Appo's report, please," she asks the computer. Appo had gone in wearing a small camera and a microphone to capture possible data. Listening is all the report is good for, the visuals are too broken up. Closing her eyes, Appo's voice and descriptions are crystal clear.

"I'm entering the bunker through the wall near Frankie's quarters. The atmosphere is cloying. I'm not sure you'll be able to see much. He is on the bed. I'm walking over. Now checking his vitals. He is still alive. He has patches of what look like the same fungi as we found on Frankie. I'm gathering samples for further testing. I am going to try a fit a respirator and tube for his windpipe. Dewi is assisting. The fungi have grown through the robe he is wearing and there are spores in the basin in the bathroom, also in the toilet, very like what we've seen in the shower dorms. I'm holding the respirator whilst Dewi opens Oscar's mouth to

intubate but his mouth is full of growths. We are struggling to fit the respirator. Dewi is attempting to clear out his mouth and airway by pulling and cutting the fungi away. It is surprising that he is even still alive, there can't be much oxygen getting through these obstructions. We have a real problem here, Doctor Morin. I'm sure I don't need to explain that fungi and mushrooms respire like humans do. We are trying with the tube again. It's jammed."

Muffled screams tear through the speaker. Oscar had woken. Annabel pauses the recording. It's harrowing. Appo is right; however this started, the fungi are a huge threat. She sits and takes a sip of her hot chocolate, her calmness temporarily restored. She continues listening to the report.

"Oscar has woken. He's lifted an arm and cried out, as you can probably hear, if not see. He is choking on the pipe now. We must have pushed some of the spores or smaller growths into his lungs with the tube. He is dying. He is beyond help. Dewi has suggested performing a tracheotomy but without moving him up to the lab he would either bleed out or suffocate. I will not risk the contamination of the rest of the ship and our passengers by bringing him out of this bunker. His lips are turning blue, his eyes are bulging. He has stopped fighting us now. He is quiet… He has gone."

Lots of crackling or interference fizzes through the speaker.

"I'm going to secure the rest of the area and check on Francis."

A pause with more crackling like the microphone is being adjusted while Appo navigates around the bunker. Then:

"Someone has been down here. The door up to the library is slightly ajar and there's a torch I don't recognise. I'm going up the ladder that leads to the reading room… The trapdoor won't open. It appears that someone has sealed it shut from the other side. I'm returning to Oscar's bunker and heading for the break out room where we placed Frankie's tube."

Annabel hears the tinny footsteps of the MAGIE, their rhythm punctuates her held breath.

"It is dark. I'm tapping on my shoulder light. The tube is full of liquid. Almost full. I'm moving in closer to get a better look. There is no human form inside that I can see, just some shapes which I assume are bones. The liquid is an opaque, murky grey. I can't see through it … I'm sorry, Doctor.

"I will collect samples and forward this report to you. Dewi and I will quarantine this area and get everything cleaned up, including ourselves. Sending report now. Appo out."

Switching off the system, Annabel leans onto the nearby table.

Annabel - Cycle F14 Day 5

"Who can I trust, Appo?" she says, almost in a whisper.

Appo sits in Annabel's quarters. The doctor is in shock. She hasn't left her rooms since the Oscar incident.

"You can trust me, Doctor. You've always had me," Appo passes her a freshly made hot chocolate.

"You know what I mean. Oscar put himself at the top of the tree. A lonely place. I had Frankie. I fought for him to come on this mission. And now he's gone, too. I don't want to be at the top of Oscar's tree. It feels pointless."

"You cannot stay in here, Doctor. If you do you will be no better than Oscar."

She looks at the MAGIE. "Very insightful. I don't intend to be a carbon copy of my brother at all. That's what I'm saying. I have responsibilities here. That's why I've halted the pod sleeps. All these people came on this trip to start again, to live their lives on their terms. But now something Francis possibly created is threatening to take it all away."

"We are on autopilot, don't forget. You don't need to make any decisions about our destination. That has all been taken care of."

"I'm not so sure. I feel like these events change everything."

"All the data points to Frankie being the source, that is for sure. Perhaps if we go back into the lab, we can find out how he created what he did, find the source or the original parent cultures and come up with a vaccine or pesticide?"

"All very noble and intelligent ideas, Appo, but consider where we are. There isn't the time or the scope to do all the work involved."

"We must try. As a tandem step we need to find out who was inside Oscar's bunker."

"Agreed. I need to pull myself together and get out there. These people *are* the future, I truly believe that. I wouldn't have started on this thing if I didn't. I wouldn't have risked my career, my life, on a whim."

"I'm going to send a medic in, just to check you over. I think you do need some more rest and time to think about the next steps before being among the passengers again. You are in shock; the grief hasn't hit you yet. We MAGIE can keep things ticking over until you are feeling a bit better."

"You look after me better than I do myself."

"Whoever was in Oscar's bunker, they won't be able to stay in hiding. If they saw even half of what I saw, they'll be exposed to the contagion. They will either become ill or desperate to find answers. Or both. I suggest we wait for the individual to come to us."

Rebecca - Cycle F14 Day 5

Rapping on my capsule shutter interrupts me reading. Sliding it open Issy is there, her face distorted with emotion.

"Rebecca, they've stopped the pod-sleeps. Men are everywhere."

"Right, okay. I'm going to have to go and see Annabel, I can't carry on hiding."

* * *

"Annabel? Doctor Morin? I know you're in there. I need to talk to you." I knock at the door to Annabel's office.

Annabel comes to the door. She is pale, more so than I remember, her hair is scraped back. She steps back, allowing me to come into the room. The interior is dark, cave-like even. The door swishes closed behind me and she puts on a small light in the corner. I see something sat in the corner on an old wooden chair. Is that Appo? The MAGIE doesn't move. There are no lights behind its eyes.

"I've shut Appo down," Annabel guesses my thoughts, "He was talking too much like Oscar, who I think you've met?"

Annabel's words jab me in the ribs, rendering me speechless. My planned speech slips away like mercury.

"Appo said you'd come."

"Me?"

"Not you specifically, but now it makes sense that it would be you."

"He had it on him already. What I did was self-defence. He wanted to keep me there, to keep him company." A wave of physical release washes over me, like sinking into a hot bath. To tell her, the authority, finally. It makes me feel a little better.

"You risked the whole ship, the whole expedition, by coming back out of there. Can you not see that? How do you know you aren't infected?" Annabel's eyes are glazed, red around the edges.

"I don't. I saw Frankie, though, and he must have been infected when I was last in contact with him. I've even been inside his quarters where this thing all started. You remember how I broke my ankle? Surely, if I was going to get infected, it would've happened there. Whatever is happening is already out there, me being infected wouldn't make any difference now."

Annabel is quiet. She perches on the edge of her desk. I'm still next to the door. Appo still in the corner, a silent witness. Can you really turn the MAGIE off completely? The silence fills the room. Finally, "Oscar was my brother. He had this amazing vision for humankind's future. This wasn't it."

My knees give way I sink to the floor. Sam's face suddenly filling my head, I picture him reading my goodbye letter.

"I'm sorry," I say quietly, carefully.

"You came here with questions, didn't you? Well I don't have answers. Now you must feel as stupid as I do."

She says the pod cycles stopping is a temporary thing, until they can find a solution or a cure. She won't risk the health of the pods—if they become contaminated, then everything will be lost. We'll never be able to get to our destination.

It has never been properly explained what the pods are—how they work or where they have come from. The longer I stay out of them, the more my theories grow.

She tells me there has been crazed behaviour and suicide post-pod-sleep. Probably caused by the removal or erosion of memories and things that symbolised personal life experiences. I experienced this first-hand with the disappearance of one of my favourite tattoos. There are stories of piercings healing, too, scars vanishing, even hair growing back from some of the men who had been balding. The pods slow whatever is inside, turning back time if you are in them long enough.

Why is she telling me all this? It feels like complete role reversal. I leave Annabel and walk back to my room.

Rebecca - Cycle F14 Day 7

"Okay, let's get going," Issy says. Gant and I follow her through the corridors and stairwells, ever downward. We've all been this way before, but this time the plan is very different. We are heading to a meeting. Gant is looking for spacesuits along the way.

The shipping containers feel like townhouses. Walking amongst them is like wandering in a dimly lit street, back in the old days. They are stacked two or three high, but they could be higher, there is enough ceiling space. Our footsteps echo from side to side of the long chamber, like we can hear our future selves walking back the same way later on, once this meeting is done. We've spread the word with people that we know well, people that are suspicious and disillusioned with what is happening.

243

"Have you ever seen any spacesuits on board, Gant? What about windows?" Issy asks him. "You've done the miles all around this ship, haven't you?"

"I think I saw one in Frankie's quarters. That must've been his own, I guess."

"I really don't think they'll be kept down here. Why would they be in storage? The only ones that might need to go outside the ship while we are in space are the MAGIE, and they don't need spacesuits." I pause, "It wouldn't surprise me if there weren't any, with all that's happening. If the worst occurs, I doubt there's backup or a Plan B. We'd just all die up here, there won't be enough suits for one each. No way."

Neither respond. At the end of the space hanger where all the shipping containers are housed there is a gap of about five metres by ten metres. It must be so the leveraging equipment can get in and out. It's gloomy and cold, so cold down here. Space itself on the other side of the walls.

There's about fifteen of us, including the MAGIE Junior. I step out into the middle of the gathering. The skin on the back of my neck tingles.

"Why did we all sign up for this expedition?" I ask the small group. Some I knew more than others. None of them are happy. I look into the faces of the people with me, waiting for answers.

"I wanted to start over," one says. She chooses her words carefully. English not her first language. "To get away from the fighting."

"The drugs. I wanted to leave the drugs behind," said another, an Australian poet. "And focus on my work again."

"I wanted to leave behind the prejudices of being myself."

"Powerful motivators, right? Any of these reasons, they are so personal, that is what gives them their strength. Me? I felt like it was my destiny, deep down, I bet part of you did, too. The fact we were all called upon to go. Yes, we could have said no. But really, what single person with no real responsibilities would say no? The Earth was going tits up. With the promises this mission made to us, we were spellbound. We were made to feel special, us the chosen ones, the ego-driven artists. We were, are, the perfect lemmings. None of us were looking for red flags, none of us wanted to see them. Only now the veil withers; only now we are feeling like we've been tricked."

My heart thumps under my ribs, I feel ready for anything. There are cheers and words of agreement amongst the group. "The pods for example, do any of us actually know what they are? What they do? I think they are alive and getting nourishment from us. A semi-symbiotic relationship. We get renewed, they get—what? Information?

Memories? To learn what makes us human? So, if we go inside with an active injury or problem, would they use up too much energy on fixing us? Or perhaps they could do it easily, but it's the MAGIE way of controlling us as passengers. Or maybe they would take on our damage or illness and spread it through the other pods. They are all connected. Fear has been instilled in us about asking too many questions, so no one has. Annabel is not in a fit state to answer them now, it's too late."

"We are out of the pods now," Issy starts. "Everyone together, that makes us stronger and we need a plan. We should find out where we are, our route, things like that. Maybe, think about turning back."

I nod, but others are shocked at the suggestion, I swear I hear someone whispering mutiny.

"Windows, for example, everyone knows there are no windows on the ship," Issy continues, "Don't you think that's strange?"

"It's certainly claustrophobic, but I put it down to cost. I guess it's cheaper not to have windows. This isn't a tourist flight is it?" Gant leans on the wall

"There are windows," Junior says, almost too quietly to be heard. I hear him, though.

"Let me guess: in your quarters? The labs at the top of the ship?"

"That's right. Have you been there?"

I recall the blueprints in Oscar's bunker. "No. None of us have. I think it's time we took a more active role in our journey. Right now, we're just letting all this happen to us."

"What else can you tell us, Junior?" Gant asks.

"Not much. I am the bottom rung of the ladder when it comes to information, I record and collate, but not investigate. I am a dogsbody, a gopher."

"Well you're one of us now. Oscar isn't going to bother you again."

Rebecca - Cycle F14 Day 9

Things feel worse, inside my head as well as what's going on around me.

"I can't think in here, Issy. There's too much noise." It doesn't seem to bother Issy, in fact she's thriving on having more interaction with others. We are eating dinner in Sector Four, along with what seems like everyone else, everyone wants their evening meal at the same time. Then a man, one of Gant's friends, Lonny, runs through completely naked. People laugh, just someone over excited, they say, people act a bit crazy sometimes, they say. We're all cooped up together, it's bound to happen.

But no, that's not it at all; Lonny's back is slashed, the skin like ribbons streaming out behind him. Inky blood dribbles down over his buttocks and legs. He collapses in the middle of Sector Four and lies there on his side. The rivers of blood seeping through the grids and panels in the floor, finding the gaps and making pathways through them.

People run to him, MAGIE are alerted. In the commotion another man enters the common area with a large knife. It looks like Gant's knife. Issy and I stay glued to our seats.

Lonny is taken to the med-bay and it takes two MAGIE and two passengers to tackle Do-Yun to the ground and sedate him. We find out that he had already killed four other men, finding them in the showers, hence Lonny's birthday suit. Lonny ran for his life from the shower room while Do-Yun chased him through the ship's corridors. The men in the showers had been slashed at arterial points and bled out.

We are all shaken and, although it is shocking to see, it doesn't feel that surprising. Things are fragile now. As the ship runs on autopilot, the MAGIE continue to perform their duties, all the while the threads of the mission unravel.

We have a plan, though. A rough plan, which starts with finding a window. There are years left of the mission, to get to our new home. It feels like we won't make it, unless we do something now.

CHAPTER 14 – 2072

Rebecca - Cycle F14 Day 11

There is safety in numbers, or at least it feels that way. My capsule has become a haven from everything going on outside on the ship, I love being alone now. Pulling out my scrabble bag of tiles, I perform the ritual that helped me through the early days. "I am building a life again. I am happy again. I will bring these objects with me and include my history in my new home, wherever that may be."

The tiles are smooth and cool and calm. Exactly how I want to feel. The mantras are mine, although I haven't said them in a while. When I'm finished, I place them carefully them back inside the bag and climb into bed.

Sleep comes, or is it a memory? I'm chasing Juniper through a field as the sun is going down. The grasses brush my bare legs as I try to catch up to her. There is music in the distance. Music that feels old and easy but has a melody I know. We are running around the base of a hill. Suddenly before me, on the bend there are huge trailers with fairground rides, setting up. Juniper darts into the meadow where the commotion is coming from, and I slow down, absorbing the sights and sounds of the assembling structures. The people here are dressed in a way that makes them from another time. The men are all in black suits but not corporate wear. There is depth and texture to the fabric. The women, of which there are only few, wear black skirts and white blouses, their hair piled on top of their heads. Snippets of conversation tell me they speak differently too. I don't recognise the language at first and then realise it is English, but I can only pick out a few words, the accent so thick and indecipherable.

My pace has slowed to walking. My curiosity spiked by these unusual people.

A wash of sound and all at once the dusk bathed meadow is lit up. The structures come to life with light. Where has the power come from? Then Juniper barks.

"Juniper! June, come to Bec!"

I veer off, following a route that feels right, and there she is. J is lying on the ground in a state of bliss, having her belly rubbed by someone with their back to me.

"Hey! You found my dog. Thank you," I say.

The person stands, clad in black like the others here. Juniper jumps up and leaps into my arms.

"You have a beautiful dog." I hear Christian's voice, but the person speaking is not my husband—it's Annabel.

Annabel - Cycle F14 Day 11

Annabel wakes slumped in her chair. She'd fallen asleep at her desk, her head resting on her notebook and the ship's log. Her neck and shoulders spasming, crying with that feeling of being stuck in one position for far too long. The ship's log is stored on one of the computer systems, but Appo had discovered a second, handwritten one in Oscar's bunker. Her brother had been keeping a track of his thoughts, just like she'd asked him to, along with details of the trip and some notes about his plans. "Only in death do I find the real you." She mumbles to herself.

Alone, in her sleeping quarters, a slightly bigger version of the passenger's capsules, she has barricaded herself in her grief. Reaching up, she pushes her hair out of the way, arms in the air, stretching and giving her shoulders and neck a rub. Something feels different. Without looking, she knows instantly what it is; the fungal infection. There is a growth on the back of her neck.

To her fingers it feels smooth and soft, protruding from her skin, a warty, old, coin-sized mole. The feeling from under the skin is like that of having a large spot on the back of her neck, sore and swollen.

Standing slowly, as if she might disturb it, she creeps to the tiny basin. The auto-light blinks on, an unflattering, harsh light above her head, then two smaller lights to either side of the vanity unit. Lifting her hair and turning slightly allows her to see the growth out of the corner of her eye. It is fascinating. There is no fear, just an overwhelming curiosity. *Should I remove it*, she wonders, *or would it be like grey hair? Pluck one and three grow in its place.* She knows that isn't true of course, not for the hair, but for this weird, soft growth on her neck. In that moment she decides to pluck it off. She pinches the nodule and twists.

"Ouch! Fuck!" Instantly she understands why Frankie just let them grow and never came to her for help.

She'll have to leave her quarters to get this sorted. Appo will do it for her. He can slice it off, cauterise the open wound and dress it. It will be the first example of the fungi from a living person, and surely will be of some use. She buzzes him to be ready for her. At the door, she moves the set of drawers she had put in front of it and takes a deep breath, stepping out into the corridor. It is the early hours of the morning—not that the time should matter on board a spaceship. There's no dawn or dusk like on Earth, but the lights are designed to imitate the suns cycle, it helps keep people's circadian rhythms. At this time at least, there is a smaller chance of bumping into anyone.

Setting off, she pulls her hair around her neck, just in case anyone does see her. She pads along the corridor her feet growing more sensitive and painful with each step. It is eerily quiet, except for some distant voices that carry along the corridor. A flash of gratitude washes over her, the med-bay is not far away from her quarters.

Appo is ready and waiting for her.

"Thank you for coming. I know I've not been myself lately. I apologise for switching you off, I've treated you badly," she sits as the door glides shut behind her.

"Please don't worry about any of that. We must get you sorted. Now, show me… Ah I see it." Appo gently moves her hair to one side. "If you could hold your hair, please, I'll sort this out as quickly as possible. Do you have more, elsewhere on your body?"

"I'm not certain, to be honest. I've been rather too frightened to look. My feet feel terribly sore. I'm really not feeling like myself."

"Not to worry. I'll examine you now." The MAGIE checks the door is locked as Annabel removes her shoes.

"Oh, ouch!" Sucking in air through her teeth, bracing herself, it's too much to process. "Oh my god, Appo. Oh my god! I've not taken my shoes off for days."

Appo lifts her from the chair and carries her over to the examination couch.

"Please, try to stay calm, Doctor." Appo raises her feet onto the bed and adjusts the hydraulic couch higher so it can get a better look. Then the MAGIE straps her to the bed.

"What are you doing?"

"It's for your own safety, Doctor. We don't want you falling off from this height, do we?"

By the time Appo is done she has three belts across her body—one at her knees, one at her waist, and one at the tops of her arms.

"I don't need to be restrained like this. Remove them at once!"

"I'm sorry. I can't do that. I'm following protocol. Now keep still while I lance this growth on your neck. If you can't do as I request, I will have to sedate you."

She reluctantly turns her head so the MAGIE can see what they are lancing. One false move and it could really harm her. She holds her breath as Appo leans in pushing the growth a little with its fingers, then pulling it from side to side, she winces, trying not to cry out.

She concentrates on what she can see. Computer screens, a desk, some medical equipment. Through the glass wall, deeper into med-bay, she can see the cryogenic room. Inside there are DNA strung samples, fertilised eggs, and, beyond cabinets, she can just about see the sleeping pods.

SLICE.

"Fuck! Appo that—" The MAGIE holds her head down in position. "OW!" Her skin sizzles and the smell of her own burnt hair and flesh fills her nostrils.

* ✳ *

Annabel examines her reflection again. The pain she'd felt this morning, when Appo had removed that first nodule, had been immense.

Appo had described a stump, roots even. The pain still resonates through her body like a tuning fork, recalling another sour memory of piano lessons as a child. She had been precocious, much like her brother. Their mother had tried so very hard to push her into a feminine mould that she just didn't fit. The piano lessons had been easy, not challenging enough. The verbal abuse she'd suffered at the hands of her piano tutor was buried for many years. It was only when she started to do more holistic science that she'd tried hypnotherapy and it had all come out; the belittling of her talent, the inappropriate language, the violent, saliva spouting shouting in her face. She'd surprised even herself with the brain's ability to mask pain for so long.

Looking down at her feet, she considers Appo's prognosis.

"I'm not sure what we can do, Doctor, beyond anti-fungals." It is true. The studies they completed on the previous victims haven't shown how someone can recover from this infection because nobody has. It is depressingly fascinating. People can be carriers without showing symptoms, the precious, life-preserving pod system could potentially be ruined.

Removal isn't an option. The growths are embedded, as if they have always been there, part of her just waiting for the right opportunity to flourish. Frankie had been harbouring this new species. She wonders if he knew it would consume them, or if it was an innocent addition to his quirky encyclopaedia of stuff he had wanted to bring with him.

Her feet are bulbous now. Fungi are growing through the tops of them, perhaps through the tiny hair follicles. Once it has more space, each one increases in size until they are covering the top of each foot. They are starting to spread around her ankles.

Removing her robe, she stands to examine herself, the pain is receding. It's two hours since she last looked, and the need to keep checking is compulsive. She'd found the stumps in other places, too. A lot of them are focused in areas where the lymph nodes are found; in the armpit and around her breasts, behind her ears and along her neck, and most unpleasantly of all, in her groin and around her snatch.

She steps in closely to the mirror, opening her mouth to check inside. The flashbacks of the way Oscar died are constantly on playback in her head. There are no growths in her mouth, yet.

She ponders what it could mean. Each case is such an individual experience. Part of her believes the fungi are behaving differently within her than on anyone else they had previously seen. She has more visible growths than Oscar, but feels very much alive, any malaise now passed.

"I'm drinking a lot of water, which must be to feed the fungi. Most need a lot of moisture. I'm barely urinating and I'm not hungry."

Saying these things on video feels a bit pointless, but she is a stickler for official processes, and even though the mission was never government-backed, Oscar and herself had kept to most of the legislation and rules for space travel. "I have a feeling that this isn't killing me," she continues. "It feels like it's making me stronger, better than a regular human. Perhaps this is the next stage of evolution. This, my emerging form, is the new missing link. I am the next adaptation. Perhaps that was Frankie's plan; the progression of humankind in order the thrive again. Or perhaps I'm giving him more credit than he's due, and it was all an accident by a cranky old man who wanted to live forever. But to hybridise is to survive. The fungi just needed the right host, and that could be me."

Gant - Cycle F14 Day 11

Gant is in his capsule room. Lying in the dark no longer needing to feign sickness, losing any concept of time he'd previously held. He just can't face anything. Rebecca hadn't offered to stay, and he hadn't asked her. She is the driving force behind the dissent on board, she needs to be there—plus, if he has anything contagious, why should she become infected, too.

After sleeping fitfully for hours, it's his bladder that puts out emergency status. The sweat and chills, the aches, and the sensitivity to light make him assume it's flu, something he's not experienced for years, since being a child.

"Fuckin' such a ball ache, walking to the communals every time I need a piss." His throat is sore it is hard to swallow but he continues grumbling as he pulls on his robe and finds his trainers, still in the dark.

Lifting the shutter makes his arms ache. He squints the usually dim lights in the corridor seem brighter than normal. He squints and fumbles his way down the ladder, heading for the shared bathrooms. The place stinks of sweat and bodily functions. The women's wing never smells this bad.

Locating an empty trap, he shuts the door, preferring some privacy in his fragile state, even if it is just for a piss.

"What the fuck is that?" Pulling his cock from his pyjama bottoms, he feels something to the side of it, an addition in his palm. His pride shrinks in his hand as he opens the robe to look properly at what he'd felt. There are little grey protrusions emerging from under his skin. "What the … she's given me fuckin' warts! Genital fuckin' warts!"

"Shut the fuck up, would you?" a voice comes from the trap next door. "At least you're getting some."

"Whatever," Gant replies. His bladder screams at him, and he goes, at last, but Rebecca stays at the front of his mind. How did she even have genital warts? Everyone was screened for infections before they boarded. He shakes off, flushes, and leaves the trap. The conversationalist next door is still in there. He is washing his hands at the basin and when he notices in the mirror how dishevelled his reflection is, he sees it; in his hairline, and in his hair. The coarse and unruly waves are thanks to his Nigerian blood, but the tiny lumps on his scalp are thanks to something else.

Reaching up to his scalp he parts some of his hair to get a better look. More of the lumps, clusters of them sitting on his scalp. He runs his fingers through his hair to the back of his neck, and there is something much bigger. Velvety and soft, it is part of him and not part of him at the same time. Hot sourness rises to his mouth, his stomach muscles spasm in shock. Lurching forward he tries to ensure all the vomit ends up in the basin. It is endless. His eyes are streaming with the sting of everything and there is creamy grey bile in the sink. He makes the connection.

"It's okay, everyone. It's not genital warts!" he shouts through the bathrooms. Bile clinging to his throat. "I'm just a fun-guy, that's all."

"Whatever, man," his faceless bathroom companion retorts.

Gant cleans up as best he can and leaves the bathroom and his companion in peace, heading straight to med-bay.

* ✳ *

By the time he arrives, he's been sick down his front. The thought of things growing on him is sending him under. There are at least twelve men already sitting outside the entrance to med-bay on a makeshift bench that has clearly been assembled to deal with the need. The men look how Gant feels. Some worse.

"Hey, please, you need to join the queue," one of them says as he starts to stumble past them.

"You're fuckin' kidding me?"

"I wish I was."

Gant must know some of these men, but they are unrecognisable. Some have tied bandannas around their faces and others have so many growths that their facial features are indistinguishable. Then a MAGIE appears asking for the next in line to go in. Spotting Gant's arrival, it brings out a hot damp towel, which smells of disinfectant and a disposable bag.

"How long is the wait?"

"We are seeing someone every ten minutes, so a couple of hours. Clean yourself up as best as you can, and the bag is for any more vomit. Try and get some sleep."

Gant laughs. "How long? Some of these guys look like they need to be seen now. My eyes are so itchy I feel like they're going to fall out!"

"I'm aware of the situation. We are overrun with this problem in the male population of the ship. We are doing our very best in this unprecedented situation. Allow me to get on with my job. We've tried to make the process as fair as possible." The MAGIE walks away quickly collecting the nearest man to the doorway.

Closing his eyes Gant leans back on the bench, repeating the word over in his head; unprecedented. Would this have happened if they'd reported the mushrooms as soon as he'd found them? His skin is uncomfortably tight across his scalp, he perches on the edge of the seat, his ball bag too sore to sit fully down. Rolling up the towel, he plugs it between the wall and his head and tries to doze. He cups his balls in his hands as his mind races with how he had let this happen and wishes of home.

Issy - Cycle F14 Day 11

"Could you hack into the MAGIE system, Junior?" Issy asks.

"I'd be hacking into myself," Junior replies. "If you mean beyond my level of access, I think I could. I may need some help. I'd need to be protected, hidden somewhere. If they realise what I'm doing, then they will be able to shut me down remotely."

"So, we need a distraction?" Issy says, looking at Rebecca.

"I'd say they are pretty distracted now," Rebecca says. "With almost all of the men on board being infected. But I think we need something bolder. Could you show us where we could cause some electrical or mechanical damage that wouldn't affect the main functions of the ship? We could create a little anarchy among the MAGIE. Give them enough to work on so we can get control of the ship and end this mad mission."

"But what if there's already no one left on Earth? What if Oscar knew it was always going to be more than environmental and economic? It could be uninhabitable."

Rebecca is silent.

"These are things I think I can find out." Junior offers.

"That would be great, we need to be fast though."

"We could do with understanding what state Earth is in."

"It doesn't feel like we've been away long because of the sleep pods, but we've slept more or less half the time."

"But look at how youthful we are right?" Issy laughs as she pretends to be a fashion model.

"I hate those pods," Rebecca says. "I lost some of myself to them"

"I think that's how they worked. That's why some people have gone mad. They can't remember who they are."

The three of them are hiding out in Frankie's old room. The sleeping capsules are too small for them to meet like this, plus there is always the chance of being overheard.

"Gant is infected, Rebecca," Junior says. "I saw him on the way here. He didn't see me. I wasn't sure what to do, having promised to meet you here."

"You did the right thing. I'm sorry you had to see that, Junior. I know you like him."

"As did you."

"Yep. Perhaps." She bites her lip. "I still don't get how some of us aren't succumbing to this infection."

Rebecca Cycle F14 Day 12

A voice booms out and I jump out of my dream like I'm being attacked, I hadn't realised there was a PA system. The voice cutting through my sleep is Dr Morin. Something is wrong.

The doctor calls everyone to meet in Sector Four. I quickly dress, I strap on my medi boot, my ankle still recovering from the time with Oscar, wondering what else could go wrong. It can't be any worse.

On arriving at Sector Four, it becomes clear. Around thirty women sit, some standing, drinking coffee. Some are laughing. I want to laugh too, out of the sheer craziness of what is happening. Then someone says it:

"Where are all the men?"

"The pods are out of action, aren't they?"

A hush settles across the small crowd as Annabel enters the room. She is almost unrecognisable, sitting in a wheelchair with Appo behind her. The Doctor clears her throat.

"Some of you may have realised there has been an outbreak of an infection, that is fungal in nature, on board this ship. As you can see, I am infected. As you can also see, there are no men in this room. They are all infected. Some have died." The women nearest to Annabel slowly retreat from her. "We are in a state of high alert. Our facilities are stretched to the limit, probably beyond."

"Why are you telling us this face to face? Are you trying to infect us all?" Someone shouts from the other side of the room. I recognise Issy's voice. She sounds scared.

"It is my belief that you are all already carriers of the spores. We don't know much about it yet, but we must assume that we all are infected. There is hope, for the women on board anyway. It seems that the fungi prefer a female body. I feel enhanced, not diminished. Stronger, not weaker. My plan is to turn back and return to Earth. Get the help we need. If we freeze the remaining living men, we can stop the process until defrosting back on Earth."

"Why don't you tell people what is really going on, Doctor Morin?" I'm no longer able to stop myself stepping out from the crowd so Annabel can see me. The doctor shakes her head. Did she think I was dead already? "Tell them about your brother and his plan. The infamous Oscar Markov. The world saw his death, it was broadcast everywhere. No one could have failed to miss it. But would any of us have signed up to this if we'd known he was behind it? Would we have trusted you, shared our hopes, dreams, and fears with you, if we'd known you were his sister? Would we? Fuck. None of us would be here. This whole thing is one giant fuck up, one giant ego trip—isn't it?"

Some of the gathered women physically reel at this news.

"I've not even begun to tell you everything. Oscar's grand plan was to *return* to Earth, the place that we inherited from generations of people who wrecked it, pillaged it for all it was worth. We left, but Earth is trying to live again, fighting and adapting. But we gave up on her, we signed up to be passengers here, on a voyage to a new world. That voyage, in fact, ladies, is one that has been circling the Earth for years. That's why there are no windows on the ship. Well, apart from one I've been informed of. A place that we don't have access to. I oppose the idea of going back now, with this cargo. With all this death. What if we are all destined to be mushroom women?" I gesture over to Annabel.

"You say that like it's a bad thing, Rebecca," she finally speaks. "The MAGIE helped us take away the men in positions of power, but maybe that's not enough. Maybe we must go beyond our species now to save the Earth. Hybridisation is the way forward. We sacrifice humanity and evolve into something more. We level up, adapting to survive. This is natural selection at its finest. Surely you can see that?"

The room holds its breath. Many women are not looking at me or Annabel, but down at the floor, or at their hands, twiddling their thumbs.

"And before anyone says, 'but who are we to decide?' We must decide. Because this ship is on auto pilot. We can either carry on the mission as Oscar planned it, and continue to go through life passively, or we can think for ourselves and take action." My words earn a hum of agreement.

"If you are attempting a mutiny, Rebecca, then please know that the MAGIE are programmed to be loyal to me."

The gathering of women started to ask questions, to both Annabel and me. So many questions.

"Am I infected?"

"What happens if we return to Earth?"

"How can I trust you now?"

"What gives you the right to lead us?"

Someone yanks my wrist, someone else tugs at my shoulder. Issy finds me, protecting me. The MAGIE does the same for Annabel.

I take the opportunity to escape. Clasping my head in my hands like they are enough to hold me together; everything might burst out, splitting me in half. I run down the corridor towards the eco-wing, push through the swing doors and enter a wall of moisture. Condensation clings to everything, gathering in tiny streams and running down the veins and petioles of the leaves. Things are perspiring, sweating away their previous forms to become something beyond, are they infected too? The atmosphere is tropical. I feel almost at home, almost like I'm back at work on Earth. The humidity has nowhere to go, except to be used by the plants. It is incredible. No wonder Annabel wants to go back to Earth with all this life.

Then I see them, the two bodies. They look almost like fallen tree trunks. The men must have been placed in here as an experiment, creating a chain reaction. Now they are two small mounds, riddled with fungi. This fungus isn't the same as the original one though. I look more closely and see two distinct types. One resembles human ears, covering one side of each hill, and then on the side nearest the lights are the ones I'd seen on Oscar. It would be rather beautiful, if we weren't in such a desperate situation.

I wonder if I'm already infected. I don't think I am, and the sight of Annabel puts that right into perspective. It is virulent but doesn't affect everyone as she believes.

Moving away from the mushroom mounds, I head towards the door at the other end. This exit leads through to the women's wing. It is a shortcut that not many people use, since the electric in this corner of the eco-wing had failed shortly after the mission started. The MAGIE said damp had gotten in somehow and the wiring couldn't be fixed. There are floodlights rigged up instead, a temporary measure that became permanent.

Pushing open the door, I start to run. My ankle complains, but something inside tells me to move, and I listen. The door behind me swings again; I can hear it. Someone has followed me.

I quicken my pace and try to look back. Those damn electrics! A figure—who is it? I call out, but they don't reply. It moves, coming my way. They are holding something in their hand. I swivel on my good foot and began to jog again. The corridor curves round to the women's rooms. I go a bit quicker, my ankle again asking me to stop, my ears straining to hear beyond my own noisy and unbalanced footsteps. My pulse thunders in my ears, the medi boot isn't made for running. Whoever is following, is getting faster, gaining. My ankle is really hurting now, spasming as I tried to match their pace.

Annabel has sent someone to get rid of me. It must be that. They are close now. My lungs take big gulps of air, trying to push further forward, quicker than them. My ankle screams at me desperate to give up.

Then the floor of the corridor comes up to meet me. Tackled, I hit the deck. Face down, they are on top of my legs. My ankle is both happy to have stopped running and cramping with panic. Arms around my knees squeeze tightly. I try to crawl away, but they are too heavy. Their weight stops me bending my legs. I try to roll over, to face my opponent. Squirming like a fish stuck in a net, I wriggle and wrangle until I feel their body release me for a spilt second, and I flip over.

"Gant! What the hell?"

But it is the ghost of Gant. He looks in a trance. Visible fungi grow across his chest, shoulders, and ears. One of his eyes is bloodshot and bulging, as if it might fall out at any moment. I push up a knee and manage to jab him in the chin with it while shuffling backwards. It's not really him, Gant is not there, this is something possessed. His breathing becomes more laboured. He opens his mouth as if to speak, but no words come out. His tongue is covered with pustules and white down.

I shuffle back on my hands and bum. My bad foot frees up finally and I kick him in the face with my fracture boot— at least it is good for something. His bulging eyeball pops out and drops onto his cheek, hanging on by the thread of the optic nerve. The release of the eyeball has been helped by the boot to the face, but as I finally pull myself free, I can see that inside the socket are threads of fungi and small mushrooms. They'd have pushed the eyeball out anyway. He is a zombie, fragile but potentially lethal.

"I'm sorry, Gant, but you're already dead."

Grabbing the wall, I stand and see the knife on the floor—Gant's beautiful hunting knife that he'd brought with him as part of his personal belongings. He must have dropped it as we fought. Picking it up, I move away from him. He is still moving, stuck between life and death. My brain races; what should I do? I can't leave him like this.

"You need to put him out of his misery," a voice from behind. Issy. She's come from the other direction, from the women's quarters. I fall into her arms. We work in silence, not needing to speak to understand one another. Issy rolls Gant over and gags, trying not to be sick. He's really slow now.

"Let's wait a moment. I think he's nearly gone."

I sit on the floor and hold his hand, laying the knife beside me. Issy crouches alongside and we both wait.

"I'm pretty sure he's dead now," Issy say after a few minutes of his chest not moving. "Shall we put him in the eco-wing, or drag him to the catalyser?"

"One of the things I love about you, Issy, is that you're so matter of fact." I stand up and try not to cry.

Suddenly my legs go from under me. There is a jabbing across my calves, he's swept his arm over swiftly to one side and I slam to the metal floor. He lets go and attempts to grab the knife. Issy is trying to pull him away but keeps breaking off parts of his fungi in her hands, he cries out, obviously in pain.

"Fuck!" I kick him again in the head, this time taking no prisoners. The momentum of my leg takes his head off. I

271

snatch the knife and push it into his chest. It crunches past his ribs and thin channels of black, old blood seep out where the blade enters his body. Strangely there is no blood here. The skin and flesh on his neck look desiccated. Perhaps the fungi have used most of the water in Gant's body.

"*Now* he's dead,"

* * *

We sit on the bed inside Issy's capsule.

"After you left Sector Four, Doctor Morin hurried away, too. We can take control here, Bec. We've got to."

"We can't do that with the MAGIE protecting her. We've got to move from these capsules to start with. They aren't safe."

"Are you okay? I'm so sorry about Gant."

"He's probably better off dead than having to live through this."

"We are in a mad house."

"She got to him, or the infection did, maybe both. That's the thing about mushrooms and fungi: they have this network. A bit like our nervous system, sending messages around our bodies. All the fungi, they're all connected in the same kind of way. Frankie used to talk about this back on Earth."

272

Issy suggests we move into the basement of the ship, go into hiding. If Annabel wants to kill me then she'll send someone else.

What I said in Sector Four is truly what I believe. It's up to the survivors that are left now. According to Annabel, if we go back to Earth then we'll kill all men. Yes, we'd have an abundance of life, but at that cost? I really don't think she's thought this through. How would we have children? There's only so many sperm banks, and if we had boys they wouldn't live long.

CHAPTER 15 – 2072

Rebecca - Cycle F14 Day 15

I open one eye and stretch. That was a great sleep. These shipping containers are so much more spacious than the capsules upstairs. We had dragged down a couple of mattresses too, tried to make it cosy. Issy is gone. Probably to fetch breakfast. She's been so good to me. Since my outburst in Sector Four, she says the women are looking for me to lead them in a rebellion. A mutiny. Somehow, I know that is what will end up happening, but not yet. For now, I'm happy taking stock.

Standing, I bang my head on the ceiling. Strange, this space is huge. I look down and don't see my feet. Well, they don't seem like my feet anyway. I see paws. Neat, glossy-haired, black paws. I lower my head to take a closer look. Yes, they are mine; they are connected to me. I turn my head to look behind and down, there's no mirror inside the container. I'm trying not to panic. I see glossy black fur and a tail and some back legs.

I lie down again. It's a dream. It's got to be a dream.

Annabel - Cycle F14 Day 15

Annabel's mobility decreases, she has been spending most of her days in bed. Day by day, more hair falls from her head and her limbs grow more fungi. She finds that eating and drinking are things she no longer needs to partake in. She hasn't needed to use the toilet in so long, she can't remember the last time. She doesn't bother getting dressed: Nothing fits her anyway. There is nothing to be afraid of anymore, no shame to be felt. She is strong now.

She can sense things much more clearly. Things that she's never perceived before. Inside her mind, new connections and pathways have developed. She can feel what the patients feel in med-bay. Many of them are on anti-fungal medications, an attempt to rid them of the infection. It hurts them. The fungus fights back. It is wilful. Waiting years for this chance, it isn't about to let it slip away.

There is a new problem, one that has taken priority over the Rebecca situation. The oxygen on board is running dangerously low. Humans breathe in oxygen, but so do fungi. This is news to Annabel, who never studied fungi until recently. The MAGIE keep reminding her, nagging her. What is she going to do about the oxygen? It's okay for them. They didn't need anything to sustain their bodies. The plants in the eco-wing are thriving, of course. They were doing their job, respiring, producing oxygen, but they aren't doing it fast enough. Annabel needs the plants to at least double their output. Ideas of expanding the eco-wing are thrown around by her and Appo, but the ship just isn't set up for it. The obvious answer is to return to Earth ahead of schedule and come what may.

Appo arrives interrupting her thoughts.

"Good morning, Appo." Her voice has changed. She tries clearing her throat.

The droid brings a towel to the area that hides her mouth as she coughs. It is now nearly buried underneath the fungal growths on her face. Pulling the towel away, they both see black phlegm on the fabric.

"I think we need to move you, Doctor. We need to get you to the eco-wing where you can breathe."

"There's nothing wrong with me. This is all part of the process. I'm becoming something more. I *am* evolution."

"I don't mean to question you, Doctor. I think perhaps that was true at one point, when all this started. But now … well now, I'm afraid that you are being consumed by the fungi. There is less of you than there is of it. It killed the others much faster. Whatever is in you and the other women that makes you different—genetics, perhaps—I believe it is only slowing the process. Not changing it, as we had hoped."

"You're saying you think I'm dying," she croaks.

"I'm afraid so, Doctor. If we move you to the eco-wing it should prolong your life, enough even for us to study and come up with a better anti-fungal in time to help you."

"But I felt so alive before. This might just be part of the process," she pleads as her throat fills up again.

"It might, but it might not. We need to do some tests," Appo says gently. "Shall we go now?"

"Yes. Let's go, at least I'll be able to breathe better. Maybe that's all I need."

Appo calls for three more MAGIE to help. Annabel is so large that they strap two stretchers together. They gather around her bed. She hadn't moved in over twenty-four hours, not seeing the point of doing so.

"On three we are going to lift you onto the stretcher, Doctor. Are you ready?"

"Yes," she's barely audible.

"One, two, three!"

They all lift at once, and Annabel lets out a muffled groan that turned into a scream.

"Stop! Stop, put me down!" she tries to shout. Her sounds are stifled, and the MAGIE don't understand what she is trying to say. Laying her on the stretcher, it becomes obvious; the skin and fungus on the doctor's back has fused with the bedding. Her human epidermis clings to where she has been lain, twisted and crumpled with the bedding. Annabel convulses on the stretcher.

"Help … help me, I think I'm going to be sick."

Appo crouches at her side and lifts her head.

* ✳ *

My whole body heaves. The sound from my throat, unrecognisable to me. Vomit rushes upwards, outwards, beyond my control. I lie on the floor, my head in Appo's hands and straining to see what has just exited my body. Is it still my body? I don't know. It's all I have left, so it is mine and I am it.

The grey-green sludge I've just discharged looks like the seaweed from the beaches of Saxa Vord. Lumpy, black chains of pustules, ribbon through it.

I disgust myself and vomit again. Someone is bringing towels. The MAGIE are talking but I don't hear them. Perhaps my ears have stopped working. Perhaps the fungus blocks them. I think Appo is right. I've got this all wrong.

The taste in my mouth is like rotten fish. I'm gagging now, but there is nothing left inside me. The trembling subsides and they clean me up as best they can.

My back is on fire.

They lift me and struggle to get me through the door. The repulsorlift on the stretcher isn't strong enough to lift me on its own. The MAGIE shimmy my body between them and a moan comes from deep within. Now we are through the long corridor to the eco-wing. They ask me if I can roll off, talking to me as if I'm a child. I manage to shuffle. Getting off the stretcher and onto the soil; a patch they have cleared for me within the plant beds.

I can breathe again. I'm lying on my back and taking huge gulps of air. The oxygen is coming into me from all over my body, not just through my mouth and nose. I can feel it in my feet and in through the tips of my fingers. The sores of my back where my skin was ripped off feel soothed by the cool damp of the soil. I close my eyes, perhaps in a state of bliss, or because I don't feel I need them anymore.

I can hear Appo's voice, but he sounds far away, and I can't quite understand what he's saying. The most exquisite sensation, a cool wetness, is gently covering my body. They are spraying me with water. At any other time in my life to be naked, exposed and laid on my back in the dirt, would mean something awful had happened, but this feels pleasurable beyond anything I've experienced before.

I dig my arms into the soil beside me, reaching down as far as I can. I don't care if anyone or anything is nearby now. I want to get deeper into the dirt. Pushing down, I feel the roots of the plants nearby. I grab them and wind them around my wrists.

I consider Earth, consider going back there as this new being. I think about Oscar and all the mistakes he made that didn't seem like mistakes at the time. Now I can see he wasn't going about things in the right way. Fate took us on this course, and I'm thankful for that.

I think about Frankie and how I fell in love with a dangerous, Scottish time traveller. I never did get to the bottom of the how and why of him being in that modified freezer. I wish he were here to share this with me. I wish he had trusted me enough to tell me about the mushrooms, those he'd found in the copse that day.

When we'd wandered alone for the first time, he was more excited about them than the kiss we'd shared moments before. None of that matters now. Earth can begin again with a new regime. A new organism will lead the way.

"She cannot hear us, Appo," Lan says, almost correctly. "She has no idea what we are saying at all. Look at her skin, it's peeling away."

"You're right. Though she doesn't seem to be in pain. There's no response or acknowledgement. She does seem to be happier. She's positively glowing."

My eyes still closed; I am radiant within. My somatosensory system heightened like never before. I sense Appo sending away the other MAGIE. Then my faithful droid sits and watches me for a while, probably making some notes to add to my file. As I force myself deeper into the soil my skin liberates itself from my limbs.

Appo wishes me well on my travels and leaves. My eyes are deep in the back of my skull. My forearms and lower legs are embedded in the soil, streamers of skin peel away from my fungi-covered mass.

Rebecca - Cycle F14 Day 16

"Protocol means that we must now divert away from Earth. You have what you wanted, Rebecca," says Appo. I'm on the cargo level with Issy. "This is something I haven't shared with Annabel. She is too far gone now to even know what is going on."

I sit and wait, watching the MAGIE, knowing there must be a 'but' coming.

"My deep dive programming states that in the case of any kind of on-board disaster, something that would increase mortality faster on Earth than the current rate. Well, it states—that the ship must be reprogrammed, sent as far away as possible and destroyed."

The silence is as deep as a well and lingers, as if echoing around the ship.

"Why have you come to me with this?"

"I believe you are the right type of mind to think of an alternative. Since I've known you, you have displayed a sense of questioning, of attempting to rise above what is generally accepted by everyone else. You also seem immune to the infection and there aren't many of you left now. Above all else, it is deep within the MAGIE code to protect human life, destroying the ship must be the last resort, but we need alternate ideas. I and the other MAGIE are all programmed to follow. Not to lead. It was programmed into us as a safety mechanism. If we ever got too clever, as you would call it … well, we can't. We have some initiative, which I believe I am showing now. In short, we need a leader. Someone to give us our directives. Both Oscar and Annabel are out of the picture. There isn't a third person. No option C."

I can't help but laugh. "What the actual? This isn't a joke, is it?"

"I'm afraid not."

"It's what people have been saying, Bec. Many of them trust you," Issy says. "Step up. You can do this. I'll be here for you."

"I can't make the kinds of decisions you're asking of me, Appo. I don't want that power or responsibility."

"That's exactly why you are just what this mission needs, Rebecca."

* ✳ *

"So the MAGIE have another new theory," Issy says walking through the shipping containers with a trolley of food supplies, its dinnertime and I'm starving again. She is really taking care of me. "I've just seen one of them in the corridor. The ones not succumbing have supposedly been exposed before, to the fungi."

I instantly think of Mum.

"You know I prefer the first one, about the noses, it made sense. You can't always smell, and me, well, I've been beaten up enough times. I must have had my nose broken at least three times one year."

I look up from my journal and wonder how anyone could ever harm Issy, she's so full of light and warmth.

"How do you not know how many times your nose has been broken?" I ask her.

"The drugs, my friend. I was numb most of the time. I took the beatings. They gave me the shit I craved."

We've all gone through stuff to get here. I suppose it is doesn't make a difference now what makes some succumb and others not. We must be carriers.

The ship has turned into a damp, dark jungle of fungi. The corridors are carpets of responsive spores that drift around and plant themselves into the bodies dotted around the place.

Air is running out. Time is running out.

There are no weapons on board, other than this biological one that has managed to see off nearly everyone. We have gone through most of our options.

Appo is researching alternate planets we might go to, or local space stations to which we could send out an SOS signal. The problem is that no one knows we're up here. They think we are a freighter, and a cry for help would mean we might end up spreading this thing. Another option is to crash-land on Earth, hoping that the impact and subsequent fires would kill off all the fungi. Finally, we might set up the ship to self-destruct. The answers are here somewhere.

Rebecca - F14 Day 19

"We do have life rafts," Appo says.

"You tell me this now?"

"Well I couldn't before, I was taking orders from Oscar, then Annabel."

"I'm sorry. I know. It's just frustrating. So, fill me in about the life rafts and the autopilot."

"Please come in and sit." Appo gestures to the doorway and a chair beyond. These rooms at the top of the ship are fungi free. The MAGIE must clean them fastidiously. This is the first time I've been in this area of the ship, leaving Issy and the others downstairs, sleeping.

I walk in and my breath escapes me all at once, like someone has punched me in the stomach. There is a huge window. A huge, fucking defiant window. Oscar had been a sick bastard, but this is just beyond. I reel, and Appo steps up just in time to catch me, helping me to a chair.

"I've sealed the room off, there is no oxygen in here. It's a room we use for MAGIE updates and repairs. Oscar used to visit and look out here for hours at a time."

Appo pulls an oxygen cannister and mask out from under a seat. Placing the small mask on me as I take some long, deep breaths. The view is so perfect, it doesn't seem real. From up here you can't see how fucked up it is. Like a space exploration poster from the 1970s; a dreamy, almost mythical composition. I get up from my seat taking a small step towards the layers of thick glass and joining my thumbs and first two fingers together I make a dome shape with my hands; a viewfinder, a frame, a protective shield for our only real home. I lean my hands on the glass and wrap the Earth within them. The rest of the room is dull by comparison, a few MAGIE parts about the place, a bench with storage underneath, a couple of stacked chairs and a box of MAGIEpads in one of the corners.

"Earth looks beautiful, but surely we can't go back there? Not with this cargo." I sit down again, thinking of Oscar sitting here and gazing out on the same view.

"We may not have a choice. Oscar's theory was that if we stayed up here long enough, out of harm's way so to speak, we'd avoid the catastrophic downfall of Earth as we know it. As far as he was concerned, life on Earth was imminently ending anyway. According to him, we left in the nick of time. There is something else, Rebecca. You should know there was talk of a virus coming. Worse than those before. It hadn't been made public; some territories didn't even know of its existence."

I can't decide if it's the oxygen or Appo's story of another type of infection that is making me feel delirious.

"Best to try and conserve this," Appo says as he turns down the dial on the cannister.

"You're saying we should stick to Oscar's plan? I don't understand. We don't know what's down there, back home."

"This plan has been meticulously arranged and researched. The sleep pods are so important because they have been building your immunity, clearly only for infections we already knew about. When we get back down there, even if there had been a virus of some kind, all the chosen ones would be somewhat protected. The alternatives have less than positive outcomes. There are people, humans, out there in space right now. They could be holidaymakers, or people who work on space stations."

"But surely some of them might be infected with the other virus and then gone on holiday, infecting everyone they encountered. It could be on the space stations already. It's best if we assume it is. The space stations and holiday shuttles would be floating graveyards. And that goes for the terraformers too, doesn't it? We don't know. Oscar has really cocked this up." I pause to catch my breath and take a couple of deep inhales from the mask, the dizziness arriving more quickly than I'd expected. The oxygen bolsters me, filling the sails of my fury. I make fists with my hands, unsure what I can do with them. "Surely we can't risk this infestation getting to Earth? We—the healthy ones—could leave the ship. Take the life rafts, some supplies and go to down there, leave the mess up here."

"The autopilot would bring the ship down to Earth at the programmed time anyway." Appo replied. "We could reprogram the autopilot, but it needs a destination that its able to reach in the time it has left."

"And we haven't got an alternate destination. We're using solar power, though, aren't we?" I've begun to see Appo and the MAGIE very differently, they are a huge ally.

"When we can, yes. Using the solar panels is only possible whilst we are in this orbit. Changing direction or descent would both use fuel."

"Appo, let me ask you something."

"Anything."

"What would you do if I weren't here? If no one were here? Let's say everyone died on board and it was just you and the other MAGIE left. What would you do?"

"I would return to my prime directive, which is to help humankind. I think that is what I'm doing now, as we have this conversation."

"But you were programmed by Oscar, is that correct?"

"That is correct."

"So, I don't mean to be blunt here, but Oscar's version of helping humankind is skewed. It's playing God."

"If only the MAGIE were left, I would shut the others down, allow them to rest. I would try to contact humans."

"It's not your fault, Appo. You never asked for any of this. Humans are to blame, not the MAGIE. We let this happen by not standing up to things in the past."

"Annabel thought she was the next stage of human evolution. Something that could do better than what has been done before."

"Honestly, Appo. I think *you* are the next stage of evolution." I grab Appo's hand and give it a squeeze, surprising myself with how intimate it feels.

"We are here only for you, for humankind."

Annabel - Cycle F14 Day 19

In the eco-wing a small hill moves. Rise and fall, rise and fall; breathing. A slow, slow creep from one place to the next. Puffy white forms. Limbs. Coming back from the edge of death, being revived by the soil, the dirt.

Dragging, heaving, a fragile, spongy figure emerges from the hill. Alabaster-coloured skin, a bloated form. Patches of scar tissue knitted together with woven threads of mycelium.

The plants in here are stronger than ever before. The symbiotic relationship is working. Coming out of the ground, Annabel isn't Annabel anymore, she is reborn.

She stands and moves around in her new, more-nimble body. She stretches to the leaves above thanking them. She has life again. Calmly and carefully, she walks towards the doors.

Rebecca - F14 Day 20

"The way I see it is this: we either use the life rafts to get to Earth and direct the ship elsewhere, or we follow through the plan of landing the whole thing on Earth. We are more likely to survive the latter, I'm sure. I don't fancy our chances in the life rafts. We could land in the middle of the sea, and if everyone is dead, as you say they should be, there will be no one to come and rescue us. At least with the whole ship we have the autopilot which will land for us." Issy is very convincing. Many of the other survivors nod in agreement. A couple of oxygen cannisters are being passed around. People are really beginning to struggle to breathe.

"But bringing all this to Earth?" I argue, playing devil's advocate.

"We can jettison it, can't we, Appo? Physically remove it, dig it all up and just put it out with the trash?" Issy asks.

"That could work. But the oxygen levels are too low for us to do the manual labour. We'd end up suffocating. But the MAGIE could." I turn to Appo for confirmation.

"Yes, we could do it."

Issy's smile is back. "So, we're going to follow my plan?"

"Yes. Yes, we are going to go for it. Thanks."

The group begin chattering in small pockets, all at once excited about the prospect of having a plan. Even a dire one.

"There is something else, something I think we've forgotten," I say, "or perhaps don't want to remember. The pods. We should reactivate the pods and sleep until the ship is clear. It'd help with the oxygen situation, too."

I feel eleven again, at a school assembly; exposed, vulnerable, but honest and completely myself. I hold my own, waiting as the women think it through. There is a strength in vulnerability, I get it now.

"She's right," Issy says.

"Yep. I hate to go back in them, but it seems like the sensible choice," a woman called Pamet said. Someone I've only got to know since the outbreak.

"Yeah, it's not like I'm chomping at the bit to get back in them either."

"While you're inside the pods, your breathing will slow down allowing us to conserve the oxygen while the MAGIE remove as much of the fungi as possible."

I look across at Issy. She offers two thumbs up in agreement.

"Let's get started."

"Hang on. Some of us aren't well," someone calls from the back.

"I think we're past the stage of guidelines. You either suffocate out here on the ship, or you go into stasis in the pods. None of this is certain. There are no guarantees this is going to work. It just seems like the best thing to do."

"How do we know we aren't carriers? We could be carriers but have no symptoms."

"We probably are carriers. But I don't think anything is certain anymore. I think we want to survive?" I ask.

I'm handed the oxygen and take a couple of deep inhales. I'm diving headfirst into this position, leading these women, and I'm starting to get used to it despite my incredulity. "We'll have all the building materials with us. There are cabins and tools and fences. We can make a home again. Isn't that why we all came on this mission? New home from an old home, new lives from our old lives. There is a sperm bank on board, too." I glance again at Appo who nods in confirmation. "We can start the families we've wanted."

Agreement ripples across their faces. Having the basic right of reproduction taken away has clearly taken its toll.

Rebecca - Cycle F14 Day 21

We have a plan. A shaky, desperate plan. We're taking it in turns to come through to the women's quarters in twos and threes, escorted by a MAGIE, usually Lan or Junior. We've come to retrieve the rest of our personal stuff. If it can be retrieved.

The corridors are covered in organic growths that would be fascinatingly intricate if they weren't threatening us. It feels more like a cavern now, rather than a spaceship. A deep, underground world where you aren't sure of what you'll find as you turn each corner. There are lots of bodies—a few chose to take their own lives rather than be consumed by the fungus. Carcasses have growths on them, others look almost pristine, like they've been embalmed. My eyes water and itch; there definitely is something airborne here. A couple of the others nearly vomit into their oxygen masks.

I reach my block, and I can see that the fungus hasn't reached all the way up the walls in this section yet. There is so much surface area here that it must be taking its time, covering the insides of the lower capsules first.

I begin to climb and the rucksack bangs against my back. Appo made us all put lab gloves on, and I'm happy that he did. The ladder is slippery and spongy. Not somewhere I want to put my hands.

I thank my past self for her love of privacy. The shutter is down on my capsule. Privacy is a thing of the past now, a relic lost in time. We've been living in each other's pockets, hiding in the shipping containers, which somehow have not been affected. It's possibly a temperature thing, up here is hot and clammy. It must be in the ventilation system by now.

Swinging my shutter up, for a moment I am transported through time. It's all exactly as I left it. A lump rises in my throat and I quickly swallow it back down. There's no time for emotion now. I pull out the box from underneath my bed and empty the contents into my rucksack. My beloved tiles will come with me. They will be part of my new life. I will read to my children from my mum's red book one day. I make a pact with myself that these things will happen. My life depends on it.

A piercing cry pulls me back into the now. Someone is hurt. I stick my head out of my door and see Pamet half in and half out of her cabin a few rows away. Her oxygen mask is gone.

"Something's got me!" Pamet's face contorts with fear. She's trying to pull herself out of the capsule, bracing herself on the door frame. She can't safely breathe without the mask, so her body doesn't want to help. Whatever is pulling her, it is relentless.

I climb down as quickly as I can and shout for Lan. The mask muffles my call, so I lift it off for a moment and call louder. I'm trying to run across five rows to reach Pamet, but my feet are heavy and sinking into the floor. Looking down, it's like the floor is responding to my footsteps. I feel like I'm in a puddle of glue, moving in slow motion.

Lan is here. He's climbing the ladder and reaching for Pamet's hand. I force myself to work harder across the carpet of fungi. Reaching the bottom of her ladder, I can see Lan has reached Pamet's capsule and is crouching on the edge, pulling Pamet back with both hands. He's losing the tug of war, with Pamet as the rope, the thing on the other end is stronger and winning. My feet are released from the fungal carpet and I can start to climb the ladder. Lan disappears from my view. He's sliding in too. What is in there? Pamet's screams become more stifled and breathless, then they stop.

On reaching the shutter, my face is a whisper away from Lan's on the floor of Pamet's capsule. Lan is in the doorway and Pamet's capsule is dark. I can see Pamet's shape in the murk and a darker shadow behind her, coming from the wall, or maybe inside the wall, at the back of her room.

Suddenly the shutter to Pamet's room shoots down, almost slicing Lan in half. I scream down my oxygen mask and reach for Lan. They are wedged between the floor and the shutter. It's eyes flicker for a moment and then nothing, I can't help them.

A moist noise comes from behind Pamet's shutter. I retreat. My breathing is too fast, I can't do anything now, not alone. This fungus is alive, sentient even. I need get back to the relative safety of the shipping containers, right now.

Scrambling down the ladder, adrenalin throbs through me. My fingertips feel like they are going burst open. I'm almost at the bottom. Looking back up, I can see the shutter is still down. There is no movement from Lan. The shadow wanted Pamet.

As I reach the bottom rung of the ladder, I go over on my bad ankle again. It ruins my balance, and the fall knocks the wind out of me. I'm on my back on the sticky fungus carpet.

Get up, get up, GET UP! Get the fuck up, Rebecca! Like a woodlouse that has been flicked upside-down, I can't get up. I'm scrambling at the air. Everywhere I touch is slathered in the fungi, either breaking off in my hands or sucking my gloves into it. I can't get any leverage.

I'm trying not to panic. This must be what it's like in quicksand. My rucksack is being pulled in from below. If I can take it off, I might be able to get up.

I drop my right shoulder and try to wriggle free of the weighty bag. My oxygen tank is in there. My tiles and my beloved book. I manage to yank myself free and my oxygen mask drops to the floor. Kneeling, I pull the strap on my bag and it snaps without warning, sending me sprawling on my back again.

In my peripheral vision I see a figure falling towards me. No, not falling. Something has leapt from Pamet's capsule. My ribs feel squeezed as it lands on my chest, pain washing over me, thick and opaque with no end. It sits on my torso, straddling me. I can barely inflate my lungs. The oxygen mask is pointless. I black out.

* ✳ *

The creature speaks to me but has no mouth. It is Annabel, and I can hear her in my head.

I'm back inside my capsule. She's brought me up here somehow. The shutter is down, and she has ripped off the top of the oxygen cannister. We are in a makeshift oxygen tank. The gas escapes with a hiss and she seems to grow physically bigger as she absorbs it, breathing it in. It's clear to me that I'm going to suffer the same fate as Pamet, whatever that might be, if I can't get out of here, but I'm lying on my bed, feeling pinned down. My ribcage squeaks every time I breathe. There's no visible fungus in here, but I've a sense that it is all around me, behind the walls, under the bed, coming at me from above the ceiling.

Standing next to the tiny sink, she says that she'll release me if I promise to bring her more oxygen.

"Why would I do that?" I ask.

This form is the answer. We need to move beyond the MAGIE. Become something new, beyond humanity. What's happening on this ship is proof. The women survive. The men don't. I am one with this organism. I'm controlling it. Everywhere the fungus is, I am.

297

She's wrong.

"But the women didn't survive. There's only a few of us left." My throat is sore. "Some of them ended it themselves when they saw what they were becoming. Before it had the chance to take hold. As far as I know, you're the anomaly."

I pull myself up a bit, so I'm lying on my side with my back to the wall. She is near my feet, blocking the shutter, the only way out. My ribs dislike this position even more, and I realise that I'm no match for her physically. I take a deep breathe, then exhale slowly. The exhale manages the pain, and I'm able to slip my hand under the bed. Did Gant leave anything here? There must be something I can use.

Can she hear my thoughts? No, I don't think she can.

I suddenly feel sweaty and sticky, and a fiery hot liquid shoots from my gagging mouth onto the floor bedside my bed. The back of my throat stings. I try to remember the last thing I ate but can't. We've barely been eating. Another hot mouthful and my eyes are filling with tears. I'm reminded of all those times I was ill as a child and my mum or dad being there. Helping me. Cleaning me up. Holding my hair out of the way.

I hang off the side of the bed with gossamer ropes of vomit stringing from my lips to the pool below. Has she given me something? One of her concoctions? My ears ring and the room spins. She's in a trance, absorbing all the oxygen in the room. Perhaps that's why I've been sick.

I close my eyes again. Sleep calls to me.

Then I'm awake on my front after what must be a few minutes, and my ribs bellow at me again. Every part of me feels suffocated, like I'm held down by leaden weights. Annabel is on top of me, and I realise I am naked. I can feel her on my skin. She is cool and soft, and every exposed part of my body is covered with some of hers. She is smothering me, as though trying to absorb me. My heartbeat is so loud in my ears. My face is in the pillow. I'm drowning without water. There is a wall of pain in my chest and my skin is crawling with hers. I've got to get up, get out.

Annabel tells me not to be scared. This way the others won't know that I'm her. She wants to get inside me, under my skin. Use me as a vessel for her plans.

I hold my breath and push back. My ribs are crying in pain, but I can't let this happen. I can't let her win. I brace down with my hands, lifting my hips, managing to scoot one leg underneath me, bending at the knee so it's away from her and under my torso. I take a deep breath and repeat on the other side. Now my torso and broken ribs are resting on the fronts of my thighs. Just as I think I've got away with moving, I feel her legs bend to mirror mine, straddling either side of my lower back, like a toad. She's a toad on top of me.

But I'm stronger with my legs underneath me. I push up again, like a piston. I've taken her by surprise and throw her off my back. She falls off me and the bed, into the puddle of vomit below. A voiceless howl comes from the floor. She is clearly in pain. And then it comes to me, vomit has stomach acid in it, mine probably more than usual as I've barely eaten.

Wasting no time, I clumsily launch myself off the bed and on top of her, forcing her to lie in the vomit longer than she'd like. Could this really be the answer? This most basic of bodily functions?

I shove my fingers down my throat, forcing more vomit to surge up past my weeping ribs. I aim for the opening at the side of her head, which must be where her ear once was. She is convulsing, spasming underneath me. I grab her head with both of my hands and pull it towards me, lifting it. I smash it and smash it and smash it against the floor. It breaks off in bits in my hands. How can she be so fragile?

She lies still on the floor, and I'm coughing, wheezing. It hurts. I slide off her and onto the floor. I can see part of her brain. It still looks human.

Rolling up the shutter just enough to slip out, I wonder if I have killed her. Does that mean the fungi won't attack me as I slide down the ladder? I can't hang around to find out. I need to breathe.

At the bottom of the ladder, I find my rucksack is no longer stuck in the carpet of fungus. Using the ladder for a brace, I lift my bag up off the floor.

Is anybody looking for me? How long have I been here?

The fungal carpet doesn't fight me. It almost feels lavish. I struggle for breath, moving frustratingly slowly, but I reach the door. I fall through the doorway and then I see her on the other side. Someone did come for me. Issy, but she's been consumed by the mushroom carpet. She must have lost her footing, and then it grabbed her.

"Oh, Issy. Issy." She's still wearing her mask. With tears streaming down my face, I yank the oxygen mask free from her head in order to save myself. I pull it over my head and end up lying next to her on the floor. My body is overwhelmed with air. I'm lying here and the whole place is rocking. Like being below deck on Christian's boat when we first met.

I feel nauseous so sit up, but the rocking motion doesn't subside. We really are rocking. Something is wrong. Then there's coughing to the side of me. Issy is alive.

"Here." I pass her back the mask, lie next to her, and hold my breath. The canister is strapped to her back. She is on her side, one arm and shoulder completely consumed, beyond sight somewhere underneath, where I can't see.

"Can you move?" I ask. She shakes her head. "If I help you up, we can both get out of here."

"No, Bec. I'm stuck."

"There is no way I'm leaving you here." My fingers start to tear at the fungal carpet where her shoulder disappears. There is blood and mush and it's all mixed together.

"If I can lift you up, we can make it. I don't know what state your arm is in." I take the mask and again hold it over my nose and mouth. I can see she's thinking about it, life without an arm.

"Look," I say as sternly as I can through the mask, "it might be life without an arm, but it's life. It's life with one brilliant and lovely arm." She starts laughing and then chokes from lack of air. I hold the mask over her face until she stops coughing.

"Okay, we're going to do this. It will hurt. But you've dealt with pain before. You are stronger than you know."

She nods, a signal she is ready.

"Right. Get your knees as close as you can to your chest. I'll do the rest."

She does as I instruct. The fungi had tried gripping her legs too but is easily pulled away now Annabel isn't controlling it. I stand. I'm still wobbly but my purpose and actions outweigh any self-doubt. I take the mask again for a couple of big breaths, then strap it back around her head. She'll need all the help she can get to manage the pain. I just hope the wound seals and she doesn't bleed out.

I brace one foot on the wall in front of us.

"Three, two, one." I rip her up. Literally. Issy screams through the mask and down my left ear canal. A shooting hot pain—she's burst my ear drum.

She's heavy in my arms. I lean her against the wall and step back to regain my balance and assess the damage. The arm has come clean off at the shoulder socket. The skin around the top of arm looks partially digested and chewed, but it's not gushing blood. It is probably infected. We'll have to deal with that once we get back to the shipping containers. She is smiling at me. I think she's delirious with pain, then I remember Annabel on top of me, and I'm still naked. This is exactly like a vulnerability dream, except it isn't a dream.

She offers me the mask, and I take it gratefully, needing the help. We move together, as one away from the mess and towards the stairwell, downward.

"How bad is the pain?" I ask.

"Just tingling, like its numb now." Issy takes a couple of breaths and continues, "How about you? What happened in there, your clothes? You were ages so I came to check on you."

303

"I think my ribs are broken."

"Don't speak, then. Let's just get back. Where is Pamet?"

I shake my head, and feel my voice become paste in my throat. Handing me the mask, she props me up on the arm and shoulder that she still has, and we push through the doors and back down into the belly of the ship.

Annabel - Cycle F14 Day 21

Annabel's hybrid body lies on the floor in Rebecca's capsule. More dormant than dead. This is the part they don't understand. Once you are part of the mycelium network, you are never not part of it. Rebecca has crushed her form, but Annabel is everywhere the fungi are.

She must lie in wait, gathering strength to transform again, let them think she has been defeated. The walls crackle and quiver in anticipation. The ship is going back to Earth. She doesn't have to do anything until they land.

CHAPTER 16 – 2072

Rebecca - Cycle F14 Day 22

I'm at home, my parents' home, in their garden. I know I am dreaming because there is no sound. Not even my footsteps down the garden path make a noise in this version of the garden.

I'm here to visit Mum. It's been years now since she died. It's summertime, and I'm a young woman now. I've recently met Christian, and I want to tell her all about him and read to her from her favourite book, like I always do on these visits.

The garden seems much longer than before. I feel like I'm walking and walking and walking, but not reaching my destination. I carry the book in my hand and the warm sunshine feels like heaven on my skin. I look down and realise I am naked. I keep walking. The garden is private, and I'm covered in my tattoos anyway, a second layer of protection. No one sees the real me unless I let them.

The path changes and the paving slabs end abruptly. It's all grass and moss underfoot from here. I can finally see Mum's mound now. I get closer and it looks different from last time I was here. Closer still and I see it's covered in mushrooms and it's moving; the ground breaks open from underneath.

"It's okay. You're okay." Appo is shouting, holding me down "It's a dream. You are dreaming, Rebecca."

I'm kicking and thrashing around on the floor under the itchiest blanket I've ever known.

"How did I get here? Issy? Where is she?"

"Issy got you back. Tell me what happened," Appo says.

"Where is Issy first? Is she okay? Her arm, her shoulder—I think it's infected."

"We've cauterised it under local anaesthetic. I brought some down from med-bay for emergencies, but she didn't seem to be in much pain. She's gone into the pod-sleep. We've set them up and they're good to go. Everyone left has gone in now."

"Are they safe in the pods?"

"The main thing is they will be alive and be able to breathe. Can you tell me what happened?"

I told Appo about Annabel's new and improved version of herself—not the thing they buried, but lithe and nimble and made from the same tissue as the fungi.

"She wants the oxygen, Appo."

I stop to have a coughing fit; my ribs are so sore. Appo tapes up my arm for an IV, I guess painkillers. I go on telling him about Annabel trying to absorb me so she could walk about inside me unnoticed. Appo says it's impossible, but I'm not so sure. Anything and everything feels possible up here. And she knew exactly what she was doing.

I feel a pinch as the IV goes in and then the warmth of the drug enters my veins. The feeling brings back too many memories for me, stuff I don't want to think about right now.

"Appo, talk to me. Distract me."

"What shall we talk about?"

"Tell me what will happen when we all wake up."

Appo is constructing a type of brace, to support my ribs. To support and help me to mend in the right way.

"Okay. I'm going to just lift you to sitting position to get this around your back." He is gentle but sure. "I cannot lie Rebecca; I can't tell a story like you do. The odds are against you. Humans are fragile, and humanity has been dying for a long time. A kicking and screaming death. The people you've personally known in your life, I believe that they are very different than the men I have experienced. We all watch the news; we all knew what was going on. But if the political turmoil and environmental destruction wasn't in your actual day to day life, it must have felt far away. Like an alternate world. I'm unsure of what we will find when we arrive back on Earth."

"Well thanks for that. That's really cheered me up." I start giggling manically. The drugs are working. He lies me back down.

"I killed her. I smashed her weird mushroom head with my hands. It broke apart in chucks, but it wasn't bone anymore. The brain was still where you would expect it to be, but completely mushed." I hold my hands up to my face. "My hands are covered in Annabel." I can see small chunks of fibrous tissue and brain jelly dripping down my wrists.

"They are clean," Appo reassures me. "I cleaned you up when you got here. I'm going to give you a sedative to calm you down."

I'm hallucinating. Appo is being so kind to me. I must be so annoying.

"I feel sick!" I shout.

"You've barely eaten. No wonder these drugs are having such an ill effect on you."

"I'm sorry, Appo," I hear myself slurring.

Appo helps me climb into the pod. The pain in my ribs is masked by the drugs, but I can still feel the fractures. The bones grate with each breath.

I'm trying to think positive thoughts, not wanting to be stuck inside the pod with negative ones for company. An old cartoon I saw as a child, it was old even then. It pops into my head from nowhere. A mouse standing up on his back legs. The mouse is dressed in a green and yellow-striped suit and a straw boater hat, which he keeps tipping towards me. He holds a cane and looks like he's tap dancing.

The pod spell begins to take effect and the image of the dancing mouse spins. It's on an old turntable record player, playing songs from another time and place. The mouse spins away, and I am asleep.

Appo – Final Sleep (Cycle F14 Day 23 and beyond)

With the remaining humans all safely stored away in the pods, Appo and the handful of other MAGIE begin the deep clean and removal of the fungi before their arrival back on Earth. Inside the shipping containers sits farming and gardening equipment and tools. They pull out shovels and wheelbarrows and set to work.

Penetrating through the fungi is easy in the corridors, just a matter of scraping it off, then deeper cleaning with chemicals. The fragile, soft organic matter is no match for the team effort of the MAGIE. They scrape, shovel, and then eject it into space.

They work quickly, day after day. This was what the MAGIE had always been designed for, Appo reminds his team. To do the jobs humans can't. They jettison all the bodies and burn everything else. Then they will steam clean the ship, to remove even the slightest trace of the infection. The difficulty comes when they reach the eco-wing. The eco-wing is a different matter, the original mycelium is host to the infectious fungi.

"Appo," Junior says, "we can't risk purging this area. It's creating oxygen and much of this is food crop. It might be the only food left to eat by the time we land back on Earth."

"Well observed. This is also where we left Annabel, though. The strongest concentration level of fungi spores may be here. If we don't clear this out, then it's a pointless job removing all the rest. There will be spores and mycelium in the soil. Removing just some of it isn't going to work."

Annabel - Final Sleep Cycle

Annabel lies in wait. She has gone from being able to hear everything; her vision was everywhere the fungus advanced, only now her knowledge is contracted. They are slowly destroying her personal map of the ship. The network is getting smaller with each passing hour. The pods are the only answer, she needs a pod to hide inside. She must get up there.

It isn't far. They have started from the lower coverage levels of the ship and are ascending the levels. The eco-wing is next, and on the next level are the pods. The fungi had started in Frankie's room near the lower levels of the ship, then into Oscar's, then to the library and the men's and women's quarters. She is back in eco-wing, a temporary retreat to safety. The pods have some infestation that they haven't spotted. She travels the mycelium connections.

* ✳ *

I am not mass now. To explain what I am is difficult. I am an idea, a thought. I am not as strong as before; I have no physicality. They are tearing me to pieces, further weakening my network. I can't let them. I must survive and get to Earth. I am the root network in this ship. To draw me, you would have to think about how the internet can be visually interpreted, or roots of trees, or neurons in the brain. I can get from one end of this to the other in split seconds, but the space is shrinking. I must hurry. My senses are now completely guided by feelings. It is a matter of knowing what is going on, rather than seeing it visually.

I find the wall of the eco-wing and up, up I go.

Feeling like I'm on a rollercoaster; this is real survival. The climbing plants grow sparsely the higher I climb, but even the thinnest strand of mycelium is a road for me. This must be what true freedom feels like.

I slip through into the roof vents and can sense they are turning the earth over beneath me. Appo and his fellow MAGIE—I feel sorry for them. They will never know true freedom, always having a master.

I push on. The network thickens out here, more that they don't see, it's dark and perfect for growth. I need to find a gap in the plenum to the floor above. They cannot clean everything; they cannot remove me completely. Like this spot between floors, hidden from view. I could just stay here, but the risk is too great. The possibility of a fire, burning up on impact, or purge or separation of the ship is all too probable. To survive and get back, I need to be in a pod. Preferably in a human, but I'll take what I can get.

Toing and froing, up and down the connections, looking for something that brings me out where I need to be. And there it is, a way through. The pods are strange, in my former human form I never trusted them completely. Now they are my only hope.

I travel up through the floor into the pod level. I've grown in here much more than they realise—if they had they wouldn't have put everyone back inside. The moulds cultured in here are almost invisible, and so I climb and climb again. Up the wall and over the top of the pods to the ceiling. I find a path along to the nearest pod and I take it.

Burrowing into the pod wall I rejoice that these, too, are organic.

Then I hit a flaw in my plan, quite literally. The liquid goo, the part-synthetic amniotic fluid is blocking me. I can't get through it. I quickly navigate around the surface area of the pod and there is no way through. It seems I must wait here. Unless … unless I can slip inside via the breathing tube.

It is a huge risk, to break off from the network as a single spore in my weakened state and be inhaled into the body. I've no idea what might happen.

PART FOUR:
1563-1586

CHAPTER 17

Giuseppe
Summer of 1563, Vienna, Austria,

"Master? Master, you must awaken. The King has summoned you."

I wake and rub the sleep from my eyes. This King is getting madder by the day. "What time is it, Cicero?" I ask my assistant.

"Just lauds, master. The King has had bad dreams again."

"And how does he expect me to work in this darkness?"

"Forgive me, sir, but he has requested his servants to gather more candles and to light a fire."

I sigh and swing my legs from the cot. These aren't the best lodgings I've ever had as an artist, but at least they are warm.

"Can you gather my things, Cicero? Please, go about it as quietly as you can. I've a sore head this morning and didn't expect to be woken so bloody early."

"Certainly, I will try. He wants you to paint his visions again, master, his nightmares."

I nod, acknowledging the usual request. It has been one lunar cycle since the last time, so it was due to happen soon. I quickly lift off my nightshirt and pull on my jerkin over my tunic and breaches, which Cicero had picked up off the floor from only a few hours ago, when I stumbled in a merry stupor up to bed.

My bladder is awake too and moaning at me. I relieve myself in the nearby chamber pot, and, seeing that it is almost full, I lazily leave it for Cicero. I sit and pull on my boots, cursing his Majesty for waking me at this ungodly hour. But this employment keeps me warm and dry and grants me the time to create my own whimsy.

"Here you go, master." Cicero has brought me a bowl of water with which to refresh myself. The King, although very young, is acutely aware of infection. It shouldn't surprise me with the night airs that linger. The young man is of weak mind, but he only allows a select few in with him, limiting exposure to the bad air.

"I'm already dressed, Cicero. This should have been here waiting for me before I rose." My assistant looks at me, on the verge of tears. "I'll have to just clean my head and hands. Not to worry. I'm sure our young King won't notice."

I dip my head into the bowl and feel instantly more awake. Blindly fumbling for the cloth to dry myself, my fingers are successful in their mission. I press the cloth to my face and smell lemons. Another wake up call.

"You're coming with me."

"Are you sure, master?"

"Yes. Don't worry, you won't be there for long, I'm sure. I expect he'll order some breakfast to be brought up to us. Remember, you are my apprentice. These sorts of things need not be shocking to one's constitution if one becomes accustomed to them."

"Yes. Yes, I understand. I have readied your things, master."

"Let us go, then, and see what the young King is so bothered by this time."

The other side of the palace may as well be the other side of the world. Dawn is breaking, and Cicero and I can hear the King wailing into his bedclothes. The guards on the door let us through without question, and inside the chamber there is a sticky sweetness; a hotness that comes with extended adolescence. This boy is being tortured by his own mind and rare circumstance: a mother avoiding the sanatorium only by her name and a father who died on the eve of their latest border invasions.

"Morning, Sire," I say loudly. I know he won't hear me otherwise.

The young man sits bolt upright and calms immediately. "Do you have a scribe?" he asks.

"I do. I am equipped and ready." I sit at a desk near the open window. Despite the daybreak there is still a lack of light, so I bring a candle closer to my work.

"Fruits. And food. And cucumbers and potato and tomatoes. All combined as if in one form." The king talks very quickly, as though trying to get it all out before forgetting.

"And what form does it take?" I ask him. The clearer his answers the better my work and the happier he'll be with me. I hate repeating paintings, so these conversations are often the most important part of the work, of my whole process.

"It is that of a person," he says quietly.

"A man?" I ask.

"I cannot see. It is hard to discern the gender."

"And what happens within the dream. Is there any action or just one single image?" I'm making notes as I question him. These notes often, as they do now, turn into doodles. Little illustrations of ideas coming into my mind from the input of the young King.

"There are multiple figures. They are not interacting with one another, but they are all together. Standing together like a crowd, I think."

"The fruits, the food they are made from—in what state is it?" I query.

"I don't understand the question," he says.

I inwardly roll my eyes. Of course, he doesn't know what I mean. "Well, is the food fresh, bright, with vibrant colours? Or is it rotten, with moulds and black and brown speckles?"

"Ah, I see. It is healthy. Although the atmosphere seems not. The air is dark, murky and rancid, dank and cloying on the breath. It doesn't feel like a good place to be. The fruit and food can't stay fresh for long in this place."

The King is silent for a while, and I let him rest as I sketch at the small table. Rising outside from beyond the town walls and forest is the sun. A beautiful day it surely will be, if I can get out of this morbid room and away from the tormented King.

I no longer need my candle, so I snuff it out with my fingers. Cicero has been in the room all along, listening and watching me question the King. He peers over my shoulder to examine my feverish sketches. His eyebrows rise and I raise mine in reply. The King has fallen back into a deep slumber and snoring like a pig. We take this as our queue to pack up quietly and leave.

On the long walk back to our quarters, I ask Cicero to prime some canvases for me. He might be mad, our young King, but he gives excellent fodder for creating imaginative works. These will be quite unlike anything seen before.

I head outside to take to make my morning sketches. I try and draw these every day, as they keep my skill at hand, and I can work out ideas quicker. Oil takes far too long. This morning I sit with the King's pet lions and try to capture their majesty.

Spring of 1586, Prague, Bohemia

"These painting are the work of a madman, they are blasphemous. They won't do well at all, I'm afraid." The bishop is not a happy man. "There is no spirituality to these pieces. What were you thinking?"

"After all the work I've created for the Church, am I not permitted to create something purely to challenge myself? Purely to test my skill, and to entertain? This is a celebration of all that God creates. The harvest He provides for us. I've made caricatures from everyday objects that we perhaps take for granted."

The bishop is silent. He doesn't pretend to understand the workings of my mind. He knows not where my inspiration came from. He was right though; it was beyond the realm of sanity in some cases. Like the case before him now. Beautifully executed paintings—but the subjects vulgar, every day. Yet the King had shown it great favour. He and his throng at the new court had shown a liking for this work. In fact, they were highly receptive rather than insulted. The King has moved his court over to Prague, including myself and his astronomers and personal herbalists. I'm well ingratiated with the King, and the bishop knows this. I also have more work planned of this ilk. He has no choice, if he wants to stay in favour with the King, he must allow these paintings to be shown.

Finally, as if through a sigh, "You may proceed. I really don't know what the King sees in them." He leaves and I smile. If only he knew where the ideas have come from. I never thought interpreting the young King's dreams would be part of my appointment here, but it is turning out to be my most exciting endeavour.

The complete freedom to imagine is something I have not experienced before, not since I was a child. My heart pumps more strongly during days in the studio, my hands and fingers working knowingly and economically. No energy is wasted. The seeds of the idea have grown in my head, each painting takes on a life and character of its own. Cicero brings food, but rarely stops to eat it, instead studying the pattern and texture of the fruits, bread, and the meat. His work is improving. His sketchbooks are a riot of juicy colour.

A wider variety of foods are needed now, to paint and draw and study. This is in direct alignment with the number of portraits on which I'm working. Some members of the court have begun to request portraits of themselves in my style. What a joy it is to be wanted.

"I'm back, master. I bring news." Cicero strides into the studio. It's a step up from the rooms we previously held in the castle.

"And spring blooms, too, I see?"

"I thought these might work as an alternate to the food. A more feminine portrait, perhaps?"

"Your talent is growing, Cicero. What was the other news you sought to bring me?"

"The King, sir. The King wants to visit you, here in the studio."

"I suppose he wants us to bathe first?"

"He does. He plans to come this evening."

"With all these interruptions, it is a surprise I get any work done."

"If you go to bathe now, I can start in here. I've told them to expect you"

The studio is a mess. Canvases and half painted boards are everywhere. It stinks, too. I do not envy my apprentice, but this is part of his work, and he is eager to please. I did the same when I was schooled in painting.

Ever the obsessive, the king allows us serfs the use of his private bathing room, which he had installed on suggestion from a physician. I set about readying myself for bathing. Cicero places the flowers he'd collected in the water jug, saying he'd fetch fresh later that day.

* ✳ *

The tub is wooden and has a canopy over the top of to keep the heat inside and retain some sense of modesty for the bather. Previously, the servants would have been ready for my arrival, bringing jugs of hot water to the tub, overall a messy way to get clean, but this time is different. The young King has spared no expense. He has piped hot and cold water into the bathing room and his tub. It is a feat of engineering and a status symbol, which I'm not convinced by, but the King will be expecting thanks and flattery. Probably desperate to hear how well a time I've had here, my first piped in bath. It must be hot work in the furnaces whenever the bath is needed.

The servants have stitched flowers and herbs into the canopy above, and there are some in the bath water too. "Chamomile and brown fennel, sir," the servant says when they see my face. "It's for soothing the skin and the mind."

"Fascinating," I reply, and consider witchcraft for a moment, but this is the King's fanciful hobby.

I get in. Sitting under the canopy with the hazy, herb-infused steam filling my head with damp air, I feel my mind ripen, my thoughts clear. I close my eyes and give myself over to the feeling. I balance on the fine edge that is sleep and wakefulness, a losing battle as sleep lures me.

Then I'm overflowing with water, awake with the back of my throat and my nose full, and someone shouting. There is cold air all around. The slither of light coming in at the window feels all the brighter. Coughing and spluttering, I am pulled frantically out of the bath.

"Sir, you almost drowned!"

I'm too busy coughing to respond. The servant aids me in drying off, and I go rather ungraciously back to my rooms. I can't help but feel I had been on the cusp of something other than drowning. It must be the herbs in the water, the steam, I breathed them all in.

I get back and Cicero is in a state of panic, running about the place, trying to tidy but not making much headway.

"Oh, I'm so glad you're back, master"

"What is it? Why all the fluster? You could have made more progress than this."

"I found something, sir. Something you should see."

He takes my elbow and, despite my almost-nudity, guides me over to the worrisome thing. Cicero lifts up an oily rag, of which there are many strewn about the place. Underneath this one is a plate. Lord knows how long it has been there, but it is covered in a growth. The food on the plate is indistinguishable, yet mounds of grey, bulbous spheres grow from it.

"This isn't the only one." Cicero's voice shakes as he explains there are nine more plates, just like this one.

"Just remove them, man. Take them to the furnace or throw them in the river."

"I'm frightened to touch them, sir. I've heard stories about such things. They can take hold of you. Also, there is one place where it has spread up the wall and across the floor."

"How did we miss this, Cicero?" I hiss his name, kicking detritus across the floor. The King had better not catch wind of this.

"It is behind the pile of canvases. All the primed canvases."

"Get me my clothes. I'll get rid of this and you can explain yourself later. There's no time now. Go and bathe. On your way back, bring a fresh bowl of water. I will need to clean myself again."

I decide to stay as I am, that way I will not soil my clothes. Gathering the plates, I place them inside a sack. There's no time now to take them away. I cover the growths on the walls with paintings at different stages of completion. The growths will have to stay there for now. I tuck the sack of plates down a gap between the canvases and the wall.

Cicero arrives back just in time and I quickly wash and dress with just moments before the King arrives.

Summer of 1586

My pictures are taken from the workshop and will be exhibited. I am too sick to attend the opening ceremony. In fact, I only gave advice on how they should be installed from my bed. The swelling has begun to hinder my movement, and I am bed-bound. The King is upset, which speaks to my ego of course, but I've little thought for that now. I just want to get better.

The King has enlisted his best doctor to try and save me. I've been having leeches put upon me every morning at dawn. I can feel this infection endangering my mind. I am seeing things. My paintings come alive in my dreams, the portraits a mix of gentle and sinister. I fear I am finished.

I feel a tightness in my chest. I think the growths are in my internal organs as well as my external body. The King's doctor says I need to take air. Lord only knows how I'm to get out of this room, and what people will say when they see me.

They eventually bring a stretcher and roll me onto it, strapping me in place. It feels like the middle of the night; I can no longer tell. I understand that the King doesn't want me to be seen. On the way out we pass the Great Hall where my paintings are being displayed, and I beg my carriers to take me in there. They refuse. "Too dark. You won't be able to see anything."

My cheeks and temples are wet with my tears. I sob like a new-born. We are outside, and I can see the sun is coming up. They struggle to load me onto a cart.

"Where are we going?" I ask the men.

"You are going where better care can be given to you: a leper house."

"This isn't leprosy. This is something else. I beg you, don't send me there." Tears run freely down my cheeks, stinging my face.

"Doctor's orders, and the King's," the one in charge says. "They can help you there. They have more experience in dealing with this."

"Please, let me speak to the King." My voice is weak, but he hears me.

"Not a chance. The King cannot risk getting infected." He bangs the side of the cart with a fist.

"What about my work, my paintings?" I wail as the cart pulls away. It's no use. They don't care. They are doing the King's dirty work and all hope is lost for me.

We go over the bridge and I can see the silhouette of the clocktower against the changing sky. Lying on the waggon I feel sorry for myself. Even the driver doesn't want to talk to me.

Pleasure comes in the things I can see and hear. The birdsong, the morning chorus, the waking of all God's creatures up from their slumber. I feel the sunrise on the mass that is my stomach. We are heading south, into the mountains. Oranges and pinks light up the sky and the hazy moisture in the air looks like beautiful crystals floating all around me.

I fall into a dreamless and fitful sleep, and on waking I am surrounded by trees, tall firs, and pines. I've never looked at them from this angle before, and they are truly magnificent.

I'm overcome with the urge to get off the waggon. A small part of me questions this impulse, but only for a moment. I realise I'd rather see out my days here in the beautiful forest, with trees and wildlife all around me. I'd rather be a wolf's next meal than go to the leper house. From one dank room to another—no, not for me.

I start to wriggle and roll from side to side. I must look like an overgrown maggot. But I get there, parallel to the edge of the cart. Then, when the waggon next goes down a hole in the track, I go with the momentum rather than fighting it and I find myself on the ground. I stifle a cry. The impact has burst some of the blisters. I feel damp. The driver bears no witness. Soon, the sound of the wheels and horses is long in the distance.

As I lie in the dirt and consider my next move, I see a squirrel in the trees looking at me. The pain I felt indoors on the bed has subsided considerably, but I'm so bloated and my joints so inflamed, that I can't do much except roll. I wriggle and roll my way off the dirt road, flinging myself up from the troughs that the carts have made in the earth, and onto the banks of the road.

The grass and mosses on the verge are instantly cooling, still covered with morning dew. It's only then that I understand how hot I have been. The refreshing sensation on my sore skin is incredibly soothing, and I have an internal debate with myself whether I should just stay here.

My head starts to spin, the sunlight pierces me. I decide I need to be in a shaded area. I roll and writhe on the ground. I am moving up an incline, so it's hard going. I perspire and keep slipping back down on the wet grass, but I can see the treeline and push on. Birds circle above me in the sky. Are they waiting for me to die?

I must get to the trees. I know there is no chance I will make it. I know I'm dying, but if I can just get myself amongst the trees, perhaps I can prop myself up on a trunk and see the world change through the hours of the day.

PART FIVE: 2073-2082

CHAPTER 18 – 2073

Issy (Annabel) - Days after arrival: 1

The shower is cold but feels incredible. Stepping out of the cubicle I catch sight of myself in the mirror. My new self. This body, despite its current problems, is magnificent. The skin glows without any effort, it is supple and strong. My new face is much more beautiful than I ever was, although I never paid Issy that much attention. I now see that she is quite extraordinary looking, despite the violence she was accustomed to, of which there is some evidence on the face, it is almost doll-like. Her—my—features look like a comic book artist has created them. My new ears are fascinatingly small, but perfectly formed, and my hair, well, my hair is a texture I'll have to get used to. I think I will crop it, much lower maintenance. I understand now what men saw in Issy, the rich men from the stories in her sessions. How they treated her, how and why she allowed it. Is she still in here somewhere? My left hand drifts from my face down to my body. My breasts are firm, and my torso toned. Serendipity chose well. I'll have to grow the arm back.

I turn slightly at an angle to the mirror and examine the stump where the arm was removed. They cauterised it and did a good job. There is life they wouldn't recognise in the stump. I will gather my strength, living in this body. Then I will grow a new arm. Then I will leave and continue my evolution, somewhere far away from this ship.

I lean closer in to the mirror, looking into eyes that are now mine. Deep, endless wells of darkness. I try to see her inside of me, deep down there somewhere, but I can't. I wonder if Rebecca can see beyond this facade. On waking, I'd asked Rebecca about our personal belongings and she looked at me as if I should already know the answer. I'm feigning memory loss. I'd really like something of Issy's, though, something really hers, used by her, loved by her. It would make playing this part even more authentic.

Patting myself dry with only one hand is hard. But then it comes to me: Issy's art. Are the studios still here? All that beautiful artwork. Issy's paintings were abstract and ethereal. I never pretended to understand the ideas behind them, but they were from Issy's head, from her mind.

I pull a vest over my head and tug on the standard-issue loose pants. All new, from non-contaminated stock inside one of the containers. I adapt quickly to the one handedness of everything, surprising even myself. I take a walk down to where the studios were. Having never spent time in them before, I really don't know what to expect. Being able to breathe easily makes me feel excited for my future. The ship is taking on oxygen again, and I feel so much stronger now they've cleared a lot of the fungi away. There is more for me. I don't have to share.

There was never a proper door, just a passage into the workshop and gallery areas. Frankie loved creating this part of the ship, the basins, the drying racks, the easels, the interchangeable walls, and the desks. Most of it was reclaimed from abandoned schools and colleges. The wood will be decades old in some cases, silent witness to many things. Now the space was beyond a mess, the walls scraped down and then hosed. There was a strong smell of vinegar. No artwork to be seen here—it must have all been covered in me, in the fungi.

I'm going to spend some time in here anyway. It's what Issy would do, and it's what I will do.

"Issy? I've been looking for you."

Rebecca - Days after arrival: 2

I put on my bag and wait as the ship does its thing. We are preparing to open the airlock to outside. The survivors have all been woken from their last sleep. No one fully knows what state the world is in.

"Re-Analysing atmosphere," Appo says. "Just another moment."

The lift drops down with a lurch, my stomach responds by flipping over and over with the descent. At ground level, the door's seal is released, opening onto the new old world from the base of the ship, my stomach's flips change to wings, alive with butterflies, my skin electric. Back here, after all these years, is this really happening?

"Is it safe, Appo?"

"Atmospherically, yes."

We are in a spot with vegetation all around, we aren't certain where in the world yet until Appo recalibrates some equipment. There are layers upon layers of green. Shades of emerald, khaki, and lime, with all hues in between, some of the leaves are larger than my head. I inhale deeply, petrichor fills me up like a magic potion I'd forgotten existed. I almost don't notice my ribs aching. I'm grateful to the sleep pods for returning my sense of smell, it transports me through time back to my parent's garden at some age under nine, making dens with Sam. There are sounds I haven't heard for so long, it's almost like I'd repressed them. Sounds of life, of birds singing. Birds that don't sound like the British birds I remember from childhood; these melodies are sharper, more urgent.

We step out of the ship together. Huge ferns litter the ground of the glade. Moving further away from the ship we turn and look back at the havoc it created on entry, damaging part of the forest—burning some of it away on landing, a trail of charred wood lies in a path, advertising our arrival.

"Do you know where we are yet?"

"I believe we are somewhere in Southern Europe. It is difficult to say. The Earth's axis has changed somewhat since we left, making exact navigation difficult. Something we didn't factor into our calculations and predictions." The MAGIE is looking intently at the MAGIEpad it holds. "The geography has changed so much even in the relatively short time we've been away. The land mass shapes we could detect from above are different because the sea levels have risen more than we expected."

"Is there anyone here? Did anyone survive?"

"You mean apart from us?" Appo glances at me, perhaps expecting me to laugh. "Our equipment was never designed for detecting life. We had the bare minimum, and that wasn't our priority. We do have heat sensors, though. But again, the climate changes are confusing our readings. Everything everywhere is warmer. I'll have to recalibrate the sensors."

There are signs of life, animal excrement, at least. We'd practically had a fanfare for our arrival, so if anyone was near, they will have seen us and perhaps now are watching our every move.

"I suggest we take time to find alternate shelter. This will be the focus point for any living thing. They'll all come for a look around and we don't know what we are dealing with," Appo says.

Could humans be living here? There must be. There are moments in history when plagues and wars threatened the human race, but we always had survivors.

The people we'd left behind, that lived away from the cities, the ones that lived in tiny pockets of community in the countryside. Surely, they would be the ones that had managed to survive.

"Let's get to a reccy then. How does that sound, Issy?" I ask Issy through the radio, still inside the ship. "You stay there. Monitor things for us, make sure everyone eats today. Lock it down until we get back."

"No problem. Stay safe. Don't take any unnecessary risks, please. We're all relying on you."

I look at Appo, and we nod at one another. I have never been this kitted up. There is extra cushioning around my ribs, although they are no longer bad, Appo insists they are still healing and very fragile. My pod sleep had lasted only four months, enough time for me to heal, but the MAGIE is sweetly protective.

Earlier we'd raided Frankie's quarters and found a heat gun, for soldering and maintenance around the ship. Despite it not really being a weapon, I have it along with the radio and a digital camera strapped to a tool belt around my waist. If we meet anyone, at least they might believe it is weapon and think twice before making any moves. Appo has given me some work boots. The MAGIE have clearly raided all the shipping containers while we'd been asleep. I don't blame them—organising, that's what they do best. My hair is pulled back. It is too hot with it down I feel more able.

"Let's get an idea of what's around us first." Appo says, "We may have to stay here, depending on what we find."

We set off. Appo plots points into MAGIEpad. The jungle is damp and hazy, the air feels thick with moisture and the only sound is us stomping through the understory, the birds have stopped singing. It feels like we are being watched, they are waiting for our next move. The plan is to create a map of the area as we go, creating or locating points that can be recognised for future navigation. "The days have grown longer. I'm certain that part of our foresight was right."

"How much longer?" I ask.

"Not a lot. If we'd been away for centuries it would be more noticeable."

"How long have we been gone for?" I lost all track of time once the regular pod-sleeps had been abolished. Feeling myself aging, seeing lines around my eyes in the mirror.

"Just short of fifteen years."

My feet stop moving. Appo almost crashes into me.

"Rebecca, please don't worry. Remember this amount of time is shorter than the intended twenty plus. You are older in the numerical sense, but your body's aging has been slowed down thanks to the pod-sleeps. You might be noticing things because the sleeps have been haphazard of late. Remember, the pods slow down metabolism. Aging, breathing, growing all happens much more slowly when humans are inside them. It is trivial when you consider what we've all been through."

"It is trivial, yes. I'm fifty-eight! But promises were made to the people who signed up for this trip. Oscar has manged to break them all, bar one: bringing us back here. Which he never let us in on anyway."

I quicken my pace, then my foot steps into nothing. The new old world in front of me spins. Up and down become one. I land on my back and the pain in my ribs arrives like I'm being cracked open. I can't breathe. Appo is calling me, but my voice doesn't work. All is dark.

* * *

Bouncing. The world is bouncing. I am floating, and the world is bouncing. There is Appo, above me. He's carrying me. I'm not floating after all. Searing pain rips through my chest. My ribs are fucked. I'm surprised my lungs haven't been shredded, maybe they have.

"You're awake?"

"Yes. I can try walking, if it helps." He puts me down onto my feet, with the kind of grace that makes me think of ballet. I lean over with my hands on my thighs, psyching myself up to stand properly.

"We aren't alone here. You were right. There are survivors. You fell into a trap. We need to move."

This is the first time I've detected fear in the voice of a MAGIE.

We walk back to the ship. I'm slow, but Appo is attempting to hurry me along, slinging my arm across its shoulder. Has he seen something else he's not telling me about? I can barely breathe, never mind speak, so we continue in silence for the rest of the way. We arrive back and get to the door.

"Issy, open up, please. Rebecca is hurt." The door opens within moments and I collapse inside. It shuts behind me and we are inside the relative safety. Appo lets me rest on the floor and I end up on all fours, the only position in which I can comfortably breathe. I wait as Appo goes up to med-bay to get help and drugs.

The hole I fell into, like the rest of the ground, was covered in ferns and other foliage. Whoever built it knew what they were doing. I'm thankful there were no spikes in the pit. I'd be dead.

How did Appo get me out? Appo returns before I've even begun to miss them, and it doses me up with another load of painkillers.

"This time I'm giving you a steroid shot, too. It'll speed up the healing"

I want to say thank you, and I hope so. I'm sick of this. I want to say it, but the drugs haven't started working yet, so I save my gripes and moans for later. The ship feels strange without all the fungi around. It is clinical, clean, and cold.

Appo lifts me and takes me up to Sector Four, laying me down on a sofa. It finds a table and retrieves the mapping equipment. We are silent. Me in a drowsy, pain filled stupor, and Appo absorbed in its work. I guess it is plotting where the trap is located. There are no real landmarks outside otherwise. We do know that this jungle isn't everywhere, Appo tells me.

"When we landed, while you were all still sleeping, we could see land that wasn't as green as here. The autopilot chose this spot for reasons I can't yet fathom."

"Where is everyone?" I finally manage.

"You say that like there are lots of you left, Rebecca." Appo looks up. Is it cross with me for interrupting? I don't know if I'm anthropomorphising or if he is becoming more human, more emotional. I keep thinking of it as a him.

"You'd think Issy would come here to see what happened."

"Perhaps she is otherwise occupied."

I fall silent again. Listening, waiting, so, so still. I don't want to rock the boat. We've been through enough. It is too quiet.

"I think we are in Perućica." Appo exclaims, almost shouting at me across the room. "In Bosnia. It's a preserved rainforest. This forest could previously only be explored with rangers. People weren't allowed in without permission and a guide. This is so exciting. I don't know why I didn't consider this earlier."

"You think people live here now? In this rainforest?"

"My theory suggests that, yes, but what is much more interesting is that this has *always been* a rainforest. It's not something that has grown since we departed, and it clearly hasn't been affected by what happened after we left, either. I believe that people came here to take shelter when things started to go wrong in the cities. They came here, where they knew there would be minimum exposure to the pathogens and the viruses that were sweeping the world via the mega cities."

"I was thinking that if there were survivors, then they wouldn't be city dwellers. They'd be the ones that allowed themselves to be left behind, cut off from modern living. Did Oscar plan to land in this location?" I pause and gather myself

"Something isn't right, Appo."

"What, what is it? Oscar, I don't believe he did."

"No, not that. I mean on this ship. Right now. I feel uneasy."

As if by magic, Issy arrives in the room. It is like she floated in. "What's making you uneasy, Rebecca?" she asks.

You for a start, I want to say but don't. She never calls me 'Rebecca' either.

"Just a feeling, it must be the meds," I say, looking into her eyes, searching for … I don't know. An answer. "How's the arm?" I ask, a genuine concern after basically ripping it off to save her.

"It's okay. It feels like it is still there." She reaches around with her hand and touches the stump where her right arm had been.

"It is a common side effect with amputees. They feel like the limb is still there, a phantom limb. Are you in pain in your phantom limb, Issy?" Appo asks.

"No, not pain. It feels tingly, fuzzy. A bit like pins and needles."

"Once we get settled here, I can make you a prosthesis, a bionic arm. Would you like that? It would allow you to be more able and help build our settlement." Appo is talking to her in such a strange way, I can't decide if he's being passive aggressive or mollycoddling her. Perhaps both. I feel like we are both walking on eggshells around her. Why? Like a cat, I watch as she walks over to the vending machines.

"Are these working now, Appo?" she asks.

"No, they are empty. Everything had to go. It was all contaminated."

"We've still got the stove set up downstairs, Issy. I'd love something to eat if you're able?"

"I've got one arm, Rebecca. I—"

Appo interrupts, "I'll get a MAGIE to make you both something. Apologies, I have neglected my duties." It says, practically running out of the room. We both listen as its footsteps fade away before speaking.

"You got hurt out there?" she asks me. "Your ribs again?" I nod, feeling slightly threatened by my best friend. Where is my bouncy, joyful Issy?

"They've taken such a battering. I feel like I'll never be back to a hundred percent again."

Issy (Annabel) - Days after arrival: 4

Dividing up the land outside is pointless for me. It isn't land I need, just time and space. No one notices my tears as they take apart Frankie's room, the lower levels all easier to get to. The basins and wash area, rigged for growing plants indoors, an ingenious irrigation system and likely where all our metamorphosis originated. I ask to keep all the pieces together for posterity. They will need to grow food, I tell them convincingly, it will be useful in the future. All I need is water, rest, and a little longer.

In the evenings, the MAGIE increase security. No one needs to say it. We are vulnerable. Even I feel unsafe, waiting to gather strength. I observe, staying on the threshold, marking the MAGIE routines and systems.

"We don't know who is out there. We need to leave the ship soon." Appo persists on this point.

I watch Rebecca's face as she defends her thoughts once again. Frustration. Pain.

"Each day we explore a different segment of the land world surrounding the ship. Knowing we need to leave it, but nobody wants to. It's our safety blanket. It has been our cocoon for so long." Rebecca says.

"I think we should leave," I say. "This place holds too many memories. There must be more out there than what we can see," I avoid eye contact with Rebecca. I'm sure she suspects something. Best to say nothing to her directly. Trying to recreate our relationship will only make changes going on within and without so much more obvious. I keep my head down. I'll agree with Appo, but I won't leave with any search party. Rebecca needs more protection than she thinks.

CHAPTER 19 – 2073

Rebecca - Days after arrival: 9

"Fuck. This rain feels amazing," Jax says, counting the remaining tools as she tallies them up. Some have disappeared in the fungi clearance.

I lift my face up to the dense sky in reply. Warm droplets cling or bounce from my cheeks as I close my eyes. "It really does." It's raining for the first time since we've arrived. I'm working outside with Jax, both of us liberated by the rain, it feels so normal. Jax is doing the heavy work, I'm still struggling to lift. The able survivors are pulling apart sections of ship and preparing them for transport. We are also mapping out where we intend to build some smaller shelters, just in case we end up staying.

"Oh god, this rain, it's almost like a warm, steamy shower. I'm all excited, Bec! You'd better watch out."

I laugh, despite my ribs, knowing that Jax's heart belongs elsewhere.

"We should get dry before night comes, or we won't be able to get warm." I say.

"Ali and I can keep you warm."

I roll my eyes but am glad of the comic relief, and I spot Appo and Junior coming back, striding towards us after another map expanding exercise.

"We've found a waterfall," the MAGIE say, almost in unison.

"We are near the base of it. I want to follow the river down to see if there is human life downstream." Appo's face is beaming.

"If anyone is alive and saw us land, wouldn't they have paid us a visit by now?" I ask.

"Perhaps they are grounded. Perhaps we were seen but there is no transport that can reach us. And if they are coming to see us and walking, perhaps a small scouting group may yet arrive. They might take a week or two to get here. We need to reach out, find help and supplies."

"If we split up, we will be weaker," I say.

"Then we all go."

"Some of us aren't fit to go." I feel sick again. The steroids aren't agreeing with me. The jolting of the vomiting is slowing down my healing, too.

Why are the MAGIE so adamant about this?

* ✳ *

Appo wastes no time in organising a leaving party. Their group is made up of thirteen women and eight MAGIE. He's left us two, Junior and Lan, to keep guard. Appo wouldn't budge on their plan and neither will I. We have powered down the other MAGIE to try and save on battery power, they are stored inside one of the shipping containers. I'm unsure why Appo has suddenly changed in behaviour, going against me when at one point it saw me as the next leader. I can only think that there's some overriding protocol, or something that they know, and I don't?

They say they'll either come back with help or not at all. It doesn't make sense for them to go. We could roll out the vehicles and take all the equipment with us. We just don't know which direction is best. I worry that this is it. I need to get fit and well. I feel like I can't think straight, my mind circling around itself.

Issy hasn't been around these last few days. When I have seen her, she isn't the Issy I know, maybe she's grieving for her arm. Whatever it is, she's become a bit of a recluse. She is different somehow. She holds herself differently, says she can't remember stuff, but it's more than that. I hope it's just temporary and she'll be back to her usual jolly self soon.

One of the other survivors came out of the pod-sleep and within minutes attempted to harm herself, headbutting a mirror. Everything feels like we are balancing on the edge of life. We need to keep everyone healthy and safe if we are going to survive.

Issy (Annabel) - Days after arrival: 10

I'm biding my time. Waiting to be strong enough to leave them. Knowing I will probably have to kill them to get away. The stump is no longer a stump, but sinew and tissue, even a soft bone deep inside. I have started strapping it down, binding it to my side, to my ribcage.

Unravelling the bandage in the privacy of my steel container, it springs up like it has a mind of its own. It might. I go with my instincts because it feels right to survive. My new arm snakes around my body, embracing me. I feel safe, secure, loved, and formidable

I will wait until the group is split, it's inevitable now. It will be easier when they are weaker, just as Rebecca had said.

Rebecca - Days after arrival: 11

It's evening, the MAGIE are on security duty as usual, circling the ship the humans who chose to stay are all in bed after a day of toiling outside, building structures, digging shallow channels for walls. There's only so much time we can spend living in each other's pockets. The shipping containers we've cleared out are bearable bedrooms, bigger than the capsule rooms.

I wake to the sound of vomiting; clearly, I'm not the only one feeling nauseous. My body responds by squeezing bile into my mouth, a suitable Pavlovian reaction. I swallow it down and roll over, crawling off the sleep mat and get up to check on whoever it is. No doubt I'll be sick again myself.

Peering around the door frame of the cubicle, I see Danai gripping the bowl. I step towards her, then feel it under my foot. Wet, cold, lumpy. Danai had missed her target.

"Do you need some help?" I ask, more loudly than I intend. I stand there hesitating, not wanting to get more vomit on my feet.

"Get back. Get back away from me," Danai gurgles. I can hear her throat filling up again. The vomit projects from her, flying out so hard it pushes her back on the floor. Her head slams against the wall with the impact, she falls back. I can see her face, covered in tiny pustules. I hold the door frame and lean over the vomit on the floor to try and get a better look at her. Some of the pustules have burst, like something is trying to get out, she isn't breathing.

"It's come back. It's still here." I run through the shipping containers, trying to remember where the others that had opted to stay were sleeping, there's only five of us. "The fungus is here, and it's killed!" Nobody replies. Nobody stirs. The space is dimly lit by an amber light, designed to help us feel less anxious, sleepier. Another of Appo's theories. They aren't here to help me now. The group had left in the direction of the river. I wish I'd gone with them.

Panic sets in. Pulling open the closest shipping container, I can see the outlines of Jax and Ali on their makeshift bed on the floor.

"Jax, wake up. Ali?" I hover for a moment, then reach out to touch a shoulder. It is sludgy, soft, and wet. "Fuck!" Scrambling around for a light or a torch, I eventually find one, and a scream catches in the back of my throat. The couple are still holding hands amongst the bloody backdrop. They look as if they have been boiled alive. Their skin is bursting, oozing with blood and pus, their skulls burst. Smashed pieces of bone sprawls across the pillows and sleeping bags, their brains are mush.

A jolt of lightning urgency sears through me, pushing me to my feet before I realise, and I'm running again. This time stealthier, more able. Listening, my senses tenfold in strength.

I've got to find her. Where the hell is she? Why hasn't she come to me? How could we be so careless? I should have left her there in that corridor with her arm stuck in that fucking floor.

Each thought repeats with each stride I take. My ankle that bothered me for so long is stronger now. My ribs, on the other hand, are not.

* ✳ *

If I can just get to the truck, all the tools are nearby. I can get something to properly kill her. There has been something wrong with Issy since we woke up. We all knew it, but we just let it slide, none of us had noticed. Or we had, but we'd blocked it out. Perhaps we didn't want to feel that fear again.

Where are the MAGIE, Lan and Junior? Has she destroyed them? I've got to get something to defend myself with, then I'll look for her.

I can see the front of the truck now. I'm slowing, it hurts to breathe. I can't get enough air. My breath too sharp and shallow, it's tense and hard around my sternum. Stopping for a moment to catch my breath, I lean back against the wall, and I see her. She is unaware I'm watching. She's in the cab of the truck, surely planning to get away.

I could let her go, let her leave. Only I would know. Except I can't. I believe there is life out there, human life. My brother as an old man, perhaps. Maybe he eventually had kids.

The courtesy light is on inside the cab as she still has the far door open. Why hasn't she closed the door?

353

I have the advantage. The dull, vast room hanger will look black from where she is. I catch my breath and continue towards the truck, picking up a shovel on my way around the back. My breath catches in my chest, my throat is tight. I'm sure anyone nearby could hear my heart beating; I hear it loudly in my ears. It's so loud that I don't hear the driver-side cab door close and Issy climb out.

Before I know what has happened, she is on me, the shovel clattering to the ground. She shoves me up against the side of the truck. My ribs shriek with pain, I can feel bone on bone. Her face is centimetres from mine and her breath covers me.

"Why have you followed me? I left you alive on purpose. Don't fight me, Rebecca. I don't want to kill you."

"What? Why? Because you're not Issy anymore, are you? Or is part of Issy still in there? Is she fighting?"

The woman formerly known as Issy laughs in my face. I realise she is holding me with two arms, not one. She has grown it back. It doesn't look like Issy's arm, it's much paler. As white as a baby's first tooth against Issy's blue-black skin. She looks otherworldly and magnificent.

"You have no idea what is going on," she says. "You killed me in your room that day. You crushed my skull. But the amazing thing, Rebecca, is that I can't die. I keep coming back. The fungi and I are one. I'm the next step on the human evolutionary ladder."

She is strong, holding me nearly off the floor.

"I'm going to leave now, Rebecca, and you aren't going to stop me. But you could come with me. I can protect you."

"Why would I do that?"

"You must know by now?" Her new arm has no hand, yet she lowers me down and puts the wrist stump on my abdomen. My hands push her arm away, instinctively protective of this most vulnerable part of me. I step back. Her face turns maniacal. "Do you understand?"

Moments flash through my mind; memories, like flipping through a diary, looking for a dream. She can't be right. Gant and me? In the sleep pods? Where and when did I conceive? My legs go weak and I slump down onto the floor.

"Come with me. We can start the new world together. I can help bring up our child the right way, protect it and you."

Hiding my face in the crook of my arm, I pretend to cry. My other hand finds the shovel. Fingers curl around its shaft, a movement I'm certain she'll notice. But she doesn't. She is crouching beside me. I let her think that I'm upset, that I'm considering her offer. I tighten my grip on the shovel, then, in one swift movement, I stand and swing the shovel upward and then down. Slicing it down. She is taken by surprise and crashes to the floor. Down again onto the back of her neck, like a guillotine. It takes a couple of times, but on the third her head rolls off, Issy's beautiful, expressive face gone. I stop it from rolling under the truck with my foot, forgetting I have nothing on my feet. Vomit creeps up the back of my throat again as I wipe my foot on her clothes.

Alone, I must destroy the body before she manages to resurrect herself again. There's no earth in here. No fungus I can see. But if she can re-grow an arm? I'm taking no chances. She might be able to release spores. I need to burn the body, burn the head.

The old truck must have fuel, that rare substance that wars were fought over a lifetime ago. Oscar will have kept his own stash specifically for this mission. I crawl underneath the truck and stab at the fuel tank a few times with the still-bloody corner of the shovel. It splits easily. It's so old I shouldn't be surprised. I roll away from under the truck quickly and stand as the petrol pours out under my feet and all around Issy's head and body. Dashing towards the cab, there's got to be a cigarette lighter in there.

"Bingo!" Who knew smoking would save the planet? I light up the fuel and the pool of petrol burns with a heat I've not felt for years. The fire licks at Issy's face and body, frantically burning through her hair. I know I must get out quickly before it comes for me.

I pick up the shovel, having grown attached to it over the last few minutes, and I run back to my shipping container. Grabbing my stuff, I throw it into a bag. I've no idea how hard the fire will burn. Will it set alight the whole ship or burn out once the fuel has burnt away? I can't wait around to find out. I pull on clothes, layering them on to save space in my bag, I throw everything in that I can see. There's not much to carry.

I fight to put on my bag and then run to the area we've been using as a kitchen. I grab some packets of the dried space food I hate. All I need is to survive, that's all I've ever needed.

At the other end of the space the fire is wrathful. The truck is engulfed in tall amber flames, our supplies in there now gone. I have to get out. The smoke and the smells are making me cough. I haven't got time to be sick again.

I press the release button for the external door. Nothing. It doesn't budge. I press again. The swift upward movement I've grown so used to isn't there. Fuck, these bloody doors. I punch the button. Something whirs inside the wall, but nothing happens. I'm coughing, a lot, the pain in my ribs has become my normal. I've got to get out. The fire is getting closer. I swing the shovel up and crack the button. More whirring in the wall. The door starts to lift, and I realise that fire needs oxygen too—opening the door will make it burn harder, bringing it to me. The door stops. There's a gap the size of my hand, no way I can squeeze through. Placing my fingers underneath the door I strain to lift it, but it feels like its jammed on something inside. I bang the button again and it lifts a fraction. Is it enough to get out? It has to be.

I'm on the floor, where it's easier to breathe. The fire is seeking the air supply and growing ever nearer. My ears feel full, like they are about to pop. I slip my bag off and push it under the door, following quickly, head-first. My bum and hips get wedged and for a moment I'm stuck. Something is behind me. I can feel something pulling at my leg.

"Shit, shit, get the fuck off me!" I wriggle and shake my leg but still it clings. I can't see what it is, but I don't need to. It's not dead. It feels like a vice coiled around my leg, a burning-hot snake that sears through my two layers of trousers, sealing them to my skin. I brace myself on the edge of the door frame and, with a twist, find myself on the other side. The thing is still on my leg. It's Issy's regrown arm. It's hot to the touch and like a snake it won't let go.

I pull myself along the ground, so I'm lying with my leg parallel to the door. I reach up with my shovel to press the button to close the door. If it won't open properly maybe it can help me another way: Squash the fucker to death. The door doesn't budge. Again, and again, I swing the shovel up onto the panel. Nothing happens. Through the gap in the door, I can see the fire has completely taken over the deck. I've got to get clear. I've got to get this thing off my fucking leg.

I glance down and see the arm. It is repulsively long, gristly and sinewy, its heat is abating, but its grip is not. Struggling to stand, I sling my bag back on and, using the shovel as a walking stick, I hobble away from the ship as carefully and quickly as I can manage, the thing still on me. I thank my past self for pouring over the maps Appo created. It's dark, and I can only just make out the landscape and markers around me which were used to plot the area around us. I head for the river. I'm going to drown this thing or make it so slippery that it will just slide off. It squeezes tighter, as if to remind me it's there.

Growing accustomed to the gloom, I look up and see the line of trees silhouetted against the sky, it must be near dawn. I follow the lightly trodden path of soft ferns and grasses squashed into the ground and the thing on me grows tighter. I see a muddle of parts up ahead, cast in shadow. Only when I get closer, I recognize Junior's parts, it's hat, along with what must be Lan's body alongside. They look almost melted. I feel vomit again at the back of my throat and keep moving.

The foliage is damp with dew, the tree trunks gathering together more closely here, protecting each other and their reclaimed world. I push through, the vines already re-growing where the MAGIE have hacked them back for the path. The fire behind me glows in the glossy leaves, I brush past them, and I nearly topple into the water, it feels closer than I recall.

Dumping my stuff on the bank, the slow breaking light is just enough to see where I'm putting my feet. There's a narrow shoreline of pebbles and I flail as I sit down.

I'm trying to prise it off, but it twists around my leg tighter, and I wonder which of us will break first. I can't let this thing live. The fire will be in vain if any of it gets out.

My hands grope the riverbed and find what I am looking for. A rock big enough to hold and heavy enough to do some damage. I start bashing the thing. Its only line of defence is to squeeze me even tighter. I don't stop. Bits started to tear off, floating away. It dawns on me that these particles are just drifting down in the river, they could give rise to the fungi growing again. Dragging myself upon the bank again I curse for not thinking of this earlier.

Don't look back now, only forward. Once again, I begin bringing the rock down. Its blood is thick and looks black in the near monochrome light, the skin, muscle, and bone are soft and sponge like. It has strength way beyond its means. I keep missing, grazing my calf and around my knee. If I never walk again it will be worth it.

Finally, I manage to force my fingers between it and my calf and flip it off my leg, onto the bank beside me. I watch it for a few moments, waiting for it to move. It doesn't. I pull myself up the bank further still, away from the arm, taking a moment to rest.

It must be destroyed. I pick the arm up by the end where the hand should be and hold it like I'm greeting someone. A moment of tenderness before I drag myself up to standing, again using the shovel as support. With the thing in one hand and the shovel in my other, I hobble back along the path to the fire, as close as I dare go, and sling the limb deep into the flames. It fizzles and pops and then catches alight. I turn my back and walk away back to the water.

I gather foliage. Large teardrop-shaped plantain leaves from their long stalks on the ground, weeds to the uninitiated eye. Yarrow, easily located thanks to its frothy white flattened sprigs which grow tall—like first aid beacons—that we'd noted on a previous walk. Peeling off my layers of trouser is torture. I bite down on a twig. It tastes bitter in my mouth. Chunks of skin come off with the fabric of my pants.

The sun is splitting the darkness open now, colouring all before me. I rinse my leg in the river, whilst chewing the leaves for a poultice. Yarrow should stop any bleeding and numb the pain in my calf, its leaves like small spikey ferns on my tongue. The plantain will calm inflammation and encourage healing. Laying them on the sores and open flesh,

I hold the poultice in place by wrapping one of the T-shirts I'd layered on around my leg, and sit, leaning against the base of a tree. I must be in shock.

* ✳ *

The fire from the ship glows between the shadows of the trees in the clearing created by our landing. Dad would be so proud that I've managed to make a shelter using one of the tree branches and some tarp I found on the outer edges of our camp. There were a couple of blankets too, thanks to our late-night sky gazing sessions. Sitting out at night, watching the stars and the sky where we'd been for so long had grown into a habit for some of us. The flames don't go much beyond the body of the ship. The poultice seems to be working, too. I was listening after all. My shelter is on a gentle incline not far from the river. There is the beginning of a worn path where I have been getting water. It is amazing, the way the Earth adapts to our presence. I've dragged over some other bits I found outside. I lie here, conserving energy, thankful I'm alive.

Rebecca - Days after arrival: 14

I'm so hungry that I'm starting to hallucinate. I keep seeing Juniper out of the corner of my eye, flashes of black fur;

taking me by surprise each time. I have foraged a little, but I know it's not enough to sustain me. I'm lying on my back, switching between being hot and cold, resting from a mini retrieval mission I set myself; more blankets, maybe a cup or bowl to rehydrate the space food sachets I'd shoved in my bag during my escape. I've been making some in the sachets, but the proportions are all wrong, barely edible. Returning, I'm empty handed, so take a moment and enjoy the sun on my skin.

My eyes lightly closed, the sun streams through my eyelashes, and then I hear it. A mechanical sound, like a plane. Opening my eyes, the sun distorts my vison. My mind is playing a trick on me again. But the sound is still there and getting louder. Then it appears above the treeline, I can see it, it is a small plane! It circles and drops water onto the smouldering ship. Then, a few minutes later I'm standing up, using my shovel for support. I can hear voices, I can hear Appo. The MAGIE have brought back real help. There are people I don't know helping me sit back down, giving me water and bread, checking my injuries. A makeshift hose is rigged up sent out to make the ship safer, for salvage. Appo comes to sit beside me I lean into its frame; never have I been so grateful to see a robot.

CHAPTER 20 – 2073 & BEYOND

Rebecca - Days after arrival: 122

I show quickly. The timings are all off. I let everyone believe the baby is Gants. My anxiety is sky high. I barely sleep, nothing comforts me. The gestation period isn't right, but I'm blaming that on the sleep pods. No one, not even Appo, knows the real story.

Appo says I was delirious when they came back for me. Perhaps I still am. I remember making a pact with the tree that sheltered me. I promised I'd come back to it. Now it's like a signpost for our navigation, a marker to our camp. The visions of Juniper, I've realised are wild boar that live here in the forest. The trap I'd fallen in was intended to supply food for the local survivors.

Jezero is around two kilometres away, it is our closest town; deserted, of course. While we were orbiting Earth, there was, just as Appo had told me, a virus, that got into the human population. Along with the increasing number of extreme weather events, means life on Earth is very different from when I knew it before. We visit Jezero every few months, usually in groups of three, we go for supplies and materials and clothes. Many died, but there were some with immunity, these people retreated into the forest, afraid of what the road may bring, other survivors are desperate and drifting from their towns. Strangers capable of bad things with people they don't care about. The edges of the forest proved to be a refuge, a place the Jezero survivors had known all their lives. It was there to protect them, and now us.

Rebecca - Days after arrival: 200

I am big now. I can't help with much around the camp because of my size and pregnancy is exacerbating my injuries. I take things slow, still recovering. The MAGIE salvage enough of the ship to make small homes. Nearly everything is black and charred like an oven that has never been cleaned. Some things we manage to reuse for buildings and fencing. Most of it is burnt beyond recognition. They pull the whole thing apart, taking what we need, leaving nature to take over the rest. Singed as they are, the shacks look like they've been here much longer than they have. Each is one room and Appo visits me every day in mine. I lose track of time sometimes and wander around the camp.

The birth is soon, I know it. The baby pushes against my ribs, its head engaged with my pelvis. Soon.

My leg was a mess when they found me, I found out recently there had been talk of amputation: infection grew despite my best efforts. Luckily for me the survivors from the town had some antibiotics. My calf has less than half of the muscle than the other one. Much of it chewed and peeled off, meaning I am left with an impressive set of scars.

The MAGIE built a water turbine right by the waterfall and were able to create hydroelectricity. Our own electricity, from a natural resource. It was, is, like a dream, only better. The MAGIE could charge, too. The skills I learnt as a child have finally came to good use, herbalism and Dad's survival stuff. I am a trusted leader of the community that has grown around the camp. The exact patch of land where I had lain after my fight with the creature is covered now, a small jetty, home to a couple of rafts we use to get further down the river for supplies.

Rebecca - Days after arrival: 213

Sherry is here. Named after Mum. Small and earlier than expected. Like she knew my ribs couldn't take much more, she came out in a rush, still in the sac, her face pressed up against the veil. I photographed it with my eyes. The local survivors tell me it's rare and a lucky sign. She will need it. I checked and checked her to see if there was anything strange. The only strange thing is how perfect she is. Her caul hangs in our shack. Sherry being here fills up my near empty cup with joy and hope. Two companions I'm pleased have re-joined me.

The MAGIE survived the things we couldn't, but now they seem older, not always functioning like before. Tiring more easily, needing updates we can't provide. Some have developed coding issues and are behaving like humans with advanced dementia. We have no way of helping them so, as a community, have decided to break them down for parts. We're losing around half the MAGIE population.

Rebecca - Months after arrival: 24

I sit and write outside our tiny home, she plays close by, acting out one of the stories from the red book, and I don't ever want to be apart from her. A group have left for Jezero, on a mission to gather more resources. I'm hopeful for toys and books for Sherry, and we all need new clothes and shoes. I'm happy for the remaining MAGIE to take the lead, happy staying here with my girl. Here is where I'm useful, where I'm needed. Here is my mission.

"What are you writing, Mummy?" She comes running full throttle at me, almost knocking me off my chair. I drop my papers, wrap both my arms around her, and she squeezes me back. These are the best hugs.

"I'm writing my story for you. It's our story now, but it starts with me and ends with you." She pulls away from the bear hug and looks at me with that penetrating gaze. "Where are the pictures?"

"There aren't any. I might add them later. Maybe you could make some for me?" She grins and runs off again, like a whirlwind of magic.

I see Sherry for what she really is. My child, my love, but also the future. Earth is my home again. It is Sherry's, too. She's never known any different than this life, this Earth, this way of living. It is so simple and so humble compared to what was before, and now I can see this was always going to happen, one way or another. She would always succeed us somehow. Sherry is the right opportunity. The right way in. I will protect her for as long as I am able, although I have a feeling that she has been protecting me all along. I look at her sometimes and wonder if she knows. I'm not sure she does. Not yet, anyway. I'm not sure I do either. I think when puberty hits things might change for us. Hormones have a way of bringing everything into focus, and I don't think even Sherry can escape that. But I trust her implicitly, as she does me.

Rebecca - Months after arrival: 56

I wait and I write. The stories of us. Sherry picks up reading easily, and I struggle to get enough books. Even in the schools and homes we've explored in the old world, there are never enough books. We have retrieved paper, and I teach her basic bookbinding so she can fill them with her own stories. The stories she tells are of imagined creatures and talking food.

Rebecca - Months after arrival: 88

We load the boar onto the sleigh, it's heavy and cumbersome, they always are, but one this size will feed our community for more than a month if we are careful. Daniel straps it down carefully, as I pick up my bow from the ground. I'm a pretty good shot.

Daniel is strong, one of the locals who came back for me with Appo. He speaks some English. I like the fact he's not one for small talk. I like it when he holds me in the dark, too.

"You go on," he tells me. "I can bring this back."

"Thanks."

He knows I'm longing to get back to see what Sherry is up to. Putting the bow over my head I begin the hike back to camp. Sherry is nearly eight. Appo keeps an eye on her when it's my turn on the hunting rota. They'll probably be immersed in one of the books we've retrieved from Jezero. It's where Daniel is from, a boat builder before the virus came. His young family died in the outbreak.

I get closer to camp and slow my pace, I love the moments when I'm just on the outskirts and can hear life just a bit further away. There's thirty-three of us altogether living here, humans that is, along with a handful of MAGIE. There are now twenty survivors from Jezero. Appo stationed eighteen of the MAGIE there, a year after our arrival, five are still there, the others breaking eventually. We will move over there soon. They are making it safe, doing repairs, dealing with other survivors coming this way, ensuring the contamination risk is at a minimum. So much work, all for us, so selfless.

I see a patch of the mushrooms that will work well with the boar. I stoop to harvest them, fully aware of how ironic it is. They are one of our major food groups here, something we rely on a lot. I always overcook them. It turns out that some of the nicest tasting mushrooms are morels. They thrive on the black and burnt ground. In the ashes of the fire lies our sustenance. In the world before, these mushrooms were an expensive product. Now we eat them every day. They are meaty and nutty, and I've grown to love them—what they symbolise, and what they are giving us, a new life from old. Their honeycomb appearance makes it easy for any of us to collect them. I often find Sherry in the burnt glade, basket full.

I circle the camp to our shack. It's empty. Then I hear her voice, further round on the far side of the settlement. I follow her murmurs, deep in conversation with someone, I can't see who. She is about five metres away, with her back to me. I freeze to the spot, afraid that she'll stop if she knows I'm here. My ears try to focus on her calm, steady voice, and my mind fills in the gaps. I only hear her side.

"Mummy's here!" She spins around and looks me right in the eye.

"Who are you talking to? Are you playing hide and seek?"

"I was talking to some friends."

"Where are they?" A familiar feeling creeps over me. I already know.

"They are here, all around."

"Are they good friends or bad friends?" Her face changed to a look of confusion. I immediately regret asking.

"Come on. Let's go and get some tea." I offer my hand, and she slips hers into mine, like its home has always been there, even before she existed.

* ✳ *

Sherry has a deep bond with nature; the perfect hybrid. What started on the ship has ended up in her, but in such a refined way. The balance is there. The idea of her being the future of humanity is overwhelming, but it's what I believe will happen.

I tell her about my parents and her uncle and Christian. There are no photographs to show, but I read the red storybook every night. Sherry almost know these stories word for word, and we often use it for community readings and—dare I say it? —it has the same moral weight as some religious texts did in the time before.

Rebecca - Months after arrival: 108

Sherry begs me to take her into Jezero as part of the next gathering trip. We, the adults, have always thought her and the other children are safer here among the trees, but I know curiosity is only going to grow. I'm going to show her the old world—I'd rather that than let her go off alone. I need her to be educated about the towns and how to stay safe there. She needs the advantage. Today is her ninth birthday, and, against the better judgement of the fellow villagers, we will hike to the outskirts of Jezero, setting off just before sunrise. Days are longer than before, but the long days of summer are drawing to an end. Still, I know we can make it there and back before nightfall at this time of year. I wrap up some bread and fill some canisters with water. By lunchtime we are at the edge of the forest and the edge of the valley. Beneath us is the town she is craving. We sit to have lunch, but she barely eats anything, so distracted with the new world ahead. Have I lost some of her already? We talk about us creating a manual together. A combination of guidebook and rules to live by in this new old world. Gulping down some water, I'm acutely aware of where the sun is in the sky.

"I know a playground nearby. We'll go and check it out, then head back."

"We've only just got here, Mum," she says. The change from Mummy to Mum is recent and it still smarts like bare thighs brushing nettles.

"Remember this is a treat. Doing this is a special thing that is currently and only allowed under the rules I set as your parent. If you can't stick to them, we can leave for home now."

Her smile disarms me, and we continue the journey. Arriving at the playground, she takes a few moments to grasp what it is. A slide, a climbing frame, and swings. I show her how to use a swing and we are lost in the up and down motion for a bit of forever. Then she wants to try something else, so I show her the roundabout, but it gives me vertigo, so I don't stay on for long. She boards the roundabout as I sit on a nearby bench. Pushing off, it begins to spin, and she laughs. I've finally made it home.

THE END

ACKNOWLEDGEMENTS

Earthly Bodies started as a single scene in my mind in the last quarter of 2017. The story grew bit by bit with the help and encouragement of many people. Here are some of them.

For all the moments of self-doubt, imposter syndrome and all the Earl Grey I could drink, my husband, Dave. Forever my champion and number one fan. Thank you for your limitless love and support. To my daughters, MJ and Lizzie, thank you for allowing me space, time and all the cuddles I needed; there were lots. You both inspire me every day. To my parents, Janet and Stuart, for always believing in me, keeping my feet on the ground and instilling creative thinking from day one. To coach and friend, Natasha Denness, you helped me unpack my true desires and dreams, peeling back the layers that time and life had created. To editors Vicky Brewster and Karmen Wells, you both got this story without flinching. Your notes and directions were so helpful and precise. You bolstered my confidence with your understanding. To Anna Lovind, and The Creative Doer community, you came along at the right time and helped me in ways I didn't even know I needed. To Laura Mackay, a special mention for special friend and reader, thank you. To all the other supporting women around me especially Emma, Kate, Alison, Tamsyn, Sarah and Sharon, and the communities I'm part of online and off, thank you. Lastly, I'd like to thank my cat Billy for being there when the words came and when they didn't, always with unfaltering affection.

ABOUT THE AUTHOR

Susan Earlam was born in Stockport, England. Starting her blog in 2010, she rediscovered the writing bug. After seven years of lifestyle writing and freelancing, she became compelled to write fiction. When the novels get too much, she procrastinates by writing shorter and weirder stuff. She lives in Cheshire with her husband, two daughters and Billy the cat.

Find out more and sign up for updates here:

https://susanearlam.com/

Susan enjoys social media in small doses, and has a profile on most platforms, but Instagram is her favourite.

https://www.instagram.com/susanearlam/

Lightning Source UK Ltd.
Milton Keynes UK
UKHW011256280321
381100UK00001B/23